THE GALACTIC PANTHEON NOVELLAS

ALYCE CASWELL

THE FLICKERING FLAME

CHAPTER ONE

'Full disclosure: yeah, I look pretty hot, but I come with baggage. A whole galaxy full of baggage. I also happen to be the goddess of fire which I understand is a bit of a deal-breaker. You mortals tend to want a marriage that lasts a lifetime, not an eternity. You'd get immortality out of it, but then you'd have to stay with me until the end of time. Shudder.'

Finara, goddess of fire (the Firine was her official title in the Galactic Pantheon), sat back in the booth and waited for her companion to respond. She lifted her glass, either painted neon pink or containing a viscous material of the same colour, and held it to her lips. The resort's galaxy-renowned drink, apparently. It had some fancy name but it clearly wasn't all that important because it had slipped her mind. In her domain there were innumerous planets with unstable volcanoes, flaming lakes and raging bushfires — she couldn't be bothered to remember every little detail about every little world that fell under her control.

If the mortals required her immediate attention, she gave it, but never any more than they needed. She looked after them because it was she had been created to do. Finara still wasn't sure the mortals deserved her assistance — or anything else from her, really.

Occasionally she indulged in some public fire dancing. It seemed to be the only thing Finara did that merited any adoration from the mortals. She was hired by hotels to perform impossible feats while wearing fun skimpy outfits and then used the money she earned from doing this to visit her favourite brothel, the Enocian Harem. Humans generally refused to supply goods and services to someone who didn't have any coin-chips to spend.

When Finara had finished her shift at this particular hotel today, mopping a towel over her forehead, she had noticed a giant vidscreen announcing a bout of speed dating in the bar. It had occurred to her that this would provide a cheaper alternative to the brothel. Her coin-chips could go into other exciting things, like flashy clothes and shiny baubles.

The human sitting opposite Finara in the booth was an improvement on the previous offerings. This mortal was well above average in height, unlike the others who'd plonked themselves onto the red leather seat in the booth. Finara was quite tall herself, so this woman pleased her immensely. She'd had short lovers and hadn't found any inadequacies in them, but she preferred their eyes to meet her own instead of her (admittedly ample) chest.

The mortal woman's skin was somewhere between bronze and tan, and her brown eyes were dark and deep, as though they held delightful mysteries. And that mouth...large and promisingly sensual. Finara hadn't seen her date's tongue yet, but she imagined its length would be more than suitable for her needs.

Finara *should* have had soothing hazel eyes, but she preferred to keep them aflame, the fire that obscured her pupils and irises held there by constant concentration. Finara had never managed to darken her olive skin through exposure to sunlight, though thankfully she wasn't as pasty as Kuja, the rainforest god. Finara had been born with brunette hair, but she kept it black to reveal her permanent mood: rebellious.

Except her racing off to have sex with mortals hadn't turned out to be anywhere near as rebellious as what her brothers had done. Sandsa, the Desine and oldest sub-level god, had thrown away his position in the pantheon to be with a mortal woman, however briefly. Then Kuja had challenged the Creator God, their father, pleading for the right to marry the mortal *he* loved.

When the Ine (the name Finara and her siblings used for the Creator God) had revealed that his children had been allowed to fall in love all along, this had caused something of a stir among the gods and goddesses — previously they'd gone after and punished any sibling who had dared to look at any mortal for too long. Finara continued to enjoy bedding anyone who was keen, but the activity had lost much of the danger and, with it, a lot of the fun.

The woman on the other side of the booth reached up and patted her hair as though to ensure everything was in place. Finara wasn't sure why. The mortal's hair was a mass of frizzy coils that looked like they would never sit the way they were told to; what the gesture did instead was make the crescent-shaped scar that ran through her left eyebrow all the more obvious.

'What exactly does a fire goddess do?' the mortal asked.

This didn't match the responses Finara had been getting all evening. Mostly people had laughed when she'd announced her identity. One man had even run with it by pretending to be a Chipper, an agent responsible for enforcing planetary laws across the galaxy, and had said that he would spank her for being a sub-level god. The Chippers worshipped the Creator God and inserted chips into their temples (hence their name) in order to reach him; these chips gave them special abilities which aided them in protecting the Creator God's mortal children.

Finara had enjoyed the accompanying images in the man's

mind when he'd tried to seduce her, but she was a little over men of late. Her brothers were always slinging insults and powers at each other, trying to prove who was the best of them, but her sisters were more reserved. Finara could simply walk up to them and begin a conversation, no exhausting ego required.

'What does a fire goddess do?' Finara mused. 'Aside from wasting my time in this dive, you mean? I do some fire dancing here and there. Shit pay, but it's something. A woman's got to fulfil certain needs. Coin-chips help with that.'

'Ms Fire Goddess — ' A disapproving frown warped the mortal's features. ' — that doesn't sound very godly. Shouldn't you be keeping mortals out of danger? Suppressing volcanoes that are about to erupt, for example?'

Finara scowled and set down her glass with an audible thunk. 'Firstly, the name is Finara. Secondly, I can't just tell a volcano to settle down. The eruption would get a lot worse if I tried to do anything. And besides, you have two legs — you can run away. You mortals don't need me to help you with that.'

Silence. Well, as much as silence could be in this place; the bar was filled with the murmur of voices and a lilting jazz tune that was just loud enough to force the couples to lean into each other to make themselves heard.

Finara was starting to wonder what she'd said to offend her companion when the mortal cleared her throat noisily, reached beneath the table and pulled out a silver prosthetic leg. She dumped it between them, knocking over Finara's glass in the process.

'You can buy those fully functional synthflesh legs, they're much more realistic,' Finara said, her lip curling up towards her nose as she surveyed the pink puddle her drink was forming on the table. 'They've been out for at least five hundred Old Earth years.'

The woman's scarred eyebrow slid up her forehead. 'We mortals can indeed get top-of-the-line models. If we have deep pockets.'

Finara grimaced. She supposed she wasn't the first person to mention it. 'Sorry — I shouldn't have said that. But still. If your warning systems are even halfway decent, they can give you enough time to hobble off before a volcano explodes.'

The woman stared at her. Unable to restrain herself any longer, Finara delved into her companion's mind, finding disbelief mixed in with indignation. There was also an unexpected spike of humour.

'I'm Grace Pendergast,' the mortal said. Her lips quirked into a smile. 'And I'm glad I am not one of your followers. This meeting would have destroyed any adoration I had for you.'

'Great, that means I still have plenty of opportunities to make you adore me.' Finara straightened her glass then brought a pink-stained finger to her lips to suckle the alcohol from her skin. 'Grace, huh? I could have sworn that name went out of fashion around the time everyone realised they could reach their creator just by sticking chips into their temples. Kind of lose the awe of the Creator God when you realise he's actually listening to you.'

'I suppose it's hard for you to feel awe for your own father,' Grace responded, picking up the leg and concealing it beneath the table once more.

'Yeah, he's pretty shit when you actually know him,' Finara said with a sigh. 'Omniscient but completely lacking in any emotional capacity. He chose a human mother for me and my siblings just to get the right mix of raw power and compassion.'

Grace leaned back in the booth, surveying Finara through narrow eyes. 'I think you needed a little more compassion in your DNA mix.'

'You think?' Finara smirked. 'Hey, you mortals don't deserve my compassion. None of you worship me, not really. You only remember me when there's a fire or an eruption and you think flattering me with nice words will make me turn nature against itself for you. The nerve.'

A siren pierced the room before Finara's companion could respond. Since a portly woman had been using an antique bell to denote the end of each speed dating session, this caused several pairs of eyes to shoot up towards the vidscreen on the wall above the bar.

Pyroclastic flow expected in five minutes, the screen announced while an accompanying voice read out the words. *Make sure you're safely within the hotel's forcefield!*

Finara clucked her tongue, irritated. She'd felt the flow coming, but she had ignored it far longer than she usually did because she had started to enjoy Grace's company. The hotel was well protected by its shield generators, even this close to the cluster of volcanoes that had made the planet Arksaw famous — apparently they resembled the face of a famous mediaist if viewed from orbit — but there were always some thrillseekers who wanted to dance with danger.

'I better go make sure everyone's made it behind the forcefield,' the goddess said, levering herself out of the booth.

'Is that concern for us mortals I hear in your voice?' Grace asked.

Finara snickered. 'Well, the more people who survive this,

the more tips I get during my shift tomorrow. You should come to my next performance.'

Three years ago, she would never had this conversation, nor would she have dared to teleport in front of mortals. But ever since the Creator God-loving Chippers from the Galactic Law Enforcement Agency (GLEA for short) had started saying that it was imperative to get along with the other gods and *their* followers, there had been less of a need to hide her existence and what she could do. Exposing herself as a goddess was no longer going to incite an ideological war.

Finara blew a kiss at Grace.

And then a swirl of fire roared up around the Firine, encasing her body before it completely erased her from the bar.

***

Grace Pendergast stared at the empty space her date had left behind.

So too did everyone else in the bar, completely gobsmacked. They'd probably had the same spiel from Finara but, judging by their expressions, they hadn't believed it. Grace hadn't believed it either, not really. Her date had been too irreverent, too improper...and she'd had little regard for mortals. Everyone knew that the Creator God loved all of them, cherished them, protected them. Surely his immortal children would do the same.

A man in the adjacent booth grabbed his communicator and said loudly, 'Put me through to the Chippers! I just saw one of those sub-level gods!'

'No, you fool!' the man's date said, lunging across the table and knocking the device out of his hand. 'Call Ton Tinel or another mediaist — they'd pay a shitload for this kind of exclusive!'

The bar descended into chaos. Rolling her eyes, Grace stood and took the only clear path to the door. Once outside, the only sound she could hear was the clacking of her heels on the tiled floor.

Immortality, she thought as she walked through the columned piazza that featured in the hotel's advertisements.

Immortality, she repeated to herself as she entered her tiny, poky room.

She sat down on the edge of the bed, detaching her cheap prosthesis. There wasn't a point in wasting her funds on a better one, because she wouldn't be alive long enough to enjoy it.

Immortality, Grace mused. *The gods have to live with their mistakes forever.*

I'm glad I don't.

She turned on her room's vidscreen. Within moments it was filled with the frenzied face of a mediaist who happened to be holidaying on Arksaw — but not without their equipment, of course. The unsteady footage, provided by a vidcam being waved from the ramp of a starship, hurt her eyes but Grace squinted, focusing on the goddess who was grabbing tourists and throwing them into rings of fire. The startled and fearful humans didn't die; they were being transported out of matching rings inside the forcefield, where they were safe from the fury the planet was unleashing.

Finara laughed throughout the entire affair. She even waved at the vidcam that was tracking her progress. Grace had a feeling the goddess could destroy the device without even blinking, but for some reason Finara wanted everyone to witness her using her powers, wanted everyone to know what she was.

When at last all the tourists had been evacuated, Finara held out her arms, welcoming the gaseous blast from the volcano. It tore through her, around her, then smacked into the forcefield before being diverted around the hotel and its denizens.

For an instant, the goddess remained visible in the pyroclastic flow. Her body became pure fire, then blew apart into a million pieces.

Grace nearly reached for her techpad, to start writing about meeting a sub-level god, but forced herself to dismiss the words that arrived in her mind, the words that begged to be Webcast to the galaxy, to anyone who would listen.

Those days were over. She was no longer a small-time mediaist. She was a cripple who deserved the fate she had inflicted on others.

Grace hopped over to the bathroom, a hand on the wall to steady herself. Once the water was running, she removed her slip of a dress, pausing to laugh at the floral pattern she had thought pretty enough to finally entice someone to divest her of her virginity. As a teenager, it had been a prize; to a woman on the wrong side of thirty, it was a burden.

A small part of her had hoped that she would meet someone at that speed dating event, someone who could convince her to forget the terrible mistakes she'd made, someone who could provide a reason to keep going.

There just didn't seem a point anymore. Grace had lost everything that had ever made her life worth living.

She had one more week until her funds ran out. One more

week until she too embraced the devastation unleashed by the nearby volcanoes.

Except her body, once vaporised, would stay that way forever.

CHAPTER TWO

When Grace emerged from the steamy shower cell, having spent a good hour in there while continuously hitting the 'start' button, she found her towel mysteriously missing. She groped blindly along the rail for a few seconds, perplexed, then nearly toppled over when the towel hit her stomach — she had caught it with the hand she'd been using to brace herself.

The mist inside the bathroom slowly cleared, revealing the source of the soft projectile.

Leaning against the door, as if she had a right to be there with her immortality, her scarlet outfit and her two functioning legs, was the goddess of fire.

'Now tell me that wasn't hot,' Finara said with a laugh.

Grace hastily wrapped the towel around herself, grimacing when she realised that she had to surrender a view of either her breasts or her thighs. There was nothing she could do to conceal the stump that had replaced her right knee.

Grace fought for something to say, but somehow the only thing that came out was, 'You could have at least handed me a bigger towel. This is indecent.'

'Indecent is what I'm going to do to you after dinner.' Finara grinned. 'But forget about that. You must have watched me saving all those mortals. How good did I look, huh?'

Her eyes scanned Grace in a way that made her feel...not uncomfortable, but confused. What did the fire goddess see that the mirror did not show? Were Grace's generous hips, wider than her cup size, somehow enticing instead of awkward?

Would Finara still look at her like that if she knew just how much blood was on Grace's hands?

Grace cleared her throat. 'Get out.'

Her discomfort must have shown — or had the goddess read it from her mind? — because Finara suddenly looked guilty.

'Sorry,' Finara said, then disappeared inside a roaring vortex of fire.

The goddess' voice returned but it was muffled; she was now on the other side of the door, in the small bedroom. It sounded like Finara was complaining about the mediaist's coverage of her appearance. Grace remained frozen in place, her breathing shallow, the soft towel sliding its way down her body and drooping onto the floor. Shaking herself out of her stupor, she threw the flowery dress back on, wishing she had brought one of her more comfortable and less revealing pantsuits into the bathroom with her.

She made herself presentable, blew out an unsteady breath and then waved a hand over the sensor on the tiled wall. The door opened to reveal Finara stretched out on the bed, taut stomach on display. Grace's techpad lay beside the fire goddess, apparently untouched, but the first thing Grace did after she navigated her way across the room was retrieve the device and slide it into a pocket. She then sat on the bed, facing away from Finara, and clicked her prosthesis back on.

Her mind raced. If the goddess had looked through the techpad, she would have seen Grace's files, those old Webcasts, possibly even the one that —

'I want to take you to dinner,' Finara declared.

'We just met,' Grace reminded her. 'I don't know you well enough to have dinner with you, let alone allow you to do *indecent* things to me.'

'That's what the dinner's for, to get to know me,' Finara persisted.

Grace looked at the door. She wasn't sure if she should make a run for it or try ordering the goddess to leave.

Finara sighed. 'You don't have to order me. You can just ask.'

'So you can read my mind.'

'Surface thoughts, mostly. I can go in deeper if I want, but it takes effort.'

'Can all sub-level gods do this?' Grace asked before she could stop herself. She shook her head, annoyed. She wasn't a mediaist anymore, she wasn't curious, she was just...

'No,' Finara answered, continuing to watch Grace with those fascinating flame-filled eyes. 'Some of my brothers and sisters can; some can't. Others are more powerful and have abilities like telekinesis and healing. Oh — and each of us has special individual powers that help us look after our assigned domains.'

Grace felt her palms itch from the need to grab her techpad and write down everything Finara was telling her. She crossed her arms, restraining the urge. 'You shouldn't be telling me this. I'm a mortal.'

'And here I thought you were a mediaist,' Finara said.

Grace flinched, a hand clasped to the bulge the techpad was making in her pocket.

'Relax, I didn't rifle through your things,' Finara assured her. 'I didn't have time. But some of your Webcasts were flitting through your thoughts. You remember all of them — word for word. That must be handy. Well, don't you want to interview me? Get a scoop? Gain viewers?'

'I did not come here to revive my career,' Grace snapped.

'Then why did you come here, Ms Has-Been Mediaist?'

Grace feared the goddess had already seen it in her mind.

Finara shook her head. 'No, you're keeping that one pretty close to your chest.'

'I came here to die,' Grace told her. The next part was harder to say, for some undefinable reason. 'Now get out. I don't want to see you again.'

Grace didn't dare look at the goddess' face as it dissolved into flames.

***

As soon as the fiery vortex that had transported Finara to her destination fell away, the rainforest began assaulting her with cloying humidity. Grimacing, Finara strode down the path leading from the waterfall, where her brother always insisted she appear so he'd have some warning of her arrival, to the hidden abode belonging to the Rforine, the rainforest god. This world, Bagaran, was famous for having been the battleground of the first and last conflict between the Chippers and a sub-level god.

Since then, Kuja had managed to establish peace with GLEA — with the assistance of one Head General Zareth Sins, who was actually the former lover of the Rforine's wife. Kuja had married Fei without telling her about his godhood and had begged Finara to help him hide his true identity. Fei had been justifiably pissed off when she'd found out what Kuja had been keeping from her (especially since he'd neglected to mention the fact that he'd made her immortal), but now she and Kuja shared a happy existence with their son, Micadei.

And Fei's mortal mother, Berale Neron.

Berale stood at the entrance to the rainforest god's residence, which seemed bigger than when Finara had last seen it, but she didn't find this surprising. The hovel grew whenever extra space was required — the rainforest was always eager to help their god with his needs.

Eyeing the Firine, Berale said, 'You just couldn't help yourself. Had to go on the Webcasts and show off to the entire galaxy, didn't you.'

Finara snorted and waved a hand towards the sky, where a GLEA vessel had once orbited, its weapons trained on the defenceless planet. 'At least I didn't almost start a war with the Chippers. Come on — hurry up and hug me before I change my mind.'

The mortal obliged her. Berale's hair, shot through with grey, indicated that she was ageing, that she would die sooner rather than later, her blood and bones feeding the rainforest. Finara did not understand why the woman was at peace with this. Thanks to Kuja, Berale's daughter and grandson would live eternally. They'd probably forget Berale, given enough time.

Finara had continued to visit Kuja in the hopes that she would learn how to make her followers love her, the way Kuja's loved him. Though this had yet to work, Finara enjoyed the company of her brother's family. There was something comforting about having somewhere she could retreat to, somewhere she didn't have to be a god.

'I need you to answer a question for me,' Finara said, carefully extracting herself from Berale's embrace.

'No time for pleasantries, as usual,' Berale noted, hands dropping onto her ample hips.

'Why would a mortal want to die?' Finara rushed out.

Berale stared at the goddess, then laughed and stood side on, opening up a space between herself and the doorway. 'That's a serious question! Come on in, dear. You look like you need a good feed.'

'You know we sub-level gods don't actually need to eat anything,' Finara reminded her.

'I spent a good two hours making this particular dish, so you will eat it and tell me it's the most wonderful thing you have ever tasted in all your centuries,' Berale said, her voice stern. The grin belied her threat.

Finara smirked in response. 'I can *tell* you anything you want to hear. You're the one who has to pretend I mean what I say.'

***

The eating area was larger than most spaces in Kuja's hovel and one of the walls was more window than it was wood, offering an uninterrupted view of the nearby waterfall. Finara suppressed a shudder at the encompassing *greenness* of her brother's domain, then turned back to her audience, which consisted of Berale, Kuja, Fei and Micadei (who was in his mother's lap). Finara had just finished explaining her encounter with Grace. Her bowl lay untouched on the low table. So far Berale had not rebuked Finara for this transgression, but it was only a matter of time.

'What did you say her name was?' Fei asked. She sealed her hands over Micadei's when he clapped too exuberantly, causing vines to shoot out of the floor. He was definitely his father's son

— and he was also why Kuja and Fei had needed to move out here, in case the mortals in the village where they had first lived became too suspicious.

'Because I can ask Ton Tinel if he knows anything about her,' Fei continued. 'He keeps an eye on any up-and-coming mediaists he thinks might challenge him and poach his viewership.'

A frown was steadily growing on Kuja's face. 'I am not sure why you're so concerned about this woman, Finara. You usually don't spend more than one night with someone.'

Finara rolled her eyes. 'Kuja, bro, this isn't undying love or anything stupid like that. She's an attractive woman, isn't as annoying as most humans, and I've decided that I want her, if she's any good at her job, to tell my story to the galaxy.'

'You do not want that much attention,' Kuja warned her. 'Ever since the mediaists started mentioning me in their Webcasts, I've had to struggle to keep up with everyone who needs my help.'

'That's your fault for proclaiming yourself the god of casualties and lost causes,' Finara told him with a snort. 'And you let everyone know you'd listen to them, no matter their faith — no wonder you're struggling!'

Fei laid a hand on her husband's arm. 'Kuja, it's her choice how she runs her domain and how she looks after her people. You said you'd help her with this, remember?'

Kuja dropped back down onto the earth-packed floor and re-crossed his legs. He didn't seem to have realised that he'd been clambering to his feet until his wife had spoken to him.

'Well? Any ideas?' Finara demanded, glowering at each of them in turn — even Micadei, though her nephew just grinned at her in response. 'Why would someone want to die? Mortals usually have a deep-rooted sense of entitlement. They think they're owed everything, including life.'

'Finara, why do you think I don't want to be immortal?' Berale asked, brown eyes gentle.

Finara shrugged. 'Because you don't want to have to put up with me forever?'

Berale chuckled and shook her head. 'No, dear. Eternity is an unbearably long amount of time. I'd rather die before things got too boring.'

'Life isn't boring if you're doing it right,' Finara shot back.

Fei hummed to herself as she began swiping her fingers over the screen of her techpad. After a few moments, the device pinged and everyone looked expectantly at the rainforest god's wife.

'Ton Tinel responded,' Fei announced.

'Already?' Kuja asked, lines creasing his forehead. 'Is he being this helpful because he thinks he might get to speak me directly?'

Fei smiled sideways at him. 'Don't worry, Kuja, Ton doesn't know who you are — he doesn't even know I'm married! He just feels that he owes me for some of his good fortune. Ever since he covered the talks on Yalsa 5, he's become even more wealthy and famous. If that's possible.'

Holding in a growl of frustration, Finara marched over and snatched the techpad out of her sister-in-law's hands. She immediately opened the vid attached to Ton Tinel's message; it was a Webcast, featuring a very familiar mediaist.

'...the escalating tension between the factions on Eransia has resulted in all-out war today,' Grace Pendergast said, dressed in a high-waisted pantsuit. The scar across her left eyebrow was missing and she stood taller, prouder, though Finara suspected this wasn't just because she had yet to wear a prosthetic leg.

Behind Grace, in a valley, sat a semi-spherical forcefield that shimmered unsteadily, clearly in danger of collapsing at any moment. Most mediaists reported from the safety of their starships in orbit. Grace was actually on the frontline.

'While the Loyalists have refused to talk to me regarding the future of the planet, the so-called Freedomists have agreed to meet with me and list their demands...' Grace looked skyward. 'What? What's happening?'

Static abruptly washed over the techpad, but not before the mediaist began to scream.

Finara swallowed. 'That's when she lost the leg.'

'There's more,' Fei said, leaning over to yank the techpad back from Finara's limp grasp. 'Ton says that Grace was small-time, trying to attract the attention of wealthy sponsors. She went planetside to get exclusive interviews, in an attempt to drum up more viewers, but in doing so she revealed the location of the Freedomists. The Loyalists attacked them the moment they saw her Webcast. As you probably saw, the shield could not take that kind of bombardment.'

'Oh, that poor woman,' Berale murmured.

'Mediaists are supposed to report the news, not make it,' Fei went on grimly. 'Ton says he lambasted her for it in one of his Webcasts. He regrets it now because she's fallen off everyone's radar. He actually looked into her to make sure she was okay, but no one knows where she went after she emptied her bank account two Old Earth weeks ago.'

Silence reigned for several long moments, broken only when Micadei bounced in Fei's lap and exclaimed, 'Aunty Finfin! No frown!'

Finara knelt beside her nephew and met his emerald stare,

twisting her lips until they formed the angle she was aiming for. 'There. Big, big grin. Better?'

Micadei's face wrinkled up. Evidently she'd failed to impress him.

'Finara, you don't need to do this to yourself, she's not one of your people,' Kuja said quietly.

Finara flung a scowl at him, ignoring Micadei's renewed complaints. 'You listen to the millions who've started calling your name — and I bet most of them aren't even in your domain. And anyway, I'm not going to talk her out of her plan, shitty though it is. I have something else in mind.'

***

The sun, filtered through the hotel's forcefield, did very little to darken her complexion. Grace was not prone to sunburn, but it was nice for the warmth on her skin to feel more like a caress than a continuous stream of lasbolts.

She had forgone the jacket of her suit today and had rolled the pants up to her thighs. A FizzWhizz, the neon-pink drink that was the hotel's speciality, sat on the table beside her, a little too sweet but potent enough to dull the steady ache inside her. Occasionally water from the pool splashed up onto her slick black heels, the unruly waves sent by children who had been unleashed by their parents.

The hotel had filled up over the past day or so, the latest bookings no doubt fuelled by the appearance of the fire goddess. Grace had even spotted a cluster of purple-clad GLEA agents. She wasn't surprised that the Chippers had arrived; they had been trying to make peace with the galaxy's array of sub-level gods for

22

the past three years, though it was difficult for them to find any gods, let alone speak to them. The fire goddess would be a top priority now.

A shadow fell over Grace, blocking her sunlight.

'I have a scoop for you, Ms Pendergast,' Finara's voice declared.

Grace opened her eyes. 'Ms Fire Goddess. You should extend your offer to one of the other mediaists in attendance. Or you could talk to the Chippers — they're even more desperate than the mediaists. I heard they're even offering a monetary reward to anyone who can set up a meeting with you. They don't drop their coin-chips for just anyone. I'd feel flattered if I was you.'

'I want to talk to *you*,' Finara said, dropping into the closest deckchair.

'I don't have time for this,' Grace told her. 'I'm killing myself in six days.'

'But don't you want to have one last big story, and all the notoriety that goes with it, before you die?' Finara baited.

Grace gave her a baleful look. Finara was yet again clad in one of her revealing dancing outfits. It was very hard for Grace to keep her eyes on the goddess' face. 'I just want to relax and enjoy the rest of my time here. I have no unfinished business.'

'Then why were you at a speed dating event? Hoping for one last fling before you take on a volcano?'

'It's not important,' Grace said.

'Ha, I disagree, your mind just got all churned up.' Finara leaned over to swipe Grace's drink from the table. She knocked it back in one gulp. 'Eugh. Filth. How can anyone get drunk on that?'

Heads were now turning in their direction, eyes wide and

mouths agape. The whispers had started and countless fingers were being pointed. The fire goddess waved at a few of the interested parties and loudly offered to sign autographs, but no one seemed to want to take her up on the offer.

'I'm not going to kill any of you,' Finara assured them, still waving. 'That would defeat the purpose of trying to gain new followers, wouldn't it?'

Grace grabbed her arm and held it still. 'If you want to give a mediaist an exclusive, you shouldn't be saying so much in public.'

'Then let me give you an exclusive,' Finara said.

'Not happening. Forget it.'

The goddess pursed her lips for a moment, then grinned. 'I won't let you kill yourself until you do this for me. I can stop anything the volcano spits out before it touches you.'

'There are other ways I can end my life!' Grace hissed. She realised that she hadn't let go of Finara's arm and hastily did so.

'I can stop you doing those too,' Finara told her. 'I'll just teleport you into a padded room.'

'You are manipulating me.'

Finara winked at Grace. 'Yes, I am. And hey, I'll even let you get something out of the deal. It's clear you want a fling, right?'

'I'm a virgin,' Grace told her calmly. There was no point pretending it wasn't on her mind. The goddess, with her abilities, would have seen it eventually.

Understanding lit the goddess' face. 'Ah! There we go. Your unfinished business. I'll help you with that, make your name great like you were trying to do on Eransia before your leg got blown off, and then let you die. Easy.'

'Easy,' Grace repeated. 'Do you know what really eats me up about Eransia?'

The goddess didn't miss a beat. 'Yeah, giving away the position of the people who trusted you enough to give you full access. That'd eat me up too, if I was mortal. At least, I think it would.'

Grace firmly rubbed her forehead, but the headache remained. 'Is nothing safe in my mind? You are encroaching on my privacy. But no! It's not just that. Eransia wasn't the first time that people died because of — '

Another set of shadows fell over Grace. She looked up at the handful of Chippers who had crept over to the deckchairs; they were viewing Finara with a mixture of fear and respect.

'Goddess of fire?' one of GLEA's agents hazarded. '"Firine" being your official title?'

'Correct, that's me,' Finara replied.

The Chipper in charge (he had many more gold strokes on the shoulders of his purple jumpsuit than his companions did) cleared his throat. 'We have been sent by Head General Zareth Sins to open up a dialogue of peace with you.'

Finara's fiery gaze slowly raked over Grace's form. 'Sure, if you don't mind doing it front of my mediaist here. This is Grace Pendergast and I'll be signing an exclusive with her.'

It took the Chipper barely half a second to respond.

'We agree to your terms,' he said.

Grace glanced away, suddenly feeling very self-conscious. She threw a towel over her legs, concealing the prosthesis. She wanted to ignore all of these uninvited guests or, better yet, demand that they leave her alone. But another part of her was desperate to see if she could prove that she was as good as, if not better than, Ton Tinel. This was the kind of exclusive he'd kill for.

Six days, she thought.

The story of a lifetime.

A goddess has offered to have sex with me.

'It seems I have an exclusive,' Grace finally said.

A grin exploded over Finara's face. 'Excellent. We'll begin right now.' She fluttered a dismissive hand at the Chippers. 'Come back tomorrow.'

Ribbons of fire swept up from the ground and swirled around both Grace and Finara, encasing them. Grace held her breath, sealed her eyes shut and then laughed hysterically when she found herself still sitting in the deckchair — except she was now high above the hotel, near the lip of one of the nearby volcanoes.

Finara glanced over, a hint of hazel appearing in her eyes for the briefest of moments. 'Are you okay?'

Grace didn't know how to put it into words. She'd been afraid of the flames, afraid they'd heralded her premature death, afraid that she wouldn't get to finish this task before her six days were up. Unable to reply, she instead chose to demand a vidcam which appeared in a similar vortex.

Once she got over her astonishment that the device wasn't burnt to a crisp, Grace got to work.

CHAPTER THREE

When evening fell on the western hemisphere of Arksaw, Finara took Grace to dinner. The other patrons in the hotel's restaurant gave them a wide berth; Grace amused herself by wondering if they did this because Finara was a goddess and they wished to show their respect, or because they were worried Finara would suddenly incinerate the closest patrons.

Mediaists had been banned from the restaurant and diners were being searched upon entry for vidcams to ensure they did not record any unauthorised footage. Grace had even heard a rumour that Ton Tinel himself had attempted to bribe his way in, but with no success.

'So the superstition that suicide angers the Creator God and causes him to refuse us entry into the afterlife...?' Grace prompted.

'Completely false,' Finara replied. 'Dead's dead, no matter which way you do it. The Ine — uh, the Creator God treats all of his mortal children equally.'

'And you can't die, correct?'

Finara frowned for a moment. 'Well, not of old age. Us gods could kill each other if we were in the mood, but so far it hasn't happened.'

'What about sex?'

'What about it?' Finara mocked, grinning right at Grace's

vidcam, which was hovering beside the table. 'Yeah, we do it. The lucky mortals don't even know what they've had.'

Grace swallowed. 'You've done it a lot?'

'Don't worry, I'll go easy on you. Or rough, if you prefer...'

'Can you procreate?' Grace interrupted. Finara's voice was low whenever she spoke of sex and it always caused something to vibrate deep inside Grace. This wasn't an unwelcome sensation, but it was distracting.

Finara paused, then performed an elaborate shrug. 'I don't know. Not sure. I guess we could always try merging DNA at one of those clinics. You know, like any normal couple does when they can't reproduce on their own.'

Grace turned off her vidcam and caught it before it hit the floor. She set the device down on the table but had to quickly move it when a team of waiters brought out some sort of sea creature. Finara retched quietly but made no other comment, so the waiters scurried off once the platter was delivered, apparently not noticing the goddess' displeasure.

'You *are* sure and you *do* know,' Grace said firmly. She was only guessing, but she had a feeling she was right. 'I'm not recording at the moment, so you can tell me what you won't say to the vidcam.'

'I don't want to mess things up for my nephews,' Finara said as she poked the engorged fish on the platter with her fork. 'I don't think the galaxy's supposed to know about them, especially the one who's — no.' She shook her head. 'I won't throw those kids into the path of some galactic shitstorm. They don't deserve that.'

'Do you want your own child one day?' Grace asked.

'Stark yes. I didn't always want kids, but when my brother...'

Finara trailed off. 'Nope, never going to happen. No one's keen on the whole eternity thing.'

Grace arranged her cutlery neatly on the table. 'But you don't need a permanent partner. You could fall pregnant and not tell the father.'

'That's a shitty thing to do,' Finara snapped. When multiple pairs of eyes flicked towards her in alarm, she twisted her lips into a smile. 'I practice safe sex. Forgetting to use caution is what got not one, but *two* of my brothers into trouble.'

'At least we won't need to worry about that tonight,' Grace murmured.

Finara's hands found Grace's on the table. The goddess' touch verged on being too warm, but it was also oddly tender. 'Can I ask you a question?'

'Alright,' Grace replied, unable to think of any reason to pull away from her.

'So I don't get it,' Finara said. 'How can getting a bunch of people killed and losing your leg make you want to die?'

'How can you call yourself a god when you'd rather dance at a resort than look after your domain?' Grace retorted, deflecting her. This time she did manage to yank her hands back to her side of the table. 'Your powers don't make you worthy of our worship. They make you *responsible* for us.'

Finara's forehead creased. 'I love fire. Dancing in it, losing myself in the flames...it's wonderful. Even a god deserves downtime because there's a starking lot of mortals to look after. You're all so exhausting, you know that? There's always some problem I have to deal with. So I dance when I can. And I have a lot of sex. That's fun. I don't want to just live, Grace — I want to *enjoy* living. Like you mortals do.'

'I don't enjoy living and I don't deserve to,' Grace said quietly. 'All I ever wanted was to become a mediaist. Because a mediaist gives a voice to the powerless. A mediaist helps people and sheds light on those who would prefer to conduct their activities in the shadows.'

Grace dropped her hand to her right thigh. 'I lost more than part of a limb. I lost all respectability. Mediaists have to stand in front of a vidcam; text reporting hasn't been popular for centuries. People want an aesthetically pleasing person on their vidscreens, not someone who can barely afford a prosthesis.'

'I'd see the leg as proof that you'd do anything to get to the truth,' Finara said.

'It's more than that! It's a reminder to everyone, a reminder of what I did to those people. That I lived, when I should have died along with them.' Grace stared down at the table, finding her fists anchored there. Her fingers ached. 'I should never have shown the forcefield on my vidcam. Or the valley. The Creator God made a mistake in letting me live. So I'm going to rectify it.'

'I could ask him if you were supposed to die that day,' Finara offered. 'If you'd like.'

Grace stared at her, aghast. 'No! No one should question our Creator's grand design.'

'But you just said he made a mistake.'

Unable to muster a response, Grace stayed stubbornly silent until the seafood platter was replaced with a mountainous dessert. Finara lit up upon seeing the 'volcano' cake that oozed molten chocolate from its summit. Grace watched, amused, as the goddess took apart the dessert with relish. Finara had told her that gods did not need to consume food to survive but clearly they could still enjoy it.

'Do you get periods?' Grace asked suddenly.

Finara set down her spoon. She looked irritable. 'Yes. Every Old Earth month. I've had more periods than any human.'

'And yet you are happy to live forever.'

Finara winked. 'I don't have a period now, if that's what's worrying you.'

Grace laced her fingers over her lap to keep them from trembling. 'I'm scared. Should I really be having sex with a stranger just to satisfy my own curiosity?'

'You should figure out the answer to that before we do anything,' Finara told her. 'I can easily amuse myself elsewhere. Like the Enocian Harem. What a place.'

'No,' Grace said firmly. 'You gave me an exclusive, Ms Fire Goddess.'

Finara smiled and the flames in her eyes faded, leaving them entirely hazel.

***

Finara watched with increasing impatience as Grace hung up her pantsuit, aligning it just so on the hanger. The mortal then moved restlessly through the room and adjusted the lighting no fewer than five times, apparently incapable of acknowledging her companion. Finara lay on the bed, already nude. Bored, she began to play with her nipples, pinching them until they sat upright. When Grace's gaze finally skirted towards her, Finara ordered, 'Come here.'

Grace sat on the edge of the bed, carefully lowering her prosthesis to the floor without bending over; she had a towel wound tightly around her body. 'This isn't fair. No other mortal has ever had to contend with the knowledge that they are sleeping with a god.'

Finara snickered. 'My brothers' wives would disagree with you.'

Grace remained very still.

The Firine sensed her hesitance, her reluctance. This was something that Grace had always wanted but had never known how to take; to her it was as unattainable as the label of 'wealthy respected mediaist'. Being suddenly confronted with the opportunity to have sex was hard for her.

Finara quashed her raging desire and said, 'Hey, we don't have to do this. We can just cuddle if you like.'

Grace's shoulders slumped. 'Doesn't that defeat the purpose of shedding our clothes?'

'Not if I get to see and feel you in all your glory,' Finara told her with a grin.

Grace visibly steeled herself, then pulled the towel away from her skin. After some gentle coaxing, Grace moved onto her side and allowed the goddess to spoon her from behind. Finara drew the sheet over both of them then lay her hand on Grace's abdomen, her other arm sliding beneath Grace's pillow. When she pressed her wet desire against Grace, she heard the mortal's sharp intake of breath, felt the shiver run through her. Finara's fingers trailed down a soft thigh, hidden from view but revealed beneath her touch.

'Can we...start and see if I'm willing to go further?' Grace whispered.

'Sounds good to me,' Finara agreed. 'Just relax.'

Easier said than done, she thought. Grace was stiff beneath her ministrations, but the mortal's thighs clenched in anticipation whenever Finara's touch skated over the wiry hair at the apex of her legs. Disturbed by Grace's thoughts, which were filled with shame whenever the goddess' fingers came too close to the stump of her right leg, Finara swept a hand over Grace's ample backside, curving her palm against each cheek and making soft noises of approval as she went.

'Stark, you're beautiful,' Finara murmured.

Grace arched against her, as though stretching, then abruptly grew lax and soft. Encouraged, Finara rolled Grace onto her back, then leaned over and kissed the mortal softly, sweetly. Though Grace kept her lips sealed, her eyes were wide and dark with lust.

Finara braced one hand against the bed, the other dancing along Grace's side before it grasped the mortal's thigh, firm and possessive. Finara lowered her mouth — she kept her gaze on Grace's — then flicked her tongue backwards and forwards across a dark nipple. There was nothing complicated about what Finara was doing, but a light touch done consistently could drive anyone to the edge. And she sensed that it wouldn't take long...

The mortal's stubborn lips parted, releasing a gasp.

Finara licked her way up to Grace's throat, then over to her ear. 'This is how I like it done to me. So take notes. Now, before I get any lower — and I will — let me know if you're comfortable with this.'

'Put me out of my misery,' Grace moaned.

'Not for six more days,' Finara whispered right before she captured a vulnerable earlobe between her teeth.

'That's not what I meant!' Grace cried, indignation swelling alongside desire in her mind.

Finara grinned. She knew exactly what Grace had meant, what she wanted. As for the Firine...she wanted, even if only for one night, to erase all dark thoughts from Grace's mind and instead fill it with pleasure.

Grace clamped a hand down over the one Finara had left on her thigh, trying to shift it higher. 'Please. I want this. I need this. *Please*, give this to me.'

Finara flashed her a mischievous smile. 'Don't worry. I promised you an exclusive. I intend to deliver.'

***

The goddess' lips left what felt like trails of fire down her stomach, which Grace would not have been surprised to actually see. Grace tilted her head back, staring up at the ceiling and clenching the sheet beneath her, hard enough to tear. The anxiety that had lined her stomach had vanished, leaving room only for excitement. When lips caressed the skin beside her hip, so gentle and tender, she gasped and looked down at the goddess. Finara's eyes, peering back at her, were filled with flames — and something much more potent.

Finara ran a quick finger down the moistening crease between Grace's thighs. Grace whimpered, somehow unable to feel embarrassed by the sounds she was making. Smirking, Finara stroked the very edges of Grace's core, a teasing touch that failed to firm, her fingers drifting over more hair than skin. Grace twisted to the side, begging, thrusting forward. But Finara continued to deftly avoid Grace's most sensitive areas.

At last, when Grace thought she could stand it no more, she felt Finara's fingers pressing into both sides of her labia — and then they pulled her apart, spreading her open for the goddess' gaze. There was a very human hunger on that ageless face. Grace's abdomen gave an impatient clench.

With agonising slowness, Finara extended her tongue and bent forward to graze it over the sensitive nub before her.

'Ah!' Grace cried and attempted to grind against Finara's mouth.

The goddess held her down, hands grasping Grace's hips. 'None of that, Ms Lucky Mediaist. I'm going to have you and I'm going to take my time about it. You'll just have to suffer.'

'Oh *God*,' Grace managed.

Finara tsked, running her fingers up Grace's folds. They met in the middle, rising, rising — then darted away before they could touch Grace's aching clitoris. 'Try again.'

Grace writhed. 'Please, please.'

'Not until you correct yourself.'

'Fine — oh *goddess*!' Grace exclaimed.

Finara wrapped her lips around Grace's swollen nub, suckling lightly, oh so lightly, but it was enough to send bolts of lightning coursing through Grace's unprepared body, bolts that seared her skin and slammed into every finger and toe.

Grace arched her back. She couldn't see. Her eyes refused to open.

So close, she was so close, and they'd barely begun —

Finara's mouth abandoned her.

Grace cried out.

When she felt Finara's weight shift on the bed, Grace frowned down at the goddess who was now propping herself up with an elbow. Finara arched one fine brunette eyebrow; it didn't match her dark hair and Grace wondered why she had not noticed before. With calculated languor, Finara licked the pads of her fingers before pressing them to her own nipples, sighing in pleasure as she began to work the moisture in.

Grace's clitoris gave an insistent throb.

'I'm considering taking my pleasure from you first,' Finara declared.

Grace's eyelashes fluttered as she pictured what the goddess would do to achieve that goal. Perhaps she'd sit astride Grace's face, her slick lips delivering a kiss far more intimate than any Grace had ever experienced. Perhaps the goddess would demand more than one release before she was willing to let Grace finally tumble over the edge.

'Mmm, you have a good imagination,' Finara said.

'You saw that.' A statement, not a question. Then Grace rushed out, 'Do you want to sit on my face?'

Finara's chuckle was low, sensual. 'I've got my own unfinished business, mortal.'

'Then get on with it!' Grace told her.

'Oh, I intend to.'

Her grin wide and wicked, the fire goddess gave her full attention to Grace once more. She alternated between licking Grace's nub and sucking it, somehow knowing just the right rhythm to use to push her lover closer to climax. Grace was already preparing to succumb when a firm finger eased its way inside her — and pressed.

Pleasure stabbed into Grace, sudden and overwhelming and impossible to resist. She pushed down hard, clenching and firmly capturing Finara's finger. Grace's entire being was reduced to the sensations exploding between her thighs and she felt like she might die from the intensity of her orgasm, but she didn't care. She would gladly die in rapture than in the path of some volcano.

After a glorious eternity, Finara's finger slipped out of her and swirled around her clitoris, eliciting an unbearable spasm.

Grace sobbed and squirmed. 'It's too much. It's too much.'

Finara released her.

Dimly, Grace was aware of the goddess rolling her back onto her side. They lay there together for a time, locked in an embrace, the room's climate-controlled air frigid against their heated skin. When Grace finally regained her senses, she took Finara's hand from her hip and brought one digit up to her mouth. Grace hesitated, wondering if she should go ahead with this ridiculous idea of hers, but then she dismissed her doubts and suckled her way from the tip of Finara's finger down to the first knuckle.

There was a soft sound in Finara's throat.

Grace moved onto another finger, and then onto the next. By the time she got to Finara's thumb, it seemed the goddess had had enough of being teased.

Finara grabbed the sheet, whirled it into a single white tentacle, then lashed it around Grace's wrists, binding her to the headboard. Grace barely had time to blink before Finara claimed her lips with a deep, demanding kiss.

Finara then spread her legs, knees either side of Grace's head, a glint in her eyes.

'Worship me,' Finara ordered. 'Slide your tongue inside me and make me moan.'

Grace obeyed, drinking in the nectar of her goddess.

CHAPTER FOUR

The mortal was splayed across the bed, sheet twisted around her naked form but doing little to cover it. Grinning, Finara stood and slipped into her clothes, then vanished inside a maelstrom of fire. Within moments, she landed on a different planet entirely, but the image of Grace dozing, legs parted just enough to offer a glimpse of the mortal's glistening brown folds, followed her. It was distracting. And unprecedented. Finara never thought twice about her lovers.

Annoyed, Finara perched on a slate-grey boulder, forcing herself to focus on the small town beneath her. Children woke and pestered their parents, older folk sat and admired the clear emerald sky, and those that could still bend their backs began to head towards their azure fields. But their animals were silent, watchful, tense. Some of the cattle, good stock descended from those that had lived on Old Earth, even broke their bonds and had to be chased down.

Finara felt the nearby volcano stirring, disturbed by tectonic plates that refused to settle. In mere days, the picturesque mountain stretching into the sky would explode, its peak smashed into a crater.

These settlers had journeyed across the stars with just enough supplies to become self-sufficient. But they lacked complicated sensing equipment — and had begun to think they didn't need it. The volcano had been quiet for the three generations they had spent here; it was part of the unchanging scenery, a feature in some of the artwork they had begun to export off-world. Their planet was making discreet seismic rumblings beneath the soil, but none of the villagers were aware, because they couldn't see or hear anything. Not yet.

They had an elaborate golden shrine dedicated to the fire goddess standing in the centre of their village. It was for show, because none of them ever bothered to worship her or even thought of her when they passed the shrine. They believed its mere presence could protect them.

'Stupid entitled mortals,' Finara said, shaking her head.

She knew that once the eruption started, they'd cry out for her instead of moving out of the way — and she'd feel compelled to save them. Older mortals she could ridicule and ignore until the last moment, but not children. They didn't deserve to die because of a decision they hadn't made. They deserved the chance to grow up and make their own stupid decisions.

In a few days, they and their parents would watch in amazed relief as molten rock flowed miraculously around their village, leaving it unscathed. After the lava had cooled, they would forget their need for the fire goddess and go back to their short, useless lives.

This bullshit was why Finara had enlisted the services of a mediaist. Some mortals acknowledged what she did for them, even if they didn't worship her, but there were others who didn't know they owed their continued existence to the Firine.

She didn't want the mortals to fear her. She wanted them to *love* her. To be *thankful*. To care about her as much as she cared about them.

Finara sneezed. Her nose picked up a salty scent, one that

was completely out of place on this ocean-less world. She sprang out of her crouch and turned towards the intruder, spurts of fire erupting from her palms. A threat for now, but the flames could easily become weapons.

Her brother stood there on the shivering grass below her boulder, garbed in tattered cloths and a cloak woven from rotting seaweed. This was Fayay, the Watine, the god of water. He offered her a carefully crafted sneer, one that was too upturned for her liking. He was going to enjoy himself, whatever he'd planned to do or say.

'Are you finally going to teach the mortals a lesson?' he hissed, his dank hair flattened to the sides of his face.

'No way, bro,' Finara said, erasing her grimace with a strained laugh. If Fayay was displeased with his followers, he sent a tsunami or some other disaster to destroy entire settlements. She wasn't sure why the Ine allowed it. 'I'm not punishing them. It's bad for my image. I've got mediaists watching my every move now.'

The Watine frowned.

'Yeah, you *should* be worried that they'll start recording your antics,' Finara said in response to what she saw in his mind. She chuckled. 'You're not just worried. You're actually afraid, aren't you, brother?'

'I can destroy you,' Fayay growled.

'You couldn't even destroy Kuja, our *youngest* brother. What makes you think you can touch me?'

Fayay's thin lips curved into a smirk. 'I can fight you and distract you long enough that these people will be destroyed when that volcano erupts. Will you be able to save them when you're too busy saving yourself?'

Finara kept silent for a moment, then burst out, 'What the *fuck* is your deal, Fayay?'

He blinked, his mouth slightly ajar.

'First you get jealous because Sandsa falls in love, so you threaten his family,' Finara said, straightening her index finger. She flicked up her middle finger to join it. 'Then you start sulking because Kuja was brave enough to challenge Father over the right to be with Fei — and it's not just Kuja that's allowed to know love, you idiot, we *all* are. So what now? I'm getting too much attention from the mortals and you can't handle the thought of your followers deciding to worship me instead?'

Finara expected the ball of water that Fayay sent her way. It disintegrated against her answering streak of fire, then misted away on the breeze. He lashed out again and again, but she parried every blow. Finara could see into his mind. She saw each move before he made it. She had an advantage.

But he had one too.

Fayay had been gifted with telekinesis, an ability that was much stronger than anything the Chippers had. Fayay could move anything, no matter how heavy, no matter how large. And Finara hadn't realised just *what* he'd been moving, because he'd kept his thoughts on one thing while doing another.

The starship drifting into position overhead was as large as one of the more generous wings of the hotel Finara had left earlier. The settlers here didn't have the sleek, small vessels that populated the richer parts of the galaxy — this was an ancient herdship, designed to move people and supplies. Its fuel cells had probably been drained dry in the last century, leaving the ship to languish on the dirt where it had landed. But today the outdated vessel had been yanked, as swiftly and as violently as an uprooted a plant, into the sky. And now it was hurtling back towards to the ground.

Finara teleported away just as the immense hulk crashed down on top of her.

When she strode out of the fiery vortex that had deposited her some distance away, she could hear panicked shouting coming from the village. She looked around to find Fayay beside her, his grin cruel and cold. He lifted his hands in a simple, synchronised gesture. The battered herdship rose back into the air, then began to hover right over the cluster of buildings that formed the village. If Finara attacked her brother now, he might lose control. The ship would fall like a stone.

'I will flatten these pathetic creatures,' Fayay told her.

Finara's tongue swiped around her mouth, moistening it. 'Unless I do what? Stop talking to the mediaists? Stop making you look bad?'

Fayay tipped his head to the side. 'You should never have done so in the first place.'

The fury churning inside Finara's stomach flooded southward, through fragile crust and flimsy mantle and then into molten core. Above them, the volcano woke too early, belching dark smoke. It had only needed a minute push.

'Shit!' Finara said.

Fayay swung a crazed look at her. He feared fire the same way she feared water. Grimly, Finara shoved aside her guilt, vowing to berate herself later for the turbulent emotions that had endangered the mortals, then forced unwavering glee into her voice as the ground shook. 'I could force a hotspot into being beneath our very feet, Fayay. Would you care to stand still long enough for me to blast your skin from your bones?'

Fayay took a whole step back, openly disconcerted.

And then he noticed what she'd be doing while *he'd* been distracted.

She had spent the last few minutes furiously turning the ship into slag, melting it as fast as a block of butter hurled into flames. Smaller, less dangerous chunks were already dropping out of the sky. The mortals were not so stupid that they didn't start running away from the deadly hail. Fayay abruptly changed tactics and tried to heave what was left of the ship onto their position instead of on the village.

Finara again used a vortex to move out of range. When her brother reappeared nearby, Finara charged right at him, a whip of fire leaping out of her hands. It lashed his cheek, bubbling and scarring the skin.

'You won't be here to save them all the time!' the Watine snarled.

A swirl of water encased Finara, smothering her and tossing her into the middle of an ocean on some distant world. Though the surface of the water glinted a mere arm's length above her, she couldn't reach it, her limbs locked in place by massive tidal forces. She couldn't breathe. She couldn't even teleport; the water was suppressing her fire abilities. This never happened in the rainforests, in the deserts or in any of the other domains belonging to her brothers and sisters. Their minions left her well alone.

I promised Grace an exclusive, she thought. *I can't die now!*

Finara's tormented scream erupted as bubbles and she lashed out with her legs, with all her might, until she was able to kick her way to the surface. Once there, Finara managed to ignite enough fire to teleport herself away. She landed on her hands and knees mere seconds later, gasping for air, cursing, her arms shaking violently. But her full recovery would have to wait.

The Firine hurtled to her feet and ran to the front of the village. Fortunately, the initial pyroclastic blast had slammed down the other side of the volcano, sparing the mortals that at least, but streams of lava were heading towards them, racing rather than flowing. There was no time for them to run. And some of them were too stubborn to have fled anyway.

Finara threw up her hands and funnelled the deadly red torrents around her, acting like the fork in a river. Nearby trees and grasses caught fire from the proximity of the lava, but she doused those by speeding up the burning process, turning the natural fuel black within moments.

The volcano eventually quietened, its tantrum finished. For now.

Finara sagged, sighing deeply, then turned around to see the villagers watching her, their mouths hanging open. She stared at them, confused. She'd completely forgotten they were there.

'You saved us!' one of the mortals exclaimed, aiming a vidcam at her.

Finara bowed dramatically, arms flung out either side of her body, relieved when the tremors that threatened didn't surface. 'Just so you know, I'm always around. Even if you can't see me. I have to make sure your butts don't get burnt off, don't I? Sorry about the herdship. Uh, I can't explain, but I had to shred it.'

The villagers fell to their knees, praising her, promising that they would never forget the goddess who watched over them.

'Much better,' Finara said, smiling.

CHAPTER FIVE

'You're saying that the sub-level gods are constantly at war with each other and we mortals have no choice but to become collateral damage?' Grace asked, looking up from the techpad resting on the table of their booth.

They were enjoying breakfast together and talking over cups of blistering strong coffein. Neither of them had mentioned the previous night so far and Grace tried to keep it from replaying in her mind, in case Finara saw it, but judging by the occasional smirk the goddess sported, she had failed more than once.

'You're making it sound way worse than it is,' Finara grumbled. 'It's not war. Some gods just get jealous and try to harm the mortals in someone else's domain. I don't do that. And I don't have an ego, not like my male siblings. They're the ones causing all the problems.'

'You don't think you have an ego?' Grace asked, eyebrows raised. 'You're now making sure there's always a vidcam around when you save people so that they give you all due attention and worship.'

Finara scowled. Her eyes, which had been hazel for most of their conversation, once more became engulfed by flames. The temperature in the bar rose steadily, causing nearby patrons to sweat. Then, just as Grace began to think she'd have to take cover beneath the table, the goddess beamed and the air abruptly cooled. 'Ms Shrewd Mediaist has seen me for what I am. Seems I can't lie around you — even to myself! Ha.'

Grace paused, wanting to bask in the goddess' radiant smile for a few precious seconds before she erased it. 'If I distribute Webcasts about you, your brother might hurt people. I can't allow that. Not after...' She looked down at her prosthesis, visible only as a strip of silver between heel and cuff.

Finara slumped in the opposite chair. 'I wish I didn't care so much about you stupid mortals.'

'Why is that, I wonder?' Grace challenged, waiting for the goddess to meet her eyes before continuing. 'Is it because you'd rather not feel guilty about risking our lives?'

Finara opened her mouth, then closed it. Fury tightened every line of her eternally youthful features. Finally, she said, 'No. I wish I didn't care because it starking hurts to lose the ones I can't save.'

Grace's stomach performed a twisting somersault. She pressed a hand there briefly, startled, then raised her fingers over the booth and made a beckoning motion. 'We'll discuss that later. Time to talk to the Chippers. I did promise them an audience with Ms Imperious Fire Goddess this morning.'

A sudden change came over Finara. She sat up straight and teetered on the edge of her chair, bouncing just slightly to show her impatience. But Grace read the wariness in Finara's fiery eyes as the Chippers approached. These were the mortals who had inserted chips into their temples in order to reach the Creator God, Finara's father. Surely the goddess had nothing to fear from a pair of GLEA's agents, whose tech-powered abilities were pitiful by comparison. Unless their connection to the Creator God was what made the goddess so uneasy...

One of the Chippers was human, though her nostrils were slits instead of holes, which indicated that she had at least one alien ancestor; her superior was a Utalian, his bipedal form similar to her own, except that his skin was radiant red and his scalp bore maroon streaks. Both of them were clad in purple jumpsuits and bore a bump on one temple, where their chips had been inserted.

The agents bowed at their waists before sliding into the booth, one on each side. Grace was just about to greet them when a bare foot walked its way up her thigh, a toe swiftly finding her clitoris even though it was covered by two layers of clothes.

'Unfortunately, some complications have arisen since we last spoke,' Grace began, narrowing her eyes at Finara.

The GLEA agents exchanged glances. The Utalian ventured, 'You said that we could have vids of the goddess agreeing to work with us. For promotional purposes. Are you saying that will no longer be possible?'

'Ms Naughty Mediaist,' Finara murmured. Her toe wiggled against Grace's crotch. 'You didn't mention that to me.'

Grace cleared her throat with difficulty. 'The Firine wanted to go public with her story in several Webcasts, set to go out next week. But it's come to my attention that doing this will anger some of her siblings. They have threatened the lives of mortals in order to silence us.'

The female Chipper snorted. 'Not exactly a brilliant idea to go public, was it.'

Finara offered the agent a fireball that danced above her palm, rotating and twisting frantically, as though it was about to jerk out of her control. Grace suspected there wasn't any danger of that actually happening; Finara enjoyed unsettling people, especially those who annoyed her.

The Chipper's eyes narrowed.

Her Utalian companion didn't seem concerned. He even held out his arm.

Finara abandoned the ball (it continued to float above the table) and took the agent's hand in hers, shaking it. 'Huh. You're not a bad man, Colonel Lon Jerrs.'

'Mind-reader?' he asked.

Finara nodded.

'Colonel Jerrs wanted me to ask you one question in particular,' Grace spoke up. All eyes returned to her. 'Why is it you don't empower any of your followers the way the desert god does?'

Finara frowned heavily. 'Fire's not the easiest thing to mess around with. You can't just make it *stop* what it's doing. I've had millennia to get it right; mortals don't have my experience. And they tend to abuse the powers they're given.' She levelled a smile at Jerrs, her gaze focused on his chip instead of his face, and closed her fist over empty air. The floating sphere of fire evaporated. 'Not all of them, but enough. Fire is a dangerous gift. I don't want anyone to get needlessly hurt.'

'Then you're exactly who we want to be working with,' Jerrs declared.

'Just what would that partnership entail?' Grace asked. 'Are you going to employ the goddess as a contractor and send her out to enforce planetary laws in your stead?'

Finara's expression soured.

Jerrs shook his head repeatedly, eyes wide. 'God, no. Head General Sins has been most insistent that we give all due respect to the sub-level gods. What we're doing is forming an alliance; the parties of which must promise to do all in their power to protect innocent lives. The Agency's numbers are too few to cover the entire galaxy, so it is better for us if the Firine continues to look after those in her domain. Only if she specifically requests our presence will we encroach on her territory.'

Finara shrugged. 'Fine. I'll think about it. But I don't see myself requesting your presence anytime soon.' The fire goddess' eyes flamed again. 'Now get out of here. I'm busy.'

Colonel Jerrs rose and gave Finara a long bow. Then he turned on his heel and left, tugging his companion along with him.

Sneering at their backs, Finara reached for her cup of coffein and downed it in one gulp. Evidently it wasn't to her liking because she grimaced. 'Eugh. Now, where were we?'

Grace held her eyes. 'Finara, I need you to promise me that you won't go to any other mediaists after I'm gone.'

'What do you care? You won't be around to see what happens.'

Shaking her head, Grace stood up, her fingers digging into a pocket. She yanked out a handful of coin-chips and threw them down on the table, even though the bartender could have sent the tab to her room. It was a more dramatic gesture and made her feel triumphant — until she heard Finara's snort of laughter. Some of the coin-chips had bounced into the goddess' lap.

'You,' Grace snapped, 'are thoughtless. And selfish. We mortals might be better off without you. I know,' she held up a hand, 'I know that you were created to help your father deal with the galaxy's expanding population. But you still don't understand your role! You are not here to be worshipped, to be admired; you are here to look after us. I am not here to worship you, I — '

'Then what good are you?' Finara demanded.

Grace held her breath until her chest ached so much she thought she was dying — but that couldn't be happening, not yet. Painfully aware of the attention they were drawing, she lowered her voice. 'You don't need to remain invisible. In fact, you shouldn't. It's a wonderful feeling for us mortals, to know that someone cares about us and wants to protect us. But so long as the one person it matters to knows what you've done, does the whole galaxy need to see it? Especially when you risk hurting those you care for? Don't deny it, Finara — I know you care!'

'Of course I do!' Finara said hotly. 'But the mortals don't — '

Grace glowered at Finara until the goddess fell silent. 'It seems that this mortal, this one standing in front of you, was created and sent here by the Creator God to make you understand your purpose. At least now I understand mine.'

Finara paled. 'Don't say that. He didn't send you.'

Grace was about to storm off, but the abject horror on Finara's face stopped her. 'What would be so bad about that?'

Once she was sitting back down, Finara told her everything, about how the Creator God had manipulated his sons by sending mortals to them — mortals they fell in love with — not to make his children happy, but to teach them *lessons*. The Creator God hadn't even let the sub-level gods know that they were allowed to love until it suited him. For millennia, Finara and her siblings had lived in fear of disrupting the grand design. They had tried so hard not to look at any mortal for too long, terrified of becoming distracted and upsetting their father. Finara's dismissive attitude towards mortals suddenly made sense. She had always cared. And she had always worried that she cared too much.

'I think I'm your lesson,' Grace said after a while. She couldn't say how she knew this to be true, but it was. She didn't

know whether to laugh or cry. Everything she'd been through —
everything — had placed her on the path to Arksaw, to Finara, to
this very moment.

Finara reached across the table, covering Grace's shaking
hands with her own. 'You're more than a lesson, Ms Gorgeous
Mediaist. You're a survivor. You're strong, stubborn, brave and
beautiful. And you deserve every bit of pleasure I want to give
you.'

'But I'm no longer a virgin,' Grace reminded her. 'I have no
unfinished business.'

Finara smirked. 'I promised you an exclusive, didn't I?'

***

This time the pantsuit ended up on the floor, several paces away
from the hanger, discarded and rumpled on top of Grace's
prosthesis. But while the mortal was keen to get started, her kisses
fast and frantic, Finara had something else in mind.

Despite the brief disappointment flitting through her
thoughts, Grace obeyed the commands she was given and lay back
against Finara's chest. Once Grace relaxed, her body growing limp
and her mind completely full of trust, the Firine coaxed her lover
to look up at herself in the mirror on the wall opposite the bed.

Nestled into the V-shape formed by Finara's legs, Grace
watched in uncharacteristic silence as Finara held her open,
revealing the moisture escaping Grace as it leaked its way onto her
thighs. Finara whispered, 'Stark, I just want to get on my knees
and taste you. But later. First...I want you to see how beautiful you
are when you come apart.'

Finara kept her touch on Grace's clitoris light and gentle,

working her way into a more steady rhythm. Grace seemed hypnotised by the movement of Finara's two fingers in the mirror, especially when they clenched the swollen nub between them. Sharing a grin with her own reflection, Finara clasped her spare hand to one of Grace's goosebump-ridden breasts, massaging the hardening nipple with her thumb and making sure to keep this synchronised with the rhythm of her fingers.

Finara took her time, teasing her lover, drawing out exasperated sighs and gasps. When Grace's eyelids slid shut, her head falling back against Finara's shoulder, the Firine tsked, 'Nope, keep those eyes open. Or I won't be finishing you off.'

Moans of combined protest and arousal escaped the mortal, but Grace did as she was told. Pleased, Finara rewarded her by letting the hand fall from Grace's breast, instead burying a finger inside Grace, curving it just so. Grace trembled and writhed, her smooth backside rising from the bed — and then Finara slid into her mind, feeling the orgasm begin as a steady pulse in the mortal's abdomen. It flooded through Grace, elevating her to an existence of pure pleasure. Her toes scrunched, then released; the fingers she had dug into Finara's thighs slowly lost their grip. Grace caught Finara's gaze in the mirror, her dark eyes shining and her lips curling.

Finara felt her stomach clench, not from desire, but from delight at having put that smile on Grace's face. The goddess asked for nothing in return, content to simply study her lover's naked form in the mirror, but Grace turned and knelt before her, balancing on one knee, no longer preoccupied with thoughts of what she had lost.

Grace grasped Finara's thighs, a touch that seemed to burn even the fire goddess' skin, and spread Finara open, baring her to the mortal. Grace's back curved and her breasts hung temptingly in front of Finara as she bent over, her tongue finding and circling Finara's clitoris before darting down to graze the well of moisture beneath it.

Finara meant to demand that Grace finish what she'd started, but all she managed to say was, '*Please.*'

Grace's laugh vibrated against Finara's slick folds, causing her to shudder. And then, without any warning, Grace slid her tongue inside Finara in one swift glide. The goddess gasped and threaded her fingers through the coils of Grace's hair, pulling her lover further into her, as far as she could go. In response, Grace moved her tongue around in a highly stimulating fashion, something the mortal had only learned to do the night before.

Finara arched and cried out — not the name of her lover, or any coherent sentence. It was a wordless plea for Grace not to walk out to meet a volcano, but to stay and worship the goddess who needed her, who needed someone to challenge her and force her to confront her own fears.

When Grace cupped her cheek and asked if she was alright, Finara said nothing.

She did not want to lie.

CHAPTER SIX

Grace dozed for hours, sometimes rousing in fitful moments to see a naked goddess watching her with a strange glint in those hazel eyes. Other times she woke to an empty room, presumably because the Firine was needed elsewhere. But Grace felt no fear in those moments. Because Finara always returned to her side.

When late afternoon light crept in through the tiny disc-shaped window, Grace found herself on her stomach, Finara's firm hands massaging her shoulders, her back, and then drifting down to knead out the tension in her buttocks. Finara's touch dipped low, almost to her front, and Grace's hips rose, presenting her slickness to the goddess; an offering, a surrender.

Her throbbing core easily accepted two fingers as Finara bent over her, whispering words that Grace couldn't catch. Grace was about to ask her to repeat them when Finara suddenly curled her fingers, wrenched a startled gasp from Grace and causing a wave of pleasure to creep through her. Her nipples brushed the sheet when she sagged against it, her skin tingling from the contact.

Grace continued to lie there, smiling, as she enjoyed another massage, one that soothed instead of aroused. After a while, when she could no longer ignore the thoughts that had ignited upon waking, she said, 'You told me your brothers were married. Do you think you'll ever follow them down that path?'

'Stark no!' Finara responded, sounding horrified.

Grace sat up, dislodging the goddess in the process. 'Is this because there was a time when you and your siblings believed that you were not allowed to fall in love?'

'That might be part of it, I suppose,' Finara said with one of her usual shrugs. 'But there's also the eternity thing to consider. How are you supposed to know if you'll still like the same person in a year, much less a century? No way am I putting myself through that. Not ever. Casual flings are enough for me.'

'I see,' Grace said.

'But hey, I'll do my best to remember you when you're gone,' Finara promised. 'It'd be hard to forget someone who makes the sounds you do when I touch you.'

'And just how long will you remember to keep out of Webcasts?' Grace asked flatly.

That shrug again. 'We'll see.'

Grace turned her back to the Firine as she slid off the side of the bed. 'You won't remember me for long. A week of your life is nothing. There'll be others, other *distractions*, for you to amuse yourself with.'

'Grace, no, that's not what I — ' Finara began.

But Grace did not want to hear another excuse — or worse, an empty apology designed to placate her until she was no longer around to call the goddess to task. She dressed quickly, located her prosthetic leg, then ran from the room. Only when she slowed to catch her breath did she realise how long it had been since she'd moved faster than a walk. She had finally adjusted to using the prosthesis.

Just in time for her to no longer need it.

***

'...so, since I'm no longer going public and all that footage got deleted, you won't need to waste any time going after the people in my domain,' Finara finished.

Waves lapped the shore. The sand between her toes felt gritty and irritating, but Fayay had insisted she meet him barefoot on one of his favourite beaches on New Sydney. Finara hadn't failed to notice the ring of topless women bowing over a shrine stowed away between some nearby dunes. She wrinkled her nose but made no comment, not wanting to anger Fayay when she was so close to appeasing him.

Fayay smiled, fungus-smeared teeth appearing between his cracked lips. 'It is touching to know that my siblings still listen to me, that they are still under my influence instead of Sandsa's.'

Finara gaped at him. 'Seriously? You're still caught up on comparing penis sizes? You do realise Sandsa hasn't spoken to anyone, including Kuja, *in three whole years*? He's not influencing anyone against you, or plotting to destroy you. You've won, if there was anything worth winning.'

'The Desine will recover eventually,' Fayay said firmly. 'And when he does, he will need repressing. He must understand that I am in charge now. You will assist me, as you did last time.'

Finara grimaced. She had attacked Sandsa along with her other siblings, because they had all believed that the Desine was not allowed a wife, that he should care for his abandoned people instead of her. Finara had regretted her decision almost immediately; Kuja had been hurt trying to protect his brother in that fight and she'd quietly helped the rainforest god recover, upset that she had contributed to his pain.

The Ine could have put a stop to that encounter in a heartbeat. But he hadn't. He'd wanted Sandsa to be forced to use his powers, forced into his godly form and forced back to the deserts, where his wife would never want to follow him.

Fury welled up inside Finara, but she wasn't sure where to direct it.

'In your dreams, Fayay,' she said. 'You only need us on your side because Sandsa would *flatten* you if you two went head-to-head. Fuck it. I'm not going to be part of this family bullshit anymore. But I also won't get in your way. So don't you dare come after my people.'

She fled to a volcano on some other world, one that was in its infancy and too volatile for any lifeforms. Screaming hoarsely, Finara vented her feelings into the roiling surface beneath her feet. The volcano blew apart, red-hot rocks exploded around her and magma lashed her form, but it wasn't enough. She was not yet satisfied.

With a snarl, she reached into the planet and ripped out its molten heart.

The world went cold, a future unmade, a dream unrealised.

'She's done what you wanted her to, Father, she's put me in my place,' Finara murmured. 'Let me look after her now. I'll make sure her last days are worth living.'

***

The days crawled by. Grace found that Finara was now unwilling to answer any questions about her immortal life. The goddess remained a generous and faithful companion, despite the permanent scowl she wore. Grace wasn't sure why Finara was in such a bad mood; the Chippers had left the planet and had ensured that all mediaists were pulled, kicking and screaming if need be, into orbit. The Galactic Law Enforcement Agency had done it as a personal favour to the fire goddess, who had told them that she considered the gesture the start of their so-called alliance.

Grace accessed a writing app on her techpad, keeping one eye on Finara who was dancing by the poolside, fire streaking over her form in a mesmerising, seductive fashion. Grace knew the goddess was doing it for her benefit, not for the many oiled, shirtless men who were paying her with compliments and coin-chips.

Smiling, Grace returned to her work. She might not be releasing any Webcasts about Finara anymore, but Grace had her own project to complete. And she didn't have long to do it.

Unfortunately, the vidscreen in her room hadn't delivered the forecast she'd been hoping for; there were no eruptions expected on her chosen day to die. She'd have to wait a whole extra week, one she could not afford to cover with her dwindling funds.

But there was an eruption expected tomorrow.

Fear slithered down Grace's spine.

Too soon.

She went deep inside herself, considering the options, keeping her surface thoughts consumed with Finara's body and her appreciation of it. She hoped the goddess would not look any further into her mind.

Temples beginning to ache from the effort of splitting her focus, Grace began to type on her techpad.

She paused to flex her fingers, but they refused to stop trembling.

CHAPTER SEVEN

Lulled by more than a few pink FizzWhizzes, Grace lay sprawled on the bed, waiting for Finara to come back to her. The goddess soon filled the doorway of the bathroom, smirking, hands on her bare hips. Something warm stirred low in Grace's abdomen at the sight of Finara and she had the uncomfortable feeling that it had nothing to do with desire. Mercifully, there wasn't time to worry about what that meant.

Finara sauntered over. 'Sorry to keep you waiting. Grass fires on Sundafar, forest fires on Ranta, factory fires on Londinium...had to deal with everything all at once, as usual. Anyway, I thought about getting one of those synthflesh toys to use on you, then I had a peek inside your head and realised you were as unfazed by those as I am. Guess you'll just have to feel my flesh all over you and inside you instead.'

Grace smiled lazily, hands resting on her stomach. 'How unfortunate.'

'Not sure what I should do to you now, since I've got something big planned for tomorrow night,' Finara went on, sitting down beside her. 'It being your last full day as my lover and all.'

'I'd just like to cuddle this evening, if that's alright,' Grace said, rushing out the words before any of her thoughts could settle for too long.

Finara's lips curved into a grin. 'No problem. I'm just as good at that as I am at sex.'

Grace's body had been starved for this kind of intimacy for her entire life and so she had nothing to compare Finara's embrace to, but she was sure she would never feel this safe in someone else's arms. They lay together on the bed, not once breaking eye contact, not once opening their mouths to speak. The hours drifted by, lost, irrecoverable. But it was exactly what Grace had wanted, what she had needed, for her last night.

Early in the morning, before the nearest star had cleared the horizon outside the tiny window, Finara left, tending to some emergency on some other world. Grace rolled over and inhaled the goddess' scent on the pillow, praying that her memories of this week would stay with her forever, just one possession she would be allowed to take into the afterlife.

Finally, Grace stopped ignoring the inevitable and pulled on her pantsuit.

Then she walked out beyond the forcefield.

***

Finara.

The Ine's voice. It was deep, commanding and immense, like an abyss. She had spent millennia ignoring the so-called Creator God, hoping it would make him ignore her in turn. She had even started to believe that she was safe from him and his plans.

She'd been wrong. But that didn't mean she had to listen to her father.

Finara busied herself by throwing flaming streaks across the shivering fields that stood in the path of an inferno. She was forming firebreaks — they wouldn't stop the oncoming devastation, but they would buy enough time for the people of the timber city behind her to flush out their clogged pipes and get their water cannons ready.

The Firine remained visible, in her human form; hundreds of mortals could see what she was doing, but not one of them owned a vidcam.

But that wasn't important. Not anymore.

If they hadn't known she was there, they would have abandoned all they'd worked so hard to build, completely unaware that she'd given them a chance. Their fear became determination. With a goddess on their side, they might just win.

FINARA.

Head pounding, Finara fell to her knees. Flames raced over her on their way towards the city, a heated caress that made her miss the warmth of her mortal lover. Slapping her hands to her ears, she demanded, 'What! What is you want from me?'

To listen, the Ine said. *To a father, not a god.*

'It's not like you're giving me a choice!'

You do not have the time to argue with me, daughter.

'Oh, really?' Finara said, sneering. 'Eternity not enough time all of a sudden, huh?'

LISTEN! he roared.

She listened. But she made sure her father felt her fury.

The Ine's voice lost some volume, but not its sense of urgency. *It does not matter if the mortal had a part to play in my grand design. You love her.*

Finara's laugh rasped out of her throat, even though the smoke shouldn't have bothered her. 'So what? She's not into the whole eternity thing. It's too long for her. Stark, a *week* is too long for her.'

I desire to see all of my children achieve happiness, be they mortal or of my blood.

'She's in so much pain because of what happened — she can't bear it!' Finara snapped. 'And you kept her alive, *living with that*, just so she could teach me a lesson! If that's your definition of happiness, I'll pass.'

There is no more time. You must go. Now!

A bar of white light slid down Finara's form, throwing her halfway across the galaxy in an instant. Disoriented by her father's method of teleportation, Finara wavered on her feet for a moment, then realised where she was — Grace's hotel room. The bed was disturbed from their night together and the vidscreen was on, displaying a warning about an imminent eruption.

But there was no sign of Grace.

The techpad lying on the bed blinked repeatedly, demanding attention. Finara gave it. Once the device was in her hands, the screen lit up, revealing the message Grace had left for her.

Finara,

These past few days with you have been remarkable. But if I let what is between us grow, then you will ask for eternity from me. If we'd had more time together, more than a handful of days, perhaps eventually I might have been able to come to terms with it. But I can't be sure of that. It would not be fair to you, to give you hope where there is none.

I may not be able to read your mind and I don't really know you that well, but I have seen a change in you — a change for the better — and I rejoice that I was the tool that implemented it.

I am so sorry.

It pains me that eternity is too long and a week is too short.

Grace

Finara vanished from the room before the techpad even hit the sheets.

Lava was already surging down the slope, towards the mortal who was greeting it with arms spread, her face set and determined. At the last moment, Finara threw herself in front of Grace, her back to the river of fire, encasing the woman she loved with safety and fresh air.

Grace's eyes were filled with tears.

Finara grabbed her shoulders, pinning her in place, and said roughly, 'Don't you dare. Don't you fucking dare. Not yet. Not until I've said my bit.'

Grace nodded mutely.

'I won't offer eternity right now.' Finara went on, 'because even though I think I might already love you, we've only just met. I want to get to know you, the you who isn't waiting to die. I want to know if we're suited for living together, I want to know if we're capable of making more out of our relationship, not just having hot, hot sex — and I mean that literally. We'll have sex in a puddle of lava and you'll love every minute of it. I'll keep you safe. Stark, I just want you to be safe.'

'But you will always want to offer me eternity,' Grace pointed out.

'If you don't want it, fine,' Finara blurted. 'Just be with me until you die, and I mean die naturally because this is stupid.'

'You don't want to marry anyone.'

Finara growled in frustration and dropped her hands to her sides, knotting them into fists. 'You're throwing that in my face now? I said that because I was upset, Ms Dense Mediaist. I was falling hard for you and you were still going to off yourself! Of course I wasn't going to marry anyone if they weren't you.'

Grace blinked slowly. Her tears were now clustered on her eyelashes. 'But if I never agree to become immortal...'

'Then I will respect your starking choice,' Finara said, scowling. 'I'll hate it, hate how I can't stop you being so stubborn, but that's *you* and I wouldn't try to change that. You challenge me. You don't put up with my shit. And I'm not asking for forever — I'm just asking for more than a few days. That good enough?'

Grace's lips answered her, delivering a fierce kiss that burned all the way into Finara's abdomen, somehow hotter than the molten rock roaring down around them. The mortal's thoughts were a turbulent mix of delight, disbelief — and excitement for what lay ahead.

They embraced, then vanished inside a swirl of fire.

***

Fifteen Old Earth years later

She was permanently frozen at forty.

Grace peered into the mirror in that same poky hotel room on Arksaw. It had taken years for her to decide that she wanted to spend eternity with Finara, but she considered it a ludicrously short amount of time now that time was irrelevant. They were forever bound together, by a ceremony that had left them with scars on their hands instead of rings.

These days Grace was an e-paper reporter, a famous one who had received a lot of attention from thousands of sponsors and *billions* of readers. Grace preferred her faceless method of disseminating information; no one could guess at her location because there were no images to draw clues from. According to the ageing but still popular mediaist Ton Tinel, her written word was strong, aroused feeling, and seemed so much more real than the breathy monologues that most mediaists delivered.

Grace turned away from the mirror, instead drinking in the sight of her companion. Finara, still a youthful twenty-something in appearance, lay on the bed, naked, smoothing out the sheet beside her: an invitation.

They were back at the hotel for their anniversary. Their daughter, Lirlia, who had been generated from merged DNA at a private clinic on Enoc, was currently in the care of Kuja and Fei. Lirlia was young and full of fire, both physically and mentally. And she was also infuriatingly stubborn — just like both of her mothers.

'So what changed your mind in the end?' Finara asked. 'You know, about eternity and all that.'

Grace eased her way onto the bed, sliding off her prosthesis as she did so. She had never bothered to replace it with one that looked more real. She didn't care what anyone thought of it — to her it was a reminder, to always ensure the safety of her sources.

Slowly, Grace removed her clothes, one piece a time, her smile growing as wicked as the one Finara was already sporting. 'Perhaps I wanted to have mind-blowing sex until the end of time.'

'Not the worst reason to marry me, I guess,' Finara said with a snort. 'You're lucky I know what you're really thinking.'

Grace lowered her lips to Finara's ankle and began kissing her way up a shivering calf. 'I could tell you how much I love you. Or I could show you.'

'You will do both, stark it!'

Grace laughed and acquiesced. They made love all through the night, once again exploring each other, exhausting each other, and finding in each other the love and support they both needed, not only to be happy, but to continue to thrive and grow.

Eternity was not so frightening when it was spent with someone you loved, Grace thought.

And yes, the sex was pretty mind-blowing.

The Shifting Ice

CHAPTER ONE

At least the vidcam will capture this, Dom Zhang thought as he plummeted to his death.

The starship that had deposited him this close to the planet's magnetic pole was long gone, disgorging the rest of its passengers half a world away at a soulless spaceport surrounded by sunny, sparkling beaches — the perfect place for tourists to add their footsteps to the millions that had come before them.

Dom wasn't interested in shooting the same tired footage that everyone else had on their personal vidcams. Nisha, his boss, only handed over the coin-chips if he captured exciting new 'scapes for the Graphic Stock Collection. Once his footage was uploaded there anyone could pay to access it, no danger required on their part.

Funny, Dom had never really thought about how dangerous his job was until his hoverboots cut out and his rappelling line snapped.

One piece of equipment failing — that's bad luck.

Two failing — the Creator God is out to get you.

If you'd asked Dom how he thought he was going die, he would never have picked 'falling off a giant freaking iceberg'.

Why bother being afraid of heights when you've got the tech to make sure you never fall? Why worry about not being able to call for help when no one can get to you in time anyway? And why entertain the thought of dying when you've survived so many times before?

At least his day hadn't started quite so badly.

***

Some hours earlier

Fingers laced behind his head, Dom kept his eyes sealed shut to better enjoy the sensations rippling through him. Sure hands grasped his hips and a wickedly hot mouth slid down his spit-slicked shaft, taking its time to reach the base — the starship's captain was certainly living up to his boast that he could bring a man to the edge and make him dance along it.

Dom's vidcam was hidden in the corner, courtesy of its miniature cloaking device. No sense wasting the opportunity to add this encounter to his own personal collection, especially since the captain was quite toned for one who spent his life darting from star to star. The onboard gym probably helped.

Dom felt the swollen head of his member brush against the back of the captain's throat for one glorious moment — and then that moment was over. Unable to stop himself, Dom angled his hips upwards, trying to increase the maddeningly slow pace his companion had set, but the captain released Dom's cock and shook his head, tutting.

Dom held in the growl. Barely.

'Told you I'd make you beg for it,' the captain said smugly.

Dom opened his mouth — definitely not to beg, of course, but to bargain — when his communicator squawked. He threw a glare at the device lying beside his pillow, knowing that he couldn't ignore it; his contract required him to be contactable at all times. Failing to answer this call might cost him his job.

He grabbed the communicator and released a hiss of air when he saw that the culprit was his boss. 'Galactic Gods, Nisha! What is it?'

'Mr Zhang, your vidcam is the property of the Graphic Stock Collection,' Nisha said flatly — hers was the sort of voice that made Dom nervous because he never knew if she was about to praise or lambaste him. 'It should not be misused in this manner.'

The captain started looking around the cabin. There was no use pretending it wasn't there, so Dom fluttered a hand and the vidcam shimmered into view. He expected anger or outrage, but the captain merely appraised the device, looking thoughtful.

Dom pressed his palm to the mouthpiece of his communicator. 'I'll totally send you a copy.'

'I think I'll have to improve my performance,' the captain said, winking.

Dom smirked and returned his attention to his communicator. It was still deathly silent; Nisha didn't waste her words.

'Now, Nisha,' Dom drawled, 'my contract states that I am free to work without any interference that might hinder my creativity. You hacking into my vidcam could be considered interfering. Which makes this a breach of contract. The Collection wouldn't want me going to the mediaists with that, would they?' He paused, raising his eyebrows at his companion and tilting his head towards the vidcam; an unspoken question. When the captain smiled broadly in response, Dom added, 'Don't worry, Nisha. You're welcome to watch.'

Nisha used a single curse word, just one, and then the connection cut out.

'Do you think she's still watching?' the captain asked.

'I have no idea,' Dom said, dropping his communicator. 'But I'd appreciate you getting back on the bed and putting on a good show anyway.'

The captain was most willing to comply.

***

Many hours later, the vidcam was aimed at empty, desolate scenery. The device would continue to hover there beside the iceberg until either the battery died or it was retrieved by the Graphic Stock Collection. All of the Collection's vidcams were fitted with trackers; it wasn't unusual for them to outlast their users and this made retrieving the tech a lot easier.

The user of this particular vidcam smacked into the ocean with enough force to snap bones and sever arteries.

Had Dom been conscious, he would not have been dismayed about the fact that his life was over — no, he would have been annoyed, because at that moment two of the sub-level gods who very rarely made public appearances were standing on a nearby chunk of sea ice. And his vidcam was pointing the wrong way.

It would have been the scoop of a lifetime, netting far more coin-chips from the mediaists than anything the Collection could have offered — not that Dom would have cared about the money. He couldn't exactly spend coin-chips where he was headed.

No mortal lived as long as a god. But fame was eternal. Dom had badly wanted to leave his mark on the galaxy before he died.

Because then someone might have actually missed him.

***

Fayay, the god of water, and Rasson, the god of ice, both watched as the mortal's body was swallowed by ravenous waves.

'Foolish creatures, the humans,' Fayay noted, then paused to spit out some of the long, dank hair that had fallen over his lips. 'How they became the dominant species in this galaxy when there are far more intelligent beings is beyond me.'

Rasson held up a hand, sending out a shard of his powers. The mortal's body, now entombed in a block of ice, rose back to the surface and fought its way across the roiling sea towards the gods. Fayay could have stilled the waves to make the journey easier, but Rasson hadn't expected him to.

'Why save him, Rasson?' Fayay asked scornfully, the scar on his cheek twitching. 'He is not one of yours.'

'He's not yours either, brother,' Rasson countered. 'He worships and belongs to no one. So I can do with him as I wish.'

Each of the Creator God's divine children had been given a domain full of mortals to rule over, a necessity thanks to the rapid spread of humans throughout the galaxy. Rasson's control was usually limited to lifeless moons or small swathes of land and sea as opposed to whole planets, but this suited him just fine. He did not need vast amounts of territory to feel superior, not the way many of his siblings did.

Fayay and Rasson were similar in build and colouring and shared the same cerulean eyes and dark hair, though Rasson kept the latter short and was fairly certain his strands were midnight blue, not black. The Iceine (Rasson's official title) was one of the youngest gods in the Galactic Pantheon, but he considered Fayay, the Watine and second oldest of them all, his closest friend and firmest ally.

Fayay smacked his lips with a pale tongue. 'The mortal entered my domain the moment his body struck the water. He should be punished for his stupidity, not rewarded for it.'

Rasson offered a bland smile. He was grateful that his brother did not possess the mind-reading abilities that some of their other siblings had been born with. Admitting to the real reason he had spared the mortal would only make Fayay assume that Rasson was turning against him — and too many of the sub-level gods in the Galactic Pantheon had done that lately. The Watine needed a brother right now, not a potential enemy.

'Our youngest brother, Kuja, has convinced many mortals to worship him in the past few years,' Rasson said, watching the waves carefully, ensuring that none of them capsized his precious cargo. 'It has made me wonder if there's a way to convince more of them to worship me. Perhaps I can glean some important insights from this man.'

Fayay's laugh was as harsh as it was incredulous. 'What do you intend to do? *Ask* him how to convert other mortals?'

'What is the harm in asking?'

'He should die for being so reckless.'

'Oh he will die, Fayay,' Rasson promised. 'But only after I am done with him.'

A cruel smile carved its way onto Fayay's face. 'Enjoy. I will pursue my entertainment elsewhere.'

Water shot up from the surface of the sea and spun into a cocoon around Fayay. When it dropped, there was no sign of the Watine. Sighing in relief, Rasson flicked his wrist and the block of ice completed its journey, stopping right in front of the god.

Rasson peered down at the broken body encased inside the transparent slab and frowned. It would take him hours to reverse such extensive damage with his healing abilities. But the Iceine did not mind. As the god of a domain that rarely needed constant intervention, he was always running out of things to do.

How did his older siblings, with thousands of years behind them, spend their hours, their days, their *centuries*? Rasson had no idea.

But now he had a plan to deal with his empty eternity, a plan that would unfold perfectly — unlike his recent conversation with Kuja, the god of rainforests.

***

Two weeks earlier

'Did Fayay send you?' Kuja asked suspiciously. Spiked vines were snaking around his arms as he stepped out of his hovel and advanced on his brother.

Despite the Rforine being so young (Kuja was just shy of eighty years old), he carried himself with confidence and his emerald eyes were fierce and determined. He was a force to be reckoned with, especially if he thought his wife and son were in danger. Coming to Kuja's home had been a mistake.

'No!' Rasson said, retreating a pace. It would not be enough to take him out of Kuja's range, but hopefully it made him seem less threatening. 'I do not mindlessly enact Fayay's bidding, no matter what any of you think — well, no more than you do for Sandsa, *your* favourite.'

'Sandsa is not...' Sorrow washed over the Rforine's freckled face. 'Sandsa is lost to me. He suffers eternally, thanks to the Ine.'

Sandsa, the Desine, had married a woman who had insisted he live as a man because she couldn't bear to be with a god. That had ended as badly as one might imagine, but the mortal served her purpose. The Ine (the name the sub-level gods used for their father) had created her to teach the desert god how to love so that he could better care for those who worshipped him.

And if Sandsa had refused to go back to his domain...his wife had borne a child that could easily replace him.

Fayay had found nothing wrong with their father's plan, because he believed that the deserts should always have a god — one way or another. Rasson had been more than happy to help Fayay track Sandsa down. Together, along with several of their siblings, they had gone after the Desine, forcing him to become a god once more. It had all seemed just at the time.

But even after they had succeeded, Fayay had wanted to continue his attack on the Desine's family. Out of desperation, Sandsa's wife had made a deal with the water god; in return for her son never using the powers he'd inherited from the Desine, Fayay would leave her and the child alone.

Rasson swallowed. 'Kuja, what happened...has never sat right with me.'

'Don't suppose you've ever mentioned that to Fayay,' Kuja snapped.

'No. I haven't.'

Kuja regarded his brother for a long moment, a frown writing lines over his features. He was one of the many sub-level gods who could read minds, but he was also one of the few who possessed an endless well of sympathy.

Finally, the Rforine sighed, as if he pitied the Iceine.

Rasson did not appreciate that. He loved Fayay and supported him by choice. So few of their siblings realised that the barbs and violence were a cloak that Fayay threw over his true self to conceal his fears and his vulnerability.

'Why are you here, Rasson?' Kuja asked, his voice softening.

'Ever since the Ine revealed that we are allowed to fall in love, I've seen the others start to develop feelings for specific mortals and I...' Rasson trailed off.

'You do not need to choose your words carefully with me,' Kuja told him.

Rasson glanced around at the nearby trees, at the gaps between them, afraid that Fayay might suddenly appear and berate him for speaking to someone no less hated than Sandsa.

'I...' Rasson swallowed. 'I want to know if it's possible to find an eternal partner for myself.'

'I take it Fayay has said it's not something worth pursuing.'

Rasson kept his lips sealed this time.

'And you have seen how happy I am, with Fei and my son,' Kuja continued, clearly reading the thoughts that Rasson couldn't bring himself to say out loud. 'Rasson, it's not easy. You can't just pick someone and make them love you.'

'But Father made it so that Sandsa fell in love with Callista,' Rasson argued. 'And he meant for you to meet your wife. That was all part of the Ine's grand design.'

Shadows flitted through Kuja's green eyes. 'I won't deny that. Yes, I was destined to meet Fei. But Father created her so that she could teach me to be a better god, not become my wife. Our love was incidental. Fei and I did that on our own.' A small smile pricked the corners of Kuja's lips, but then his gaze grew serious once more. 'Rasson, listen, falling in love is the easy part. You have to work hard to maintain a marriage. And guess what? No mortal owes you their love. They can choose not to love you.'

'But there must be someone for me,' Rasson insisted.

'Why...' Kuja hesitated. 'Why do you want this?'

Rasson turned away, icy shards hailing down around him as he prepared to teleport away. 'I've been here for too long. Do not mention this meeting to anyone.'

When he returned to his domain, Rasson dove into his duties rather than wait for Fayay to arrive. The Watine rarely visited his brother, but he always brought with him the love and companionship that Rasson craved. It was generous of Fayay to spend any time with the Iceine when he didn't need to...and yet, somehow, it wasn't enough.

Rasson needed someone to fill his loneliest hours.

***

'I have chosen you,' Rasson declared. He knew his companion could not hear him, but the words erased the awful silence that Fayay had left behind. 'You should be very grateful.'

Rasson kept a hand on the mortal's frigid coffin, ensuring that it did not drift away while their new home was being built. The skyscraper-sized iceberg knew exactly what Rasson wanted; it was hewing rooms and tunnels inside itself so that it could provide a palatial fortress, one worthy of the Iceine's consort.

The mortal's skin had taken on a blue tinge, but Rasson knew that with enough care and devotion it would return to its normal tan colour. He found himself admiring that solid frame, those strong firm hips —

Rasson looked down at his slim build and frowned. 'You will find me pleasing. I'm sure you will.'

When the last piece of their crystalline home boomed into place, Rasson teleported inside the iceberg, his consort at his side; a position the mortal would hold for all eternity.

Rasson shivered with anticipation.

CHAPTER TWO

The warmth was almost stifling.

It swarmed over every limb and every piece of meat clinging to his bones, cooking him from the inside out, but Dom was unable to wriggle away from it. He wondered if he was in the throes of sleep paralysis, as he sometimes was at dawn. He had learned to lie quietly during these moments of fright, forcing himself to remain calm until his body no longer refused to obey his mind.

Sometimes he would pass the time by studying the ceiling of his hotel room. But this didn't look like any hotel decor he'd ever seen. The gentle curves and swirls reminded him of the organic caves on the planet Nanlis, over on the Orion Spur. Given enough time, the caves would hollow out and grow steadily more translucent, until they eroded into white sand that eventually formed entirely different catacombs.

Dom made a mental note to pay the right amount of compliments to the owner of this hotel, whatever its name was. But for now...there was nothing to do but wait until the paralysis faded.

Something shifted in his spine.

'Ah!' Dom gasped.

'Did that hurt?' a gentle voice asked him.

Dom wondered if the grimace made it onto his face. 'No, it — it felt wrong.'

Soft laughter swept over him, like a caress. 'I'm not surprised. You broke your back in that fall. I am knitting your vertebrae together again.'

Galactic Gods! The panic was like a lasbolt to the heart; when it struck, Dom's chest compressed and he fought for air. His lungs gave an even greater spasm when sensation abruptly came flooding back into his limbs. Dom writhed.

'Stop struggling!' The voice was firm now. 'You will interrupt the healing process and I do not wish for your body to break again. I have put much effort into repairing it.'

Dom might have obeyed had he not realised that there were restraints on his wrists and ankles. These weren't the usual lascuffs favoured by the Galactic Law Enforcement Agency (and he'd worn a pair of those during one very lascivious evening with a GLEA agent) — no, these were like ice, cold enough to burn. He yanked furiously at his restraints, but they were hard and unyielding. He'd definitely be counting bruises later.

'Hold still or I will throw you back to the waves!' the voice snapped.

Dom went very, very still.

When a few minutes had passed, he cautiously tilted his head forward, his chin grazing his chest. He was naked, but that wasn't the strangest thing about his situation. There were two pallid hands with long, thin fingers hovering over his torso; they seemed to be the source of the white haze that was smothering him. Dom knew, somehow, that this was for his benefit. The cuffs though...they definitely weren't. Dom figured he must be hallucinating because they really did look like they were growing out of the slab of ice that formed his bed.

'Look, if you're hoping for a ransom, you won't get anything,'

Dom warned. 'The Graphic Stock Collection hires thousands of footographers. They won't care if I go missing. I'm expendable.'

'I have no need for coin-chips.' Another laugh, one that sounded like the tinkling of glass wind chimes. 'Do you have any family?'

Dom couldn't help it. He snorted. 'Same deal. I'm one of fifteen. My parents never had the time to notice me when I was there, let alone when I wasn't.'

'Perfect,' the voice said, a surprising amount of satisfaction filling that single word.

'Perfect...perfect for what?' Dom demanded.

When the voice did not immediately answer, he dropped his head to the side. A dark blur swiftly darted around behind him, evading his gaze, and the white light dimmed for a moment as the man — at least, it had sounded like man — readjusted his position. Dom tried to wrench his neck around to catch a glimpse of his captor, but he felt ice — definitely ice — grow up and over his temples, sealing his head in place.

'You're not human,' he deduced.

'My mother was a human, like you.'

'And your father?' Dom nearly laughed at himself, for being distracted when there was a much more pressing matter to deal with. 'Forget I asked that. What are you going to do with me?'

There was a distant boom, like thunder. Dom felt the ensuing vibrations in the firm surface beneath him and wondered if a nearby ice shelf had collapsed.

'I plan to ensure that your stay here is a very pleasant one,' that voice said lowly.

More vibrations, but this time they came from inside Dom.

He shivered and wasn't sure why, because the light encasing him was still close to becoming unbearably hot.

'But first you must rest.' The stranger released a regretful sigh that never quite settled, like feet skidding over a frozen lake. 'You mortals are so fragile. I'm not sure how you survived without me.'

The strange light cut out. Dom tensed, expecting to feel a chill, but thick furs were pulled over him and stuffed beneath his back. Dom would have thought this a tender gesture if he hadn't been secured to the bed. But he kept his complaints to himself while thin strips of cloth were carefully inserted into the cuffs, separating his skin from ice.

'Sleep well, mortal,' the voice said. 'I will return once you are rested.'

As his captor's footsteps padded away, Dom found that he could barely keep his eyes open. He didn't fight the darkness, couldn't fight it — and he figured that if he played along for now, he'd be able to attempt some sort of escape later.

If he could just figure out where the stark he was.

***

The vidcam yielded more treasure than Rasson could have hoped for.

After he retrieved it, he sat for several hours in the spacious antechamber, flipping through the footage on the small playback screen, entranced by the many landscapes, seascapes and skyscapes that had been captured by the device. Some mortals were happy to live their whole lives on the one planet, but it seemed his consort — Dom Zhang, according to some voices that had spoken off-screen — had seen hundreds of different horizons in his three decades of life.

Rasson had never thought the waterfalls in Kuja's rainforests anything special until he saw them lit perfectly by a star winking its way through the treetops. And he had never admired the barren desert dunes belonging to Sandsa until Dom had made them look like precious mounds of gold.

'Beautiful,' Rasson breathed, but not at the scenery. It seemed the vidcam also contained a cache of footage showing Dom sleeping with various men. 'I've chosen so well. But of course this philandering will need to stop now that you are mine.'

Rasson set the device down and instead studied his unblemished palms, envisioning the binding scars that would appear there after he married his consort. Giddiness descended, threatening to swamp him — but no, he couldn't celebrate, not yet. He first had to make sure that Dom knew the price of marrying a god.

The Iceine worried his lips together. Immortality. He would be passing it on to Dom once they were bound. It might be difficult for a mortal to adjust to the concept of living forever. Rasson wished he had asked Kuja how he'd helped his wife come to terms with it.

No matter. Dom would have all of eternity to adjust.

But right now, the mortal was awake and calling out for assistance. That husky voice would soon caress Rasson's name, those gold-rimmed chestnut eyes would fill with adoration and those travel-worn *hands* —

Rasson ran to the door dividing him from his consort, but his footsteps faltered before he could reach it.

'What if he does not like what he sees?' Rasson wondered,

opening his dark silksein robe and looking down at his too-thin, too-pale form. He had always been naked beneath it and would have gone without the robe entirely, except that Fayay...

Fayay is not here, Rasson reminded himself.

The door, which was a sheet of ice, slid aside and became one with the wall, allowing Rasson to tread tentatively over to his consort. Still restrained on the bed, Dom twisted around as much as he could in order to see Rasson. The Iceine quickly cinched the robe tighter around his body and sent a mental command to the cuffs. They withdrew and vanished, absorbed by the colossal structure.

Rasson threw a similar silksein robe at his consort. Dom was still belting it on as he stood up, his eyes trained directly on the god who was approaching him. Rasson wet his lips. What he wouldn't give to be able to read minds, the way his sister Isabis could —

'Let me go,' Dom ordered.

Rasson glanced down at himself. 'Is my form that displeasing to you?'

Dom blinked once, twice — and ignored the question entirely. 'Look, I'm grateful you healed me. I get that you might want something in return. But I won't be your hostage.'

'You are not a hostage,' Rasson assured him.

'Like I said, I'm grateful — '

The ice cracked beneath Rasson's feet, sending tiny crevices sprawling out in all directions. Dom hastily retreated to the bed.

Rasson drew a deep breath, then slowly released it. The fortress stilled.

'I will never hurt you, Dom,' he told his consort. 'But I was remiss in not explaining myself. I apologise.'

'I'd get right on that if I was you,' the mortal said flatly.

It wasn't until he attempted to move closer that Rasson realised that spikes of ice had crept up around his ankles, holding them in place. He shot a look down at the floor and switched to mind-speech. *What are you doing?*

You have frightened the mortal, Master, the ice replied. *We think it would be wiser if you stayed where you are.*

'Oh,' Rasson said out loud, feeling foolish. Now he could see that Dom was shivering and it wasn't entirely because of the cold. 'I chose you as my consort.'

Dom's eyebrows disappeared beneath his shaggy russet hairline. 'Don't I get a say in that?'

Rasson frowned. 'I will not perform the binding before obtaining your consent. But I chose you and you will bow to me on this matter.'

The mortal's eyes raked over him, lingering in a way that made Rasson tremble with excitement. 'You're a sub-level god — the god of ice, I'm hazarding.'

'Yes,' Rasson said, pleased. An intelligent mortal was going to make things so much easier.

Dom took another step back and collided with the bed. He quickly sat down, as though to keep himself from falling to the floor.

'I will never hurt you,' Rasson reaffirmed.

'No, you'll just hold me hostage and demand I marry you,' Dom snapped, then his face immediately blanched. He looked as deathly pale as he had been mere hours ago. 'I don't mean any disrespect, but the Creator God — your father, if the rumours are right — gave us mortals free will when he created us. So I choose to exercise said free will.'

Rasson's lips parted but no sound escaped them. He could not win that argument.

'I won't marry you.' Dom crossed his arms. 'So let me go.'

'But I saved your life,' Rasson tried.

Dom's stare did not wilt, but his bravado was clearly fading. He was now shaking violently and goosebumps were spreading along his bare legs. Rasson desperately wanted to drape the furs back around Dom — or perhaps use his own arms to warm his consort.

'Are you hungry, Dom?' Rasson asked, keeping his feet still even after the ice encasing them had thawed. 'Are you cold? Tired? Do you — do you require entertainment? I'm not even sure what you mortals do with your time.'

Dom gave a short snort of laughter. 'That's obvious. Well, here's my daily routine. I wake up. I go to the bathroom. If I'm lucky, there's someone in my bed I can screw. Then I eat. And then I *leave*.'

Rasson decided to overlook the jibe. 'Leave to do what?'

'Work, earn a living, see the galaxy,' Dom said. His shoulders abruptly straightened out of their slump. 'My gear — did you see what happened to my gear?'

Rasson attempted to hide the answer from his face.

Dom's eyes narrowed. 'You have my gear. Or at least you have my vidcam. That wouldn't have fallen in with me until its battery ran out.'

Rasson allowed a smile to infuse his cheeks with warmth — and subtly increased the temperature of his body. Usually he kept it close to freezing but that wasn't likely to entice Dom into his personal space. 'Yes. I enjoyed perusing the footage on it.'

'I bet you did,' Dom said wryly.

The Iceine wondered if he was blushing. Dom's smirk seemed to confirm it.

'So can I have the vidcam back?' the mortal asked.

Rasson hesitated. He could very easily hold up his hand and teleport the item into his palm, courtesy of a miniature vortex of ice. But an idea had just occurred to him. 'I will make a bargain with you, Dom Zhang. You may have the device in return for your promise to...to consider becoming my consort.'

Dom lifted a hand and twirled it towards Rasson, a gesture that invited an explanation. 'And by "consider", you mean...'

'You will be staying here — with me.' Rasson swallowed, grateful that Dom couldn't hear the pounding of his very hopeful heart. 'For one Old Earth year. You will get to know me and like me. I am sure of it.'

'One month,' Dom said immediately. 'That's all I get for vacation time per year. I have a job. Remember?'

'Yes, I remember,' Rasson hissed.

'You only get that much because I'd rather have you on hand to deal with any lingering problems from the water snapping my spine. Pretty sure you could have grabbed me before that happened, but let's not get into that.'

Rasson simmered in silence. The mortal couldn't have known that while Fayay possessed telekinesis, Rasson did not.

'Now, I'd like something a lot warmer than this robe,' Dom went on, waving that same hand from crown to hip, indicating his attire. 'And a shower. And drinkable water. And food — something piping hot. Seafood's acceptable. I'll also need a new communicator, if mine's trashed, so I can contact my boss.'

Rasson fought the urge to march over and shake the mortal by his shoulders. 'Anything else?'

'What do I call my captor?' A lift of an eyebrow. A sardonic smile.

'My title...' Rasson drew a breath. 'In the Galactic Pantheon I am known as the Iceine.'

'Ice...ine. Not terribly impressive. Or unique. The desert god's known as the Desine, isn't he?'

'I have a real name,' Rasson said, trying not to sound too defensive. He had never appeared to those few who worshipped him and given them a special name to call him by, the way Fayay had (the mortals called the Watine 'Oceania'). 'It's Rasson. But, as my consort, you may...you may call me Rass. No one else has ever been afforded that privilege.'

Dom's gaze remained level. '*Rasson*. I wish I could say it's nice to meet you, but it's really not.'

There was nothing to be said to that.

Rasson turned on his heel and marched through the tunnels of the fortress he had made for this ungrateful mortal, for the man who had been offered a rare and wonderful opportunity — and had refused it.

No, he refused you, Rasson, the Iceine's inner voice taunted. It sounded so much like Fayay that Rasson actually paused and scanned the area for his brother's presence, but 'Oceania' was still on another planet.

'He would have accepted if I wasn't so hideous,' Rasson moaned.

CHAPTER THREE

If Dom wasn't afraid of the god impaling him with an icicle or something, he would have outright laughed at the naivety of his captor.

Rasson simply took it at face value when Dom said he liked to go for morning jogs if time permitted — in reality, he hated any form of exercise that didn't yield a satisfying result. Climbing mountains and scaling walls to find that perfect angle with his eyes when the vidcam's lens failed to do it was more his kind of thing. But the jogging gave him an excuse to record the tunnels — the vidcam dutifully trailed after him, along with Rasson — so that he could attempt to form some sort of cohesive map of his prison.

It took three entire days to realise that there was no exit. The fortress seemed to have been grown rather than built. When Dom asked about this, the god replied, 'I made it for my consort. So that you would have a suitable home for this climate.'

Suitable home. Galactic Gods, it was a freaking iceberg.

Despite his opinion on the matter, Dom forced himself to say pleasantly, 'No one's ever made anything for me before. As gestures go, it's a pretty impressive one.'

Rasson smiled shyly in response, his baby blue eyes falling to the floor.

Sometimes when Dom looked at his captor, he couldn't quite believe he was standing in the presence of a god — this pale, vulnerable waif that he could easily pick up and bend over his lap for an afternoon of leisurely spanking?

Anyway, Dom wasn't going to feel bad about getting Rasson's hopes up — he really wanted to avoid saying or doing anything that might make the god kill him out of spite. Not that Rasson seemed particularly vengeful. No, just a little quiet and uncertain — and, if Dom was honest, more than a little attractive.

Stark it, Dom had forgotten how much he liked slim pretty boys, especially the ones with long eyelashes. At least Rasson didn't have the typical mop of hair that fell over his eyes. But somehow he managed to look coquettish without it.

Once or twice Dom had considered bedding the god, just to say he had, because who else could make such a boast?

But then he remembered that he was a prisoner, cut off from the galaxy in more ways than one. He had managed to contact his boss using a borrowed communicator that Rasson teleported away as soon as Dom was done with it. Nisha's dedication to abrupt conversations meant that she hadn't bothered to ask Dom why he'd wanted to take time off. He wished she had — he'd always cashed in his vacation days instead of using them before now. It should have been suspicious.

Dom had decided that he might as well keep working; he had a backlog of footage to look through. Although the vidcam was in perfect condition and its year-long battery (as promised by the manufacturer) was still going strong, the tiny playback screen wasn't ideal for editing. Part of Dom's job was cutting vids down to the best few minutes to save space and time when uploading them to the Collection.

Rasson had firmly refused Dom's request for a techpad, which would have made things easier — probably because the device would have also allowed Dom to use the Web to send for help. Apparently the god of ice knew enough about tech to remove the Web-chip from Dom's vidcam, so at least he had that. It kept him from getting bored and doing things he shouldn't even be *considering*.

Like trying to find out what Rasson looked like under that robe...

Often Rasson would sit near him, not close enough to see what Dom was doing, but close enough that the heat of his presence caused Dom's shivers to abate. Other times the god was gone for hours, tending to what he called his 'duties'. Rasson had assured Dom that during these absences the iceberg would look after him and keep him safe, as if it was some sort of living, thinking being. Maybe it was.

Any food that was offered to Dom seemed to appear out of nowhere. He suspected that his captor was capable of teleporting from world to world because he definitely recognised one desiccated squid as a delicacy native only to New Sydney, which was at least eight days' starship travel from his current location (Rasson had kindly confirmed that Dom was very nearby to where he'd fallen).

At night Dom was allowed to retreat into the privacy of his bedroom. Somehow hot water could be piped into the ensuite's shower without melting the entire structure, which was amazing and duly appreciated — not that Dom would ever admit this to a certain god.

He wasn't stupid enough to think that Rasson ever truly left him alone, so once he was done with his nightly routine he lay between the thick furs on the slab that served as his bed and did nothing to ease his mounting frustration.

Days without being able to release himself had to be the reason he eyed the god so frequently, Dom decided.

One afternoon while they were in the bedroom's antechamber, which was large enough to accommodate several ice-hewn pieces of furniture draped in furs, Dom asked, 'Have you ever been with anyone? Sexually, I mean.'

Rasson, sitting cross-legged on the recliner opposite Dom, seemed to freeze into that position. This wasn't entirely infeasible for a god of ice, Dom supposed, but he didn't fail to notice those blue eyes darting towards the nearby corridor, betraying the god's sudden desire to escape.

'No,' Rasson finally answered, sinking back onto the recliner. 'Because I only intend to be with one man.'

Galactic Gods, you're just too precious, Dom thought, unable to help his smirk.

'Only one?' he echoed. 'You have no idea what you'll be missing out on.'

Rasson levelled an even stare at Dom. 'Many of my brothers and sisters are content with the ones they have. Just as I will be.'

Dom filed that information away for later. Gods and goddesses choosing mortal spouses was the sort of information that could net him some serious coin-chips if he sold it to a mediaist. He nodded silently, projecting a look of interest, hoping to hear more.

'Perhaps they chose better than I did,' Rasson added in a small mutter.

'Yeah, this is one fish you might want to throw back in the sea,' Dom said with a laugh.

The god frowned. 'No. I would not discard you so thoughtlessly. Not as you did to all those men in your footage.'

Dom's lip twisted. 'Better to leave before they get the idea to do it first.'

'I will never leave you.'

Perturbed, because he knew Rasson meant it, Dom tossed his vidcam over his shoulder (its small hoverpad ensured that it never hit the floor) and kept his voice light, teasing. 'Promises, promises, Rasson.'

'Of course I don't mean every moment of every day,' the god said quickly. 'I have my duties, just as you have your work.'

'What about when I sleep?' Dom asked, quirking an eyebrow.

That shy smile again. 'Sometimes I remain to watch you.'

Dom felt a small, unwanted shiver of delight race down his spine. He'd been right.

'Can you turn invisible?' he asked.

Rasson blinked, apparently startled. 'In a manner of speaking. I can shed my human form, which makes it easier to spread my awareness across my domain. If I choose to, I can also merge and become one with this iceberg. And I can even stow my presence in a single cube of ice.'

'Huh,' was all Dom could think to say to that.

Later that evening, when he returned to his bedroom, the feeling of being watched intensified and the furs stacked on top of him felt heavier and more oppressive than usual. Dom stifled the groan. He knew he shouldn't even be considering this, but his balls starking ached and it wasn't like he was going to ask the god to get involved...

Dom kicked the furs away from his overheated skin, then yanked off the clothes that Rasson had teleported in from somewhere to replace the ones Dom had lost.

He definitely didn't imagine that sharp intake of breath.

Dom took a moment to look down at his body, smiling in satisfaction. Still taut in all the right places. Still a lure for the prettiest of pretty boys. And gods.

'I'm going to lose it if I don't deal with this,' Dom said matter-of-factly.

He pinched one nipple, which was already standing upright in the cold air, then pinched it again, groaning as hot sparks shot through him, tightening his already roused member. Dom's other hand skimmed along his side, over his hip, and then down between his thighs. Usually he spent some time stroking and teasing the skin beneath his balls. But tonight he couldn't wait. His hand moved straight to his shaft and encased it.

He kept the rhythm slow at first, his strokes long and even, but after a few minutes of this doing nothing for him he changed tempo. Instead of obeying, his cock began to slacken in his grip. Dom growled in frustration. He needed this, stark it. If he didn't finish now, then he wouldn't be able to trust himself in Rasson's presence tomorrow. He would probably end up doing something very, very stupid.

It then occurred to Dom that his obstacle wasn't speed, but lack of stimulation.

He blew out a sigh and opened his eyes. 'Rasson. Can you show yourself please?'

A spike of ice immediately shot up from the floor, growing and filling out into the figure of a man. Rasson was wearing that silksein robe, as always — the flimsy fabric did nothing to hide the god's obvious desire. Dom *had* wondered if it was possible for the god to become aroused when he was part of the iceberg. Clearly it was.

'Help me out here,' Dom said. 'Can you take off the robe?'

'My...why?' Rasson frowned down at himself. 'I am naked beneath this.'

'Yeah, I guessed that. But I need to have something to focus on.' Dom forced a flippant grin. 'Not usually a problem for me and I'll probably get there in the end anyway, but if you wouldn't mind...'

Rasson's fingers strayed to the front of his robe and he bit his lip, an action so mortal, so normal and so very sweet that Dom almost got off the bed and went to him.

'You want to see my naked form?' Rasson clarified.

'Galactic Gods, Rasson! Yes!' Dom said, silently hoping that he didn't sound as desperate as he felt.

Rasson shifted awkwardly, his gaze locked onto the wall behind Dom. 'I'm not sure you understand what you're asking me to do.'

'Wait, is this because you don't want to be naked in front of me until we're married?' Dom asked, catching the flicker of hope on Rasson's face. He felt momentarily guilty for using words he'd known would get a reaction from the god. 'Because I'm clearly naked already.'

'It is only fair,' Rasson murmured.

Score, Dom thought as the robe fell, puddling around the god's feet.

Dom was so used to seeing Rasson as slim and gentle, but the hardness thrusting out proudly between his legs definitely wasn't slim *or* gentle. It was a glaring contrast to the god's form and the girth promised a tight, torturous squeeze into a confined space —

'Yesss,' Dom hissed, pumping himself more vigorously.

He didn't usually submit to his partners in that way and would never have chosen it as his fantasy, but stark...!

Dom groaned, trying to focus on the physical sensations instead of the source of his unbearable arousal. He actually thought he might have succeeded — until that last, heart-stopping moment, when he looked up into the pale blue eyes that watched him with rapt attention and naked desire.

'Ah,' Dom gasped as his cock pulsed. Warm fluid pooled onto his abdomen.

He kept his fingers moving for several more seconds, until a second intense spasm wrung him dry. Dom sank further into the furs, his hands limp on his thighs as he forced his breathing to even out. His pounding heart was less willing to obey.

'Beautiful,' Rasson said softly. 'I could never grow tired of this view.'

Dom swallowed, dredging up much-needed moisture into his mouth. 'Yeah, you could. Give it a few centuries. You sub-level gods live for a while, don't you?'

Rasson laughed gently. The dark lust that had marred the god's porcelain features was gone, though his stiff, thickened member was still announcing its interest. 'Oh, we do, but the exquisite pleasure on your face just then...the way you looked at me...' Rasson's voice hitched. 'Those images will stay with me for eternity.'

'Glad to be of service,' Dom said with a wink.

He shook out his lazy limbs and rolled off the bed, staggering his way over to the ensuite. He grinned to himself, imagining what Rasson thought of his perfect arse, then stepped beneath the hot spray that helped him scrub desire and sweat from his body. He couldn't help but think of those fingers — those long, delicate fingers — trickling over his skin instead of water.

'Don't go there,' Dom cautioned himself. 'If you do, he'll never let you go. Just three more weeks and you're out of here.'

When he returned to the bedroom, the god was gone — and so too was his presence. Dom paused and tipped his head to the side. He couldn't explain how he knew he was alone, just that there was an absence...an absence of warmth, an absence of promise and protection.

Shaking his head, he pulled the furs back over himself and fell asleep.

CHAPTER FOUR

Rasson roamed the frost-crusted plains, the snow-capped mountains and the iceberg-studded seas, his insubstantial form allowing him to straddle thousands of worlds at once. He stopped to weaken the pack ice that had captured the landing gear of a starship — the vessel's exhaust ports had melted the surface when the ship landed and the decrepit engines had cut out afterwards. The repairs hadn't taken more than an hour, but that had been enough time for the ice to harden back into place.

The ship was stuck fast. And the planet was so isolated, so far from the usual shipping lanes, that it would take months for anyone to respond to the crew's distress call — months they did not have the supplies for.

All it took was a single thought to free them from their predicament. Their fearful cries at seeing the ice retreat so rapidly faded into murmurs of awe. One even whispered their thanks to the nameless ice god and Rasson paused, startled and pleased, before moving on to the next mortal who needed him.

In the beginning, under Fayay's tutelage, Rasson had helped only those whom dumb luck had afflicted rather than those who were careless. But as the decades had passed, as the mortals increasingly became the only people he saw, he'd found that he could no longer remain deaf to their pleas for help.

Rasson knew he shouldn't be doing this; he shouldn't be trying to save *everyone* the way Kuja did. The rainforest god had even started telling the mortals outright that he was their 'god of lost causes and casualties', that anyone could go to him, no matter where they lived. So arrogant, so much like the Desine, the fool who had let love lure him from his duty.

Fayay is right — we should never let the mortals distract us, Rasson told himself as his presence glided over a glacier smothering an ocean's shore on some distant world. *It is just as well that Dom rejected me. He's distracting enough as it is.*

He didn't expect the glacier to respond, but it did, in a voice that boomed and echoed, as though it was trapped inside an abyss. *You know the Watine only says these things because he is bitter about the past. Be honest, Master. Is the mortal distracting you? Or is he giving you something you lacked?*

Silence, Rasson ordered.

When night began to dwindle on the planet containing his chosen consort, he returned to linger at the foot of the bed, gazing down on Dom as the mortal slept.

'I will not keep you here any longer than our deal permits,' Rasson murmured. 'But I will not relinquish you before that time.'

Dom's eyelids flickered. Those beautiful chestnut eyes slowly slid open. And then the sated smile appeared, one that Rasson couldn't help but feel partly responsible for. Rasson curled his own lips, waiting for Dom to thank him, to perhaps even ask for more hands-on assistance...

'You left your robe here,' Dom told him.

Rasson looked at the floor, startled to see his robe there, then down at his nude form. His member was soft now, but he had enjoyed how it had sprung to attention while he'd watched Dom bring himself to pleasure.

Ducking his head to hide his disappointment at Dom's words, Rasson retrieved the robe and clothed himself.

'You showed me something wonderful last night,' he said in as calm a voice as he could manage. 'I wish to show you something in return.'

He waited while Dom dressed (why the mortal insisted on wearing poorly insulated jeans that he had to cover up with several layers, Rasson had no idea) then held out a hand. The mortal accepted and encased it — with the fingers he had wrapped around himself the night before. Rasson drew in a ragged breath but swiftly banished the images that had filled his mind, forcing himself to focus. Shards of ice shot up from the floor, sharp and deadly, causing Dom to flinch. But the mortal lifted his chin and remained standing tall, even as the shards began to swirl dizzyingly around him. He wasn't afraid. No, he looked almost...almost eager.

Within moments, they were standing on an icefield, bathed in a glorious sunset that would last for hours on this particular planet. Rusty red and orange hues painted the sky, creating a stunning contrast for the purple buns and swirls that the clouds formed beneath it. The ice at their feet, silver instead of white, was flawlessly smooth and reflective; it bounced strange, warped shadows over both mortal and god.

'Galactic Gods,' Dom breathed. 'This is amazing. Should have brought the vidcam.' He turned to Rasson, excitement sparking in his eyes and making their golden rims stand out even more. 'What planet is this? I have to come back.'

Rasson told him, watched Dom mentally take note of it, then said, 'Not as beautiful as the sight you gave me, but does it suffice?'

'Well...' Dom smirked. 'It *suffices*. But I think the sight would drastically improve if you got rid of that robe.'

Rasson swallowed. 'I'm not sure I want to take it off again.'

'Why not?'

'This...this human form...' Rasson wound his arms around himself, ensuring that the robe remained sealed. 'It is nothing special and I have no wish to inflict it on anyone else. Once you leave my domain, no mortal will look upon it ever again.'

Dom tsked and said in a voice that could only be described as a purr, 'That's a shame. Are you sure you won't show it to anyone else? Took me a lot of effort not to get up and touch you last night.'

Rasson wondered how it was possible that he could shiver. He was the god of ice — *ice!* The cold should not be affecting him. And yet it was. Somehow.

No, he had to admit it wasn't the cold. He was thinking of all the men he had seen on Dom's vidcam. Some nights he re-watched that footage, wishing Dom's lips were encircling his shaft, desperate to feel Dom's fingers plunging into him, stretching and preparing him for something so much bigger and so much more fulfilling.

Oh Father, what I would give for one night — and the willpower to release him... Rasson agonised.

'I thought my form was undesirable,' he said at length.

Dom laughed and shook his head. 'No, you're just my type. Slim and malleable. The things I could do to a pretty boy like you...'

'But you won't,' Rasson said flatly. It was a fact; he would have to accept it. 'And I promise that you will never be forced to.'

Rasson's heart clenched when relief flashed over Dom's face. But regret swiftly became delight as he watched the tension that

Dom had carried around with him for the past week evaporate. The mortal's shoulders relaxed and his stance loosened. Even Dom's smile now seemed more genuine.

Together they watched the sunset in silence for more than an hour, until Dom suddenly said, 'You're lucky, Rasson.'

'I am?' Rasson said, taken back.

'Yeah,' Dom responded. 'You have eternity to experience everything the Creator God has ever made. There's so much I'll never see. Things like this. I've got about six or seven decades left to travel this galaxy, if I really take care of myself. Which I probably won't. But even if I do, I'll never see everything.'

'Do you wish you could live forever?' Rasson asked, his tongue playing along the inside of his lips. Oh, how he desired to offer immortality to his companion. But he would be refused. The price; too steep.

Dom glanced at him, eyebrows raised.

'Of course, there are few mortals who want such a thing,' Rasson rejoined quickly. 'Needing to fill in all that additional time. Growing bored with favourite hobbies. Outliving friends and loved ones.'

'I don't know, it might not be so bad,' Dom said, a wistful smile stealing across his face. 'I've got a bunch of planets I want to see, planets I'd like to revisit — I'd need hundreds of lifetimes for that. And you know I don't have any friends or loved ones; there's no one to miss.' Dom's expression grew neutral as he looked back at Rasson. 'Do you? Have anyone, that is?'

Rasson hesitated. 'Yes. My brother.'

'See him often?'

'No, I don't,' Rasson admitted, wishing the sky would hurry up and darken so that his discomfort wouldn't be so obvious.

'Only a few times each Old Earth year. But I don't mind waiting. Most of our siblings do not understand him, the pain he has suffered, the isolation he feels. He will always need me.'

'Are you lonely?'

There wasn't any point in denying it, Rasson thought.

'Yes,' he answered.

Dom watched him closely. 'Lonely enough that you plucked a stranger out of the sea and chose him as yours.'

'Yes,' Rasson repeated, much softer this time, unable to look away from the gaze that saw right through him.

'I understand,' Dom said. 'And I'm sorry it's that way for you.'

Eventually Dom mentioned his missed morning meal and Rasson took him back to the fortress. Once he was fed, Dom asked Rasson to sit beside him and then held out his vidcam at arm's length, so that they could both watch the tiny screen. Rasson had already seen the vids that Dom was showing him, but the footage was that much more vivid when Dom added to them his memories, his husky voice and his animated gestures.

Rasson had been on countless worlds, seen countless sights. But over the past two centuries they had grown stale, uninteresting. He was enamoured of Dom's ability to treat each new horizon as a challenge — and an opportunity.

Dom seemed to find beauty in everything he saw.

Even the pale, unappealing body of the Iceine.

CHAPTER FIVE

Dom stretched, his hands held high over his head, and released a contented sigh. The furs slid down to his stomach but he waited until the frigid air became unbearable on his skin before reefing them back up. He found that he didn't mind the cold as much as he'd used to, something that bothered him, because he didn't know if he was acclimatising or if it was yet another small thing Rasson had done to make him feel more comfortable.

Dom sighed again, this time almost wistfully.

He'd been moving so fast for so long in his pursuit of the galaxy, in search of scenery that no one else had ever aimed a vidcam at, that he'd forgotten what it felt like to just sit...and relax.

Dom had run out of work to do for the Collection a couple of weeks ago and since then had found himself reliving his childhood dream of becoming a graphic artist — a dream that had withered away when needing to eat and pay his way across the galaxy had taken priority. With nothing better to do, Dom had fooled around with some of his footage, even made attempts at his own art. The results weren't great, because he was rusty and had to use a vidcam with limited features as opposed to a techpad, but he felt a certain thrill to be creating again.

This forced vacation might have had its uses, though he hoped he wasn't going to crave more time off. He was allowed one Old Earth month per year to do with as he wished and he always cashed it in to fund his exploration habit. But maybe, just once, he'd sit still and create again...

Dom burrowed further into the furs on his bed and smiled, satisfied from performing for Rasson again. He'd made it last longer than usual, teasing himself more than ever before, because it had been his last night in this fortress. Afterwards, just as Dom had begun to doze off, Rasson had promised, in a voice thrumming with unfulfilled need, that he would let Dom go in the morning.

A pity, Dom thought, that he couldn't show the god how much pleasure he was capable of inflicting on someone. He was sure Rasson would be impressed — to the point of demanding it every day for the rest of Dom's life.

Rasson had been candid about his belief that Dom was right, that even one night spent together could spell disaster. Dom wondered if he should bother to feel grateful that the god had listened to his opinion, given that Rasson was responsible for putting him in this position in the first place.

'Don't you dare form an attachment to him, *you're a hostage,*' Dom muttered to himself. 'There are docovids about this sort of thing, stark it!'

He extricated himself from the furs and began stumbling his way over to the ensuite, lured there by the promise of a hot shower. Once the necessities were dealt with and clean clothes were clinging to his form (he knew Rasson saw the jeans as impractical, but he had managed to climb mountains in them), Dom sauntered out into the antechamber that had, through laziness on both their parts, become the main space for entertainment, work, food and discussions in which Rasson proved he knew very little about mortals, despite looking after them for two hundred years.

Better get used to attracting older men, I guess, Dom mused. *I'm not getting any younger. Well, I could always lie about my age for a bit...I don't look* that *bad yet.*

Smirking, he plonked himself down on a recliner smothered in furs and made himself comfortable. He didn't have to wait for very long. Within moments, piles of crushed ice appeared, swiftly subsiding to reveal an array of food beneath them. All his favourites were there, Dom noted. He shook his head in amusement as he reached for the Butislan caviar. Not really a breakfast food, but why not.

'My brother also likes that dish,' Rasson said, dropping onto a matching recliner. The pose he adopted should have have been relaxed, with one leg propped over a knee and his arms crossed behind his head, but on the god it looked awkward. Dom had tried to teach him to act more like a human, admittedly to little success. Rasson's oddness was actually kind of cute. Not that Dom would ever mention this to him.

'Your brother — you mean Oceania, the water god,' Dom guessed around a mouthful of pancakes; their sweetness merged surprisingly well with the salty caviar. 'I know, I know, you can't tell me his real name. But you talk about him a lot. Don't you have hundreds of other siblings you can tell me about?'

Rasson's lips twitched. 'Not hundreds. And it seems only one of them can be bothered to come to my domain and speak to me.'

Dom kept his mouth stuffed with food instead of questions. He wasn't going to tangle with politics on a divine level, though Rasson had said just enough to imply it was a minefield. Dom cleared his throat and set down his plate — not made of ice this time, thankfully. He wasn't a fan of losing the skin off his fingers. On that particular occasion, Rasson had quickly apologised for not thinking and had then healed Dom, who had been trying not to burst out laughing at the ridiculousness of his situation.

'I can't even imagine the things you've seen,' Dom said, sucking a smear of caviar off his thumb. 'I'm jealous. I won't even get to see a fraction of the galaxy compared to you. And it'll get harder to charm a cheap ride out of the captains I come across once my looks fade. I'm thirty-five now, practically old enough to start haunting starship graveyards.'

Dom chuckled and waited for Rasson to remind him that thirty-five was nothing — to a god it was really *was* less than nothing — but Rasson didn't respond. The god pursed his lips, clearly on the verge of saying something (Dom knew that look now), and then shook his head.

'What?' Dom asked, grinning. 'You thought you were worse off, being forced to look that pretty forever? Sorry to disappoint. You could help me out, though.'

'How could you possibly know — ' Rasson cut himself off. 'How can I help you?'

Dom had a feeling he didn't want to delve into whatever *that* had meant. 'Well, you can teleport, can't you? So you could drop me off somewhere that would usually take me months to get to.'

'I could,' Rasson said softly.

The itch on the back of Dom's neck grew steadily more insistent. In the weeks they'd spent together, Rasson had become somewhat transparent to him. And right now, the god was preoccupied and — and *fearful*.

Dom knew he should keep his mouth shut and go on his merry way. He'd never have to see the Iceine again.

But Dom scratched that itch. 'What aren't you saying?'

Rasson hesitated, nibbling on his lip as he glanced towards the corridor. Dom half expected him to flee. But instead the god abruptly sat up, swung his legs to the side and scooted to the edge of the recliner. He then leaned forward, his expression earnest, looking a lot like Dom's siblings did when they were trying to wheedle their way out of some transgression.

'I can make you immortal,' Rasson rushed out.

Dom narrowed his eyes. 'And the catch? Don't get me wrong, the offer's nice, but there'll be strings attached.'

'Doesn't it — disturb you?' Rasson pressed. 'Immortality. It should disturb you.'

'Not really, no,' Dom said. 'We've been over this before, Rass. You know I don't have anyone to miss, that I'd have things to do with my time.' He dropped his plate and twisted in his seat, mirroring Rasson's pose. 'The catch. The price. What is it?'

'You are truly considering this?'

'Stop avoiding the question, Rass.'

They watched each other, matching stare for stare, until finally Rasson murmured, more to himself than to Dom, 'If we were to wed, in a ceremony that involves the mingling of our blood, my immortality would pass to you.'

When the ensuing silence grew too awkward, Dom retrieved his plate from the floor and this time went for the battered calamari. It was greasy and slicked his fingers, but the taste made the mess worth it. As he reached for more, he cast a look at Rasson who was now lying back on his recliner, apparently fascinated by the ceiling. Dom peered up as well and saw that the god was creating patterns in the ice above them — an array of gentle arcs and swirls, similar to the art Dom had recently created on his vidcam.

'I take it we'd have to stay married for eternity,' Dom said, lowering his gaze to Rasson's.

'If you want to continue living, yes,' Rasson answered curtly. As if it didn't matter.

But Dom saw the longing in those pale blue eyes.

He swallowed. *Galactic Gods. Why didn't he say something earlier? Unless he was afraid that I would accept...and regret it.*

'Still tempted, Dom?' Rasson asked darkly, suddenly sounding so unlike himself that Dom had to study his face for at least half a minute to be sure it was him.

Could sub-level gods take the forms of others? Dom didn't know, didn't want to hang around long enough to find out. He'd already lost a whole month that he could have spent travelling and working. And he really needed to get laid. Properly.

'I'd have to give this way more thought than I can do in the time we have left,' Dom said, tactfully (he hoped) dancing around the issue.

'I understand.' Rasson's voice trembled. 'If I was as attractive as my brothers are...best not to dwell.'

'It's not that,' Dom said.

Rasson glowered at him. 'No?'

'No! Seriously, Rass, how can you not believe me? I whack off to your naked body every night. I like what I see.'

Rasson was staring at Dom, a crease running across his forehead, likely the only line that would ever mar his skin. 'But...?'

'I'm not the type to settle down with one man — that'd be hard for me. Impossible, even.' Dom flipped the god a grin. 'Look, if anyone could tempt me away from my life of hedonism, it'd be you.'

Rasson bowed his head. 'Thank you. I will treasure those words for much longer than you live. Let me know when you are ready and I'll teleport you to a world of your choosing.'

Dom sighed in relief. He was as good as free.

But then his stupid mouth started saying, 'Tell you what. I'll think about your offer. And if I want to accept it, I'll...I'll come back here.'

'That's more than I deserve,' Rasson said, but didn't try to dissuade him.

Dom hadn't thought he would. Shaking his head, he reached for the caviar. 'You really should try some of this. I know you gods don't need to eat, but there's a reason your brother likes this, trust me...'

Barely an hour later, Dom was standing beside his bed, unable to refuse the top-of-the-line hoverboots, the flashy new techpad and communicator, the freshly folded clothes (including the jeans the god had so often scoffed at, much to Dom's amusement) and the bulging pack full of supplies. All of it teleported here, for him — and mostly likely stolen, given that Rasson didn't seem to see the need for coin-chips.

Dom looked Rasson in the eye and thanked the god for saving his life, then promised he would never go to the mediaists. He hoped Rasson knew he meant it.

'See you 'round,' Dom added.

Rasson laughed gently. 'I do not believe you will.'

Before Dom could respond, a vortex of ice rushed up from his feet, shielding Rasson from view. When it dropped, Dom was on a different world entirely, standing waist-deep in shivering savannah grasses. The stone monoliths on this planet were supposed to be something else. And better yet, no one had ever captured any footage of them.

Until now.

Dom unclipped his vidcam from his belt and tossed it into the air. He had work to do.

***

'Lost interest in your little toy, did you?' was the first thing Fayay said when Rasson obeyed his summons. The Watine had chosen to meet him inside a dank cavern that had blood-red seaweed crawling up the walls.

Rasson linked his hands behind his back, trying to keep them from trembling. He couldn't think of anything to say, because he didn't want to tip Fayay off to what he'd really hoped to get out of Dom.

Please do not let him find out, he pleaded silently, hoping his father would hear and indulge him, just as he indulged the mortals who cried out for their Creator God.

'Or did your toy lose interest in you?' Fayay continued. A wet snort disturbed the curtain of hair smothering his face. 'I am not surprised. I have often tried to teach you how to gain the respect of mortals, but you seem to lack the ability to learn.'

'I know,' Rasson murmured. 'I'm sorry.'

'But you always listen to me and try to do as I say, which you are aware means much to me,' Fayay said, his lips parting. His teeth were smeared with fungus and the gaps between them played host to tiny crabs but Rasson didn't care, because his brother rarely smiled enough to display them. This was a good sign.

Rasson managed a smile of his own. 'I *do* listen, Fayay. My eternal existence would be utterly boring without these conversations of ours.'

Fayay laughed darkly; it was an oily sound that threatened to slide down the back of Rasson's throat. 'Really? Is that all I am to you? A diversion? A way to pass the time?'

'No, of course not,' Rasson said quickly. 'Fayay, I was being funny. It's a trait I picked up off the mortal.'

'Lose that trait — now,' Fayay ordered. 'Did you learn anything of use? Or did you choose to have fun with your toy instead? I know the men are to your tastes.'

Rasson dropped his voice to a murmur, half hoping his brother wouldn't hear it. 'The mortal was not interested in pursuing a physical relationship. I did not press the issue.'

Fayay smirked. 'My poor little Rasson. You are a god. You do not need some mortal's permission for such a thing.'

They'd had this conversation before, Rasson reminded himself, but his heart refused to crawl out of his gut. He'd bound Dom to the bed with his powers at the start, not just to keep the mortal from injuring himself, but because he knew it was something Fayay did to trap his conquests. But when it had come down to it...Rasson hadn't wanted to mimic his brother. He'd let Dom go.

When Rasson failed to laugh and joke along, as he always had, he knew immediately that he'd made a mistake.

'Rasson, have you disregarded everything I've told you about these ungrateful creatures?' Fayay spat. 'They will give you nothing — you must take it!'

The ire in Fayay's tone struck him like acid. Rasson flinched. 'I am sorry I failed you, brother. I will heed your words in future.'

'Good! Now go hunt down that mortal, whom you no doubt kept alive — do not deny it, you are so predictable — and *take* what you are owed.'

'No.'

'No?' Fayay flicked his greasy hair out of his face, scowling. 'Why not?'

Rasson was already dipping his head forward to apologise before he realised what he was doing. He lifted his chin. 'I don't want to.'

'Pathetic,' Fayay sneered. 'You should have killed him, as you promised you would. Perhaps I will do it in your place.'

'*No*,' Rasson said again.

Fayay's pale blue eyes narrowed and became as sharp as icicles. 'Why should I not deal with this mortal who is in danger of rendering you impotent, in more ways than one?'

'I chose him as my consort,' Rasson said, surprised that he could sound — and feel — so calm, given that the water inside the cavern was now spitting steam. He already regretted his words, but it was the only way to keep Dom safe. A few years ago, some time after the Desine's wife had needed to make that deal with Fayay, the Ine had warned the Watine that he would be punished if he harmed any of his siblings' chosen spouses.

Rasson swallowed with difficulty. 'My consort is wrapping up his mortal affairs. Once he's done with that, he'll accept the binding.'

Fayay's nostrils flared. 'You never used to lie to me, Rasson.'

The Watine would have looked furious to anyone else. But Rasson could see that he was upset, hurt even, that his younger brother would turn against him, as so many others had. The walls in the cavern had actually started to cry.

But this was only the first time Fayay had realised that his brother was not being entirely honest with him. Rasson had frequently disagreed with Fayay, but it had been so much easier to wear a polite smile instead of arguing.

'It's not a lie,' Rasson insisted. 'When Dom returns, we will be married.'

'You are a *fool*,' Fayay told him. 'Did he promise he would return? He only said that so you would release him. They all say such stupid, transparent things.' He paused, flicking his tongue repeatedly, as though to rid himself of some sour taste. 'Very well. I will not harm your precious mortal. But you must promise not to make a mistake like this again.'

Rasson's chest ached. Yes, he and Fayay could overcome this, and in time they would heal the rift yawning between them. But oh, he missed Dom. He missed their fascinating conversations, the delight on Dom's face when they watched those sunsets, and that howl of laughter Dom would toss over his shoulder whenever he managed to outrun Rasson through the fortress' tunnels (Rasson had promised not to use his powers on those occasions).

'It was not a mistake,' Rasson said quietly.

'No?' Fayay arched both eyebrows. 'How do you know? You are so young.'

Rasson frowned at his brother. 'I know more than you realise, Fayay. It was not a mistake. I learned so much from him.'

'I see,' Fayay drawled. 'This consort of yours was sent by the Ine to teach you, just as he sent wives to Sandsa and Kuja. Do not forget, Rasson, those mortals were created only to teach our brothers lessons. You do not need to love your *lesson*.'

'No, it wasn't like that...' Rasson protested weakly.

A smirk slashed its way across Fayay's pale features. 'Poor Rasson. Poor little Rasson. You thought you'd managed to capture a mortal all by yourself, when in fact Father intended for you to meet him all along.'

No, no, no. Something squirmed inside Rasson's stomach. For a moment he wondered if Fayay had teleported a fanged Eransian eel inside him, but that wouldn't have hurt nearly as much. *It was my decision to save Dom. My decision to let him go. Not yours, Father — mine!*

'I wonder, what could you possibly learn from this mortal that you couldn't learn from me?' Fayay went on, flashing those foul teeth again.

Rasson felt sick; he feared he would throw up if opened his mouth. But he was too angry to stop the words simmering out of him. 'That I am not you. That I can make my own decisions. I do not need you, Fayay. I never did.'

Fayay stiffened. 'You are upset. I understand. Let us speak of this another time.'

'There won't be another time,' Rasson said.

'You still need me,' Fayay told him, his expression darker than the shadows around them. 'You will call for me when you realise that. I'll be waiting, Rasson.'

'That's your choice. Farewell, brother.'

There must have been some love left between them, because Fayay did not attack him. Rasson vanished unhindered, teleporting away to that same icefield he'd spent hours on with Dom. He watched the superb sunset for a time, trying to ignore the empty space beside him, then finally asked, 'Father...was Dom sent to me as a lesson?'

He didn't expect an answer. But he got one. *Yes.*

Rasson bit down hard on his lip. 'I know Fayay has done awful things, things he expected me to do, things I *couldn't* do, but I...I never meant to hurt him.'

You cannot remain in his shadow, Rasson. That position will only cause you pain. The Ine's voice was surprisingly gentle. *You needed to stand up to Fayay, for your own good and for the good of the mortals who rely on your kindness.*

'Why couldn't you just...talk to me? As a father to a son?' The wind was raw in Rasson's throat, forcing him to whisper.

This was the most effective method.

Rasson blinked rapidly, the tears on his cheeks hardening into tiny beads of ice. 'I wish you hadn't sent Dom to teach me this *lesson.* I have lost more than a consort. I've lost a brother. But at least I had them, even if it was only for a little while. I never had a father, did I?'

The Ine didn't respond. Rasson squeezed his eyes shut, pained, then shed his body and drifted away, to tend to the mortals in his domain. They thought the Creator God loved and cared for them, but they were nothing but convenient tools. The Ine's godly children fared little better.

Rasson envied the mortals their blissful ignorance.

CHAPTER SIX

Eleven Old Earth months later

'Are you going into hiding because of that price on your head, Mr Zhang?' Nisha's voice carried the hint of an uncharacteristic smirk. 'It is my duty to remind you that the Graphic Stock Collection does not provide assistance to employees who have offended local populations. Seducing a Lentarian politician's husband and breaking up her family unit counts as causing offence. You're on your own if a bounty hunter finds you.'

Lying in a cramped transportation pod and stowed away in the hold with hundreds of other people, Dom had to admit that he should have expected this response to his request for vacation time; he'd only asked for it on one previous occasion.

He winced and rolled his shoulders. If he'd wanted to, he could have seduced the captain of this particular vessel and scored himself a more comfortable bed.

But the captain had been a sturdy man with thick biceps. Definitely not Dom's type.

'No, Nisha, this has nothing to do with what happened on Lentaria,' Dom said, suppressing a small smile. His conquest had been slim, pale and oddly skittish for a Lentarian. Despite the four arms, it had been so easy to imagine someone else. 'I just...I never get a chance to work on my art. I need to make time for it now or I never will.'

'I don't care what you do with your time,' Nisha said, 'so long as you get back to work in a month.'

She had barely cut the connection when a voice on the ship's intercom announced that they were arriving at Dom's chosen destination. Ignoring the uncomfortable jolt inside his stomach, one that had nothing to do with the increasingly uneven movement of the vessel as it tore through the planet's atmosphere, Dom dutifully rolled out of his pod and retrieved his hoverbike from the bay beside it.

The ramp in the floor dropped open while he was still pulling on his visor and gloves. Cold and unforgiving wind began to batter him immediately, one gust of it so fierce that it caused the ship to juke. Drawing in a gulp of frigid oxygen, Dom strapped himself in, flicked the ignition switch and then shot down the ramp.

He fell towards the raging sea, but only until the hoverpads kicked in. Dom let out a whoop of exhilaration and darted around the first iceberg in his path. He'd bought the hoverbike a few months ago and had learned how to use it within days — it was far more reliable than the various brands of hoverboots that kept failing him. And it was fast. Very fast. It definitely beat walking. There was no time for that anymore.

Dom was surprised he even found the right iceberg. He'd only seen it from the outside that one time, thanks to Rasson's insistence on keeping Dom inside the fortress (except for those fun excursions to other planets). But there it was: the immense chunk of ice that had nearly been the death of him.

He parked on top of it. And waited.

Half an hour dwindled by. Dom paced, inwardly berating

himself. Had he expected Rasson to immediately appear and fall upon him in delight?

When two torturous hours had passed, the biting wind still his only companion, Dom cast off his pride and knelt, a gloved hand caressing the rough surface of the iceberg.

'Rass,' he said quietly. 'Rass, I've returned. To you.'

More silence.

Dom tried to swallow the guilt but it lodged at the back of his throat. Despite what he'd said to Rasson, it must have been obvious that he had never intended to come back. But he'd had eleven months to think things over. Eleven months of counting each new fleck of grey that appeared in his hair.

'I came here to marry you,' Dom continued. 'You made me that offer, Rass. If you want to rescind it, fine, but I'll be staying here until nightfall.'

He never made it back onto his feet. Twin vortices swept up around him and the hoverbike, depositing both man and machine inside the antechamber that shared a door with Dom's old bedroom. Rasson was there, in his usual silksein robe — but he was standing against the opposite wall, arms crossed and looking decidedly nonplussed. Dom couldn't blame him.

'You want the immortality,' Rasson stated. 'Not me.'

Dom winced. Laid out like that, it did sound pretty bad. 'I'm sorry. Forget I mentioned it. Don't suppose we can spend the afternoon catching up and eating caviar and pancakes instead?'

A snort of laughter from the god. The air warmed considerably. 'We certainly can. I am surprised you came at all, that you risked your freedom in an attempt to gain immortality.'

'You'll let me go, like you did last time,' Dom said, trying not to make it sound too much like a question. He leaned heavily on his hoverbike as he eased himself up from the floor.

'Yes, of course,' Rasson assured him. 'You do not need to fear otherwise.'

Dom's requested food appeared seconds later, arrayed between the recliners. Without another word to each other, they both sat down and began to eat, often making eye contact, sometimes even reaching for the same platter at the same time. But their hands never met.

Dom finally broke the silence. 'You kept the place intact.'

'You said you would return.'

'And you believed me?'

'Not entirely,' Rasson admitted, sending a shy glance in Dom's direction. 'But I made it for you. And I have...many happy memories here.'

Dom decided he wouldn't bring up the immortality thing again. The moment he came to this conclusion, smiling and swallowing became a lot easier. So too did admitting that he'd come for a terrible reason. He mentioned as much to Rasson, who then said, 'Of course the offer still stands. We can perform the binding right now if you wish.'

'But I'd only be doing it so I can keep gallivanting about the galaxy.'

Rasson's lips curled. 'Gallivanting. Yes, you seem to do that a lot.'

'You watched me,' Dom guessed.

'Yes,' Rasson said — and then the spark of humour in his eyes died. 'At first. Then it occurred to me that this was an invasion of your privacy.'

'Rass, you know I like being watched. And I pretended it was you. Every time.'

Rasson frowned. 'You're just saying that. You don't need to gain my favour. I have already offered to marry you.'

'Rass...' Dom sighed, rubbing his forehead. This was all his fault. 'I spent a month trapped here with you and I never got to touch you. Galactic Gods, thinking about you makes me come quicker than anything else. I can't help those fantasies.'

Dom watched a smile spread reluctantly over Rasson's features.

'I have conditions,' the god said after a moment. 'If you are getting immortality out of this, then I should get something too.'

'Only fair,' Dom said cautiously.

Rasson's throat bobbed. 'I want you here for...for half a year. Every year.'

'Rass, I only get one Old Earth month of vacation time,' Dom argued.

'Three months then.'

'One or there's no point.'

'One month every year,' Rasson agreed easily — much too easily. Dom wasn't sure if the god had been toying with him, but he figured he deserved it. Rasson added, 'And I will teleport you wherever you wish to go at the end of that month.'

Dom nodded shortly. 'Sounds good. Now, if you're expecting monogamy...'

Rasson's eyebrows rose.

'...sorry, but I can't spend the rest of eternity tossing myself off,' Dom finished.

Rasson's expression darkened. 'Yes, you can, if you wish to remain immortal. You will bed no one while married to me.'

'No one?' Dom repeated, smirking. 'Not even you?'

Rasson's mouth oscillated for several moments, not a single sound escaping it. But then a great hunger came over that ageless face and the god's pale eyes raked up and down Dom's form. Dom was still clothed but suddenly felt like he wasn't. Stark, he wished he was naked already.

'So, one month of me living here and driving you mad with pleasure, then eleven months of you knowing that the only one I'll ever touch is you...' Dom trailed off, allowing his gaze to feast on Rasson in return. 'Every single year. What do you think?'

'I think I could be satisfied with this arrangement,' Rasson replied.

'Great, then let's do this.' Dom paused. 'Wait, what is it we'll be doing, exactly?'

***

He returned to me, Rasson thought as they walked side by side into the bedroom.

Only so that he could gain immortality, he reminded himself as they knelt onto a rug on the floor, facing each other. *But he wants to touch me. I do not care why he does this, because he wants. To touch. Me.*

As ordered, Dom presented his palms to the ceiling. Rasson slid his own hands over Dom's, sealing them together. It was the first time they'd ever touched and the moment was electric. Tingles raced up both of Rasson's arms then plunged into his chest, causing his heart to stutter.

Rasson swallowed. 'I bind myself to you, Dom Zhang, so that you may live forever.'

'I bind myself to you, Rasson, god of ice,' Dom's voice softened, 'because I'm very okay with you being the only man in my life from now on.'

Rasson shivered at those words, knowing he should dismiss them, but he couldn't. Steeling himself, he reached for his powers. There was a sharp intake of breath from Dom as the cuts opened up on their pressed palms. Blood dripped, blood mingled, and then white light blasted between their fingers, sealing the wounds for eternity.

The light slowly receded. Their hands came apart. Each palm now bore a diagonal line of scar tissue.

Fearful that Dom might regret it already, might ask him to remove the binding scars right there and then, Rasson swiftly stood and took a step back. But Dom was inspecting his palms with wide eyes, apparently fascinated.

He glanced up at Rasson. 'Thank you. I know it's not fair to you, but...thank you, husband.'

'Husband,' Rasson repeated, tasting the word, savouring it.

'Sounds better than consort, huh?'

Rasson nodded mutely, unable to curtail his smile.

'Take off your robe, husband,' were Dom's next words. It was more command than suggestion. 'If I'm only allowed to have sex for one month out of every year, I am definitely not going to waste my time.'

Rasson trembled. He'd wanted this, desired it, but... 'I'm afraid. You know I have never been with anyone. Sexually.'

'I'll go easy on you,' Dom said, the golden rims of his eyes shining. 'For now.'

As Dom got to his feet, Rasson remembered that he was shorter than his husband, though not by much. The Iceine was distracted from making any further comparisons when Dom's fingers danced along the opening of his robe. Grinning, Dom found the cord holding it together and tugged playfully, bringing Rasson much closer to him in the process.

'I guess I'll just have to take this off myself then,' Dom said.

'I guess so,' Rasson agreed.

He remained very still as Dom disrobed him, the mortal's warm breath grazing his cheek. Once Rasson's skin was bared, Dom pressed a palm to his chest, a palm that bore an eternal scar.

Rasson gasped.

Dom chuckled as he pulled away to deal with his own clothes. He wadded them into a ball that he then set on the rug at the god's feet. Rasson glanced down, confused, but then a hand curved around his jaw and guided his gaze upwards again.

'Kiss me, Rass,' Dom said huskily.

Rasson pressed his trembling lips forward. Dom captured them, his tongue tapping tentatively at the seam of Rasson's mouth until the god allowed him in. One of Dom's hands supported Rasson's neck while the other caressed his chest, his hip, his thigh — and *there*.

Rasson kissed Dom again, desperate, unable to plead with his voice.

Those talented fingers left Rasson's straining member and moved back up his body, finding and flicking a sensitive nipple. Rasson released a hiss of air. He had never climaxed, but now he badly wanted it, needed it, would gladly die just to experience it.

While continuing to tease one nipple with his fingers, Dom bent over and licked the other, again and again. The dual sensations wrenched an impatient moan from Rasson. But he didn't move, didn't dare do more than breathe, afraid that Dom would cease his ministrations.

Eventually Dom's mouth and hands did leave Rasson's chest, but within moments they were sliding up each of his thighs, to the base of his shaft. Whispering lips began to tease Rasson's balls, making them feel tight and heavy with longing.

'Husband...' Rasson said softly.

Dom turned a knowing grin up at Rasson and lowered himself onto his knees, his discarded clothes cushioning them far more adequately than the rug. Rasson now understood why Dom had placed the mound of fabric there, though he still wondered why his husband had earlier requested that the Iceine teleport in something that Dom called 'lube'. The item sat beside the bed, untouched for now.

'It won't take you long to finish this time — don't worry,' Dom added, no doubt seeing the spasm of fear that Rasson couldn't keep from his face, 'you've got eternity to get better at this. There's no shame in it, Rass.'

Before Rasson could form a reply, Dom kissed the head of his swollen member. Rasson cried out and tried to jolt forward, but Dom's hands wrapped possessively around his hips and pinned him in place. Rasson shuddered as a deft tongue teased its way along the leaking slit on his tip, spreading the moisture already gathered there.

He never got a chance to wonder what would happen next; Dom's mouth slid right down to the base of his shaft.

'Unh,' Rasson managed, his eyes wide.

Dom's lips receded, revealing glistening skin and bulging veins. Rasson watched, fascinated, as Dom began to work the shaft up and down, his cheeks hollowing as he sucked harder and harder. Rasson groaned, pleased to feel the pressure building up inside him so quickly. He needed this. Oh, how he needed this. But his torment was far from over.

Dom abruptly released him, leaning back to admire Rasson with eyes so dark with lust that the Iceine was surprised that he didn't climax simply by looking into them.

'Husband...why did you stop?' Rasson asked breathlessly.

'I wanted to tease you a little, draw it out.' Dom winked. 'Because you definitely won't last much longer.'

Rasson thrust his hips forward. 'Please, *please*. Then you can...' He wet his lips. 'Then you can do anything to me — anything. I mean it.'

'Well, aren't you're eager,' Dom said, smirking. 'And I may hold you to that...*husband*.'

'Faster, Dom, faster...' Rasson's plea rose in pitch when that hot mouth encased him once more.

Dom dutifully increased his speed — and then paused again, his laugh sending vibrations up Rasson's shaft.

'Don't stop next time, *please*,' Rasson begged.

Dom's mouth was too preoccupied to answer, but his eyes held a promise.

Rasson dropped a hand onto his husband's head, trying to keep Dom from moving too far from his pulsing member. He could feel the fragile strands of Dom's hair snapping in his fingers — he knew he should apologise, wanted to form the words, but something was happening inside him, something much more urgent.

Sparks shot across Rasson's vision. He went blind. And then pleasure exploded inside his abdomen, forcing its way out through his shaft, a hot spurt that wrenched a startled cry from him.

'Ahh,' Rasson breathed as Dom continued to suckle away every drop of his desire. 'Ahh, Dom...I can't...'

He collapsed into Dom's waiting arms.

Dom grinned down at him, lips glistening as they parted. The kiss that followed was thick, salty — *me, I'm tasting me*, Rasson thought, dazed. He was startled to find himself lying on the rug, his head propped up in Dom's lap. He couldn't remember getting into this position, but he didn't care. He liked it.

'Husband, that was...that was...' Rasson trailed off.

'Only the start,' Dom promised. Goosebumps were beginning to spread over his body but his own member, despite the cold, was still solid and visibly throbbing.

Rasson scurried onto his feet and then lurched over to the bed, his breathing ragged. Dom followed him, telling him to slow down. But Rasson no longer wanted to take it easy *or* slow down. He wanted more. So much more.

Once the furs were smothering them and his mortal — *immortal* — lover was no longer shivering, Rasson obeyed Dom and turned over onto his stomach. The lube's purpose became startlingly apparent when those patient fingers eased their way into Rasson, filling and stretching, causing a renewed surge of desire to race through him.

Rasson refused to let himself think about why Dom was here — not now, not when Dom's hard length was pressing into him from behind, a firm, delicious pressure that soon gave way from pain to pleasure.

He spent the whole month trying to forget that he was only the means to an end for Dom. But somehow, he just couldn't.

At least he was able to earn back Fayay's love. The water god didn't make it easy — he forced Rasson to beg for forgiveness on his knees — but Rasson knew Fayay would always be there for him, even if the Watine preferred it when his younger brother was miserable.

No one else cared about Rasson. No one.

Not even the father who had inflicted a useless lesson on him.

CHAPTER SEVEN

It took three months without sex for Dom to go absolutely mad.

His nights were full of erotic dreams and memories of his time with the Iceine — sometimes all wrapped up in one delicious package. It was impossible not to reach for his impatiently aching shaft when he woke alone in the dark. Dom could barely last a minute before his member was spent and slack in his hand — and his body naked and cold. Then desire would gnaw at him again and his cock would demand more, a creature that could never be satisfied, not once it had had a god.

Dom became concerned when several weeks went by without him being aware of Rasson's presence. He knew the god wasn't tired of watching him masturbate and had hoped that his husband's self-doubt wouldn't get the better of him. Apparently it had.

He needs someone to remind him how gorgeous he is, Dom thought. *Stark it, I can't compete with his brother when I'm not there.*

There were so many men in this hotel and Dom could have had any of them — if he wasn't married and his ongoing immortality didn't rely on his monogamy. Rasson had explained that the binding scars could be revoked at any time and no starking way would Dom risk that. But he could not go this long with only his hand for company. Eleven months was an eternity itself.

Finally, when he could stand it no longer, Dom lay on the bed, completely naked, and said, 'Rass. Please come here.'

Nothing. No response. Perhaps Rasson hadn't heard him.

'Rass,' he repeated. 'Come here. Come to me, your husband.'

There, a chill in the air. Dom shivered, anticipation heating his skin even as the temperature dropped. 'Please. I need you.'

Really. Notes of disbelief and repressed desire warred and mixed together. The god was somewhere nearby, but not quite here, not yet in his fleshy form. Rasson was using what he called 'mind-speech', an ability the sub-level gods used to communicate with others when they weren't wearing their bodies (Dom had asked about it in a fit of boredom during his first month inside the iceberg).

'Rass, I really need you to...' Dom grimaced and tried again. 'I *want* you.'

A snide laugh. *You already have what you want from me.*

'Would I be calling you if that was the case?'

Don't pretend that you are not relieved to be free of my presence.

'What's got into you?' Dom demanded. 'Have you been hanging out with that brother of yours again? You know, Rass, you never sound happy when you talk about him. And don't think I didn't notice you sneaking off during our last month together. You always came back with your head down and then I'd have to spend hours convincing you that I wanted to screw you and *only* you.'

Stunned silence. Then — *I will not bother you. Not until the end of the year. Or perhaps not even then. Farewell, husband.*

Dom remained there on the bed for several moments, his body rigid (one part of it decidedly more rigid than others), then growled in frustration. He threw on his clothes and tore out of the room, heading directly for the bar.

***

Rasson remained out of sight, lurking in a cube of ice that was slowly melting in a glass beside the bed Dom had vacated.

How did he know? Rasson wondered.

He'd left Dom's side frequently after their binding and Dom had seemed to accept Rasson's excuses — he was assisting mortals, he was tending to glaciers that required redirection or he was shoring up icebergs against warming waters. But quite often Rasson had needed to depart the fortress because Fayay had suddenly announced that he was about to arrive.

Rasson regretted not standing up to his brother sooner, because the trickle of visits had risen to a flood. Fayay now came to his domain every three or four days, demanding to speak with the Iceine. Some discussions were important, involving the interplay of sea and ice, but Fayay never missed an opportunity to remind Rasson that his new husband was only there grudgingly — and for one mere month per year.

No matter how many times Rasson defended Dom, no matter how many times he accepted an equal measure of blame for his situation, and no matter how many times he told himself to ignore his brother...

It always got to him.

And somehow, somehow, Dom had pieced it together. Rasson thought back to all those days when he'd returned from Fayay's side — Dom had indeed spent hours exalting him, seducing him, worshipping him. Rasson had blamed it on his husband's seemingly unquenchable sexual appetite. There couldn't have been any other reason.

Was I wrong? he asked himself, confused.

Rasson had enjoyed his two individual months with Dom far more than his two consecutive centuries with Fayay — but did Dom really want him? Could Rasson trust his husband?

Can I trust Fayay?

Yes, he could trust Fayay — to be jealous of him, to try to bring him down. It was a constant he could always rely on, but it wasn't a good one.

Even if I lose Dom, he thought, *I can't go back to Fayay. I can't. Not anymore.*

Rasson inwardly sighed. He should release Dom from their agreement. It would be easier that way, easier to disappear forever and never have his heart broken —

Dom burst back into the room. But he wasn't alone. Another man followed him in, shirt and pants hitting the floor before the door had even closed. Dom seemed more hesitant, but soon enough his clothes were gone too.

'It's been ages since I got any action,' the stranger said.

'I know exactly how you feel,' Dom replied and hurled himself onto the bed.

Rasson seethed. Fine. He would let Dom keep the immortality, let him sleep with anyone he wanted. They never had to see or speak to each other ever again. At least one of them would be happy.

But then Dom said the words that nearly broke him: 'You can stop this any time, Rass.'

The stranger paused, frowning. 'I told you, my name is — '

'Get over here,' Dom snapped.

The man started obeying. But the order wasn't meant for him.

***

A roar of wind from the deepest, coldest chasm; the boom of distant ice shelves collapsing into the sea; icicles shooting out of the ceiling and floor, ripping fabric, splintering furniture and cracking paint from the walls.

The god of ice had arrived.

Dom could only stare, awed. He'd never seen Rasson use his powers like this. It made him that much sexier.

The Iceine lifted a finger and pointed it at Dom's companion, a mediaist who really wasn't his type, but that hadn't been the point.

'Leave!' Rasson thundered.

The mediaist half-ran, half-stumbled his way out, still trying to pull his pants up. The door slid shut with a decisive click. Dom remained where he was, arms fastened to his sides, unable to deny the fact that his arousal had just blasted into the stratosphere.

Rasson approached the bed, practically simmering, which was an achievement for the god of ice. 'You are *mine*. Did you forget that we are bound?'

'No, but this got your attention, didn't it?' Dom said, arching an eyebrow. 'Had to make sure you didn't run off without us having the conversation I'm pretty sure we should have had months ago.'

'Silence, husband.' Those thin lips quirked into a smile. 'On your hands and knees, please.'

Dom stared at the god for a long moment. He knew he should try to say something, try to make things right — he knew that, stark it — but he was now so hard it was almost painful. He'd seduced the mediaist into his room in the hope that it would get Rasson to intervene. He couldn't refuse the consequences now.

Wordlessly, Dom did as he was told. The air behind him shifted slightly and the bed dipped beneath him, but he kept his knees locked and his eyes pinned on the headboard.

Icy fingers trailed up towards one of Dom's nipples, circling it, never quite reaching the inside of the areola. Dom released a hiss of air when Rasson's other hand ensnared him, winding fully around his straining length. The god squeezed lightly, relaxed his grip, then squeezed again; a gentle caress, inciting desperation and nothing more potent.

Dom was just starting to relax when Rasson swiftly pinched his nipple. White spots danced frantically across Dom's vision and his other nipple began to ache from neglect. Panting, he prepared himself for the next attack — but it wasn't what he expected. An open palm slapped his backside.

He swore and nearly fell forward.

'Dom?' Worry threaded through Rasson's words and his hand curved over Dom's stinging rear, a soft touch that lacked any real pressure.

All it would take was a single word and the god would desist.

Dom didn't want him to.

'Yesss,' Dom managed. 'Yes, Rass. Do it again.'

He almost sobbed with relief when the next few hits came. Each slap sent a bolt of heat right through his throbbing shaft, causing his tip to weep steadily — and every time Rasson's hand connected with soft flesh, his other hand tightened around Dom's cock. The combination of pleasure and pain was having a devastating impact on Dom's ability to keep still.

Rasson paused in doling out Dom's punishment and smoothed his palm from hip to shoulder then back again, murmuring, 'I like that this belongs to me. All of it. And I like knowing that mine are the only hands that will mark the surface of your skin. For eternity.'

Dom wet his lips. 'Please, Rass. Please.'

'*Mine*, for eternity,' Rasson repeated. Two long fingers wended their way down past Dom's balls, glancing across sensitive skin, and then dipped inside Dom, but only to the first knuckle. Rasson's fingers stilled and went no further.

'Galactic Gods, you're killing me...' Dom rasped.

'Say it,' Rasson commanded. There was need in his voice, a desperate need that outstripped mere desire.

This was a god asking, *begging*, for his husband to stay by his side.

And Dom had no intention of denying him.

'Yours,' Dom promised. 'For eternity.'

The fingers slid out of him. Dom moaned in disappointment —but then they were back, this time coated with lube. The Iceine had no doubt teleported it in from somewhere and Dom would have congratulated his husband on doing it so discreetly had he not been so distracted. Rasson continued to work his way further inside Dom, his other hand braced on Dom's hip.

When he removed his fingers again, Rasson compensated for the loss by bending over and kissing each and every notch of Dom's spine, claiming the bones he had mended, the body he had healed.

Dom's hands fisted into the sheets. 'Rass...in me, please.'

He heard the slither of silksein puddling onto the floor; Rasson had disrobed. Dom was tempted to look over his shoulder at the slim lines of his lover, his husband...and could find no reason not to.

He grinned. 'You really are something else, you know that?'

Rasson's gaze dropped. 'Dom, I...'

'Don't deny how fucking beautiful you are,' Dom told him. 'Because then I might have to get you on *your* hands and knees and spank the confession out of you.'

Rasson looked back up from the floor, pale eyes glinting. His hand closed over his own hardness and began to spread the lube along each bump and bulging vein.

'Next time,' Dom promised.

Rasson blinked — then smiled slowly. 'No. I am a god. I will never be beneath you.'

'Wait a minute. I've had you under me, moaning my name and...'

'Dom. If you wish me to satisfy you, keep silent and accept that this is how it will be from now on.'

Dom swallowed, trying to rein in the groan that threatened to escape when his god's swollen cock nudged his entrance, slick and ready. But Rasson was playing with Dom, taking his time. And those frigid fingers were doing such wicked things to Dom's nipples — tweaking them, rubbing them or skating right around them.

Stark! Why had he taught Rasson to be so good at this?

Rasson pushed forward another few micrometres. Dom ground his teeth into the inside of his cheek. He would not beg. Not when his god required silence from him.

'Your obedience pleases me,' Rasson whispered against his shoulder blade.

Then, with one swift glide, the Iceine encased himself fully inside his husband. Dom's elbows dropped onto the bed and he cried out. He was too far gone to apologise for disobeying. But it seemed Rasson didn't need him to. The Iceine wound his hand around Dom's shaft, a snug embrace that only grew tighter.

'Rassss,' Dom hissed, unable to say more, unable to insert anything other than lust into his voice.

'Husband,' Rasson rumbled in response, causing Dom to spasm inside his grip.

And then the god began to move. His thrusts were excruciatingly slow at first, his strokes on Dom's thickened length matching the gentle rhythm. After a couple of minutes, Rasson shifted on his knees and pressed up against that sensitive spot inside Dom, pausing when Dom drew a startled breath.

'Dom?' Rasson questioned.

'Yeah, right there,' Dom gasped. 'Keep hitting that.'

Rasson obliged him, effortlessly finding that spot again and again, maintaining his accuracy even as he increased his speed. A heavy ache began to spread throughout Dom's pelvis, rapidly growing in urgency. Dom arched back into Rasson, forcing his husband's thrusts, not caring if he was going to be punished for it, knowing that any torture his husband might unleash on him was well worth —

Rasson grunted and flared inside Dom, triggering his own release. Intense pleasure slammed into Dom, reducing his entire focus to the heat coursing through his cock. He collapsed, his contorted expression crashing into the pillow beneath him. His thighs and stomach were coated with his satisfaction and his mind was cast adrift, an iceberg loose at sea.

He lay boneless as Rasson scooted down beside him on the

bed, thin arms wrapping around Dom's torso and holding him close.

'I...' Dom shuddered, overwhelmed by the lingering sensations of their union. 'You know I only got that man in here to get your attention. I wasn't going to betray you.'

'You don't need to do this to get my attention, husband,' Rasson murmured. 'Not anymore. Now be quiet. And rest.'

Dom forced his eyes to remain open. 'Rass, we need to talk about this.'

The Iceine nuzzled his neck for several moments before responding. 'I...I am sorry for being distant with you of late. I thought I could stop my brother getting to me, but he managed it anyway. He always does. You must understand; he's been the only one there for me, in all this time. I trust — I trusted him. He said you could never want me after I...after I...'

'You kept me hostage in an iceberg,' Dom pointed out. 'Even a cruel god like Oceania can see how messed up that is. I'm not surprised he said that.'

'Husband...' Rasson's voice broke.

Dom wriggled around inside his husband's embrace in order to face him. Those pale eyes glanced away.

'Look at me,' Dom said.

Rasson's eyelids flickered but his gaze didn't budge.

'*Look at me.*'

With a sigh, the Iceine finally relented.

'You did it the wrong way,' Dom told him. 'Let's not dance around that issue. And yeah, I did jump at the chance to marry you for my own selfish reasons, but you knew I'd do that when you offered it. No one's blameless here.'

'Dom, it does not matter, not anymore,' Rasson said, voice firming.

'Silence, husband,' Dom commanded.

Rasson swiftly obeyed this time, delight glowing in his eyes, apparently just as affected by ceding control as Dom was.

'I've never had a stable relationship,' Dom went on. 'No one ever fought to keep me around. When I said I was leaving, they just didn't care. My parents, my brothers, my sisters, my lovers — none of them cared. I guess what I'm saying is...you're my rock. My iceberg,' he corrected with a laugh. 'My stability. So while I'm off exploring the galaxy for most of the year, I'll always know I have somewhere to go home to.'

For one glorious hour, they simply entwined, their spent bodies sagging into the sheets, staining and warming them. Dom was just about to doze off when Rasson began to speak, mostly about his relationship with Fayay; it was a deluge of words that sounded as though they had been trapped inside the Iceine's chest for centuries.

When his husband had finally stopped talking, Dom brushed his lips over Rasson's, then drew back to say, 'I don't mean to tell my husband who he can and can't hang out with, but this brother of yours doesn't sound like the best person to have around. He's a black hole, sucking you in with him. I can keep reminding you how gorgeous you are, how much I want you *forever*, but it's going to get annoying if it becomes a daily thing. I like to skip straight to the sex.'

Rasson laughed. 'I am so glad I chose you.'

'And I'm glad I chose you right back,' Dom said, smiling.

CHAPTER EIGHT

'Will you return home with me after we've done this?' Rasson asked.

They were standing outside the hotel, bathed in the muddied yellow light that crept through the planet's thick atmosphere. A few paces away, parked on the dirt path that passed for a street, was the sleek hoverbike that Dom intended to ride over to some nearby catacombs which had been recently hewn by an aggressive species of fern. When Dom had asked his husband if he'd like to come along as well, Rasson had been unable to think of any reason to refuse.

Now the Iceine stood there in the open, feeling strange and vulnerable in the slightly too-large shirt and jeans that Dom had foisted on him (along with a leather belt that barely kept the denim from falling to Rasson's knees). Apparently the mortals would think it odd if Rasson wore only his robe among them.

Dom shook his head, grinning. 'You know the agreement, Rass. I get to go explore the galaxy at my leisure for eleven months out of every Old Earth year.'

Rasson sighed. 'Once I would have thought eleven months nothing compared to the centuries I will live.'

'You could visit me sometimes, and not just to have your way with me,' Dom offered. 'You'd get to see how I work, how I capture my footage. And we could get to know each other, like any normal couple.'

Rasson pursed his lips, considering. He was duty-bound to look after the mortals and the areas that fell under his control, but if there was an emergency anything from an ice cube to an iceberg would let him know if he was needed. And things tended to move at a glacial rate in his domain, for the most part.

'I would like that,' Rasson said finally.

Dom slid his riding visor on and then produced a second pair. Turning the item over in his hands, Rasson wondered if his husband had kept the spare visor for himself or in the off-chance that one day he'd have company.

'Glad to hear it,' Dom said, interrupting his thoughts. 'Now let's get moving.'

Dom rode the hoverbike with practiced ease, either swerving around obstacles in their way or leaping over them entirely. Even though Rasson trusted Dom, he held on tight, moulded along his husband's back as the vehicle bounced beneath them.

Rasson could have teleported them both straight to the catacombs, but he hadn't offered — because that would be a shortcut, leaving those two hours unfilled at some other point in their future.

And what better way to spend his time than with Dom Zhang, the mortal who still had so much to teach him?

***

Ten Old Earth years later

The odour of rotting seaweed roused the Iceine from his post-coital doze.

Rasson blinked, adjusting to the pre-dawn gloom, then slid

off the bed and grabbed his robe. Within moments he was on top of the fortress, a chilly breeze slithering beneath silksein and caressing his skin, the way Dom's fingers had done barely an hour ago.

This was Rasson's favourite month of the year — and the one he feared the most.

For while he enjoyed lying beside his husband in their home, there was always a risk that Fayay would try to intrude on his happiness.

The last time the brothers had spoken, shortly after Rasson and Dom had begun to see each other outside of their special month, Rasson had told Fayay to stay away permanently.

'You will come crawling back to me,' Fayay had declared then, so sure that he was right. 'You came back before.'

But Rasson never did.

After years of basking in the company of someone who didn't feel jealous about him being comfortable with his body and his choices, Rasson found he didn't miss his brother.

Now, a decade later, Fayay had come crawling to *him*.

'Fayay!' Rasson called. 'Meet me up here. Don't go anywhere near my husband.'

An immense tidal wave rose beside him, taller than the fortress, and dashed itself against the ragged surface. The ice at Rasson's feet formed cords that locked around his ankles, keeping him in place as the water slammed into him. When it receded, gushing down every side of the iceberg, Fayay finally swirled into being.

'Say what you've come to say,' Rasson gritted out.

'I require your assistance with a plan of mine,' Fayay said, a glint in his eyes.

Rasson tilted his head to the side, allowing the breeze to ruffle his hair into the mess that Dom seemed to enjoy so much. 'What are you up to, Fayay?'

'Accept your place by my side and I will tell you.'

'No.'

'No?' One eyebrow crept up Fayay's greasy forehead.

'*No*,' Rasson repeated. 'You are no doubt thinking of going after the Desine again. And he will defeat us. *Again.*'

'Poor Rasson, poor little Rasson. You always were slow.' Fayay's lip curled. 'I have no intention of fighting Sandsa openly. There are other ways to gain power in this galaxy.'

'I want no part in this, whatever it is,' Rasson said firmly. 'Go away.'

Disgust darkened Fayay's expression. 'That husband of yours has made you soft, *weak*. I'd be doing you a favour if I got rid of him. Any punishment Father might inflict on me for slaying your precious Dom would be well worth it.'

Rasson's heart stuttered, but he kept his voice even. 'This isn't about Dom. I've spoken to Kuja and Finara. I know how Father interferes, how he plans our lives. Do not delude yourself into thinking that you have any real choice in how your scheme finishes.'

'Coward,' Fayay snapped.

Rasson laughed, his chest feeling oddly light despite the old pain that Fayay's visit had stirred up inside him. 'It's not cowardice. I vowed never to hurt Dom and I will not risk breaking that vow. My death would hurt him.'

'Are you sure?' the Watine hissed. 'Has he ever said that he loves you? Well, has he?'

'He's never needed to.' Rasson held out his hand, a sharp

spear-like icicle growing out of it. He wasn't sure how useful the weapon would be, given that Fayay could use his telekinetic abilities to defend himself. 'I will not help you. Leave.'

Fayay glowered at his brother but remained where he was, despite the implied threat. 'You have turned against me. It is only a matter of time before you betray my confidence.'

Rasson released a sigh. 'Fayay. I can't be that miserable little brother you liked pushing around. Not anymore. But I promise I will never reveal your secret to any of our siblings.'

'You told *him*, didn't you,' Fayay snarled.

'He's my husband. I trust his silence, just as you should trust my faith in him. Why are you still here? Go away!'

Rasson threw the icicle, but it was a half-hearted attempt. The translucent shaft dropped and skidded, missing Fayay completely. The Watine could have easily deflected the missile, but it seemed he hadn't even tried.

Something akin to relief spasmed across Fayay's face. Then the water god turned and ran to the edge of the iceberg, launching himself off it. Rasson didn't hear a splash.

The Watine was gone. Hopefully for good this time.

Rasson spent several minutes up there alone, watching the sunrise poke its way through fading mist, then descended into the fortress. Dom was now awake, a fur sliding down his back as he lay on his stomach and worked on a large techpad he had propped up against his pillow. Above him, a vidcam hovered, its lens aimed down at the bed.

Dom had ceased to work for the Graphic Stock Collection some years ago. He now spent his days as a faceless but popular graphic artist who manipulated raw footage taken with his own vidcam. He'd even had a widely read e-paper article posted on the Web about him, written by the similarly anonymous Grace Pendergast, wife to the goddess of fire and thereby Rasson's sister-in-law. Rasson still wasn't sure what to make of Dom's association with Grace, but he was pleased that Dom had someone he could talk to about his loss of mortality.

Rasson bit his lip. Fayay was right. Dom had never said that special word, but neither had the Iceine. In all this time.

Rasson was well aware that the emotion hadn't been there to start with (the lust had been their strongest tie then, not their binding scars), but his feelings had matured slowly over the years, until they were so strong they drove the beating of his very human heart.

Dom looked up at him. 'Good, you're back. I need to show you this — '

'Silence, husband,' Rasson said. Once Dom had dutifully quietened, a smile tweaking his lips, the Iceine continued, 'I have neglected to tell you something. Perhaps I feared how you'd respond. But...' It was now or never. He ploughed on. 'I love you.'

The laughter he did not expect.

Wiping the mirth from his eyes, Dom waved his husband over. Rasson obeyed and crouched beside him, eyes on Dom's techpad. Its screen was displaying another of Dom's masterpieces, beautifully rendered through the device.

And the caption beneath it...not just a title, as usual, but also a dedication: *To the love of my very long life.*

'I thought I was going to beat you to it,' Dom said, still chuckling. 'Anyway, since this is my best work yet — it's *perfect* — then it is worthy of my husband.'

Rasson kissed him, hard, then stole away the techpad, hiding it beneath the furs. When Dom twisted around in search of the device, Rasson surged forward and pinned him down on the bed. The vidcam dropped lower for a better angle, its lens refocusing.

'*Perfect* is that look I put on your face when I'm inside you,' Rasson whispered.

Dom smirked. 'I'll judge that for myself when I watch the replay.'

Rasson growled his approval.

The Whispering Grass

CHAPTER ONE

'Sanyul! What are you wearing?' Malikar Bello cried. Her hands fisted around the edges of her son's jacket and she yanked him inside before the neighbours could see him. 'You look like you're going to a funeral, not visiting your mama!'

'And here I thought he looked like an assassin,' Ablar, Sanyul's older sister, remarked as she moved forward to greet him, a beer already extended in her hand. While her mother had paired two matching pieces of kanga to create a fashionable green dress, Ablar wore only one piece as a skirt beneath a simple cotton shirt. She had chosen a kanga with a lined pattern that brought to mind golden grasses waving in the wind.

'Ablar, no, don't say things like that.' Malikar scolded. 'Someone might *hear*.'

Sanyul Bello accepted the beer from his sister and took a pull. The mbege, made from his family's own banana trees, was a balm on his sore, dusty throat, an annoyance he had been afflicted with while riding in from the cave where he'd stashed his starship. His hoverbike was an older model and he hadn't yet found the time to fix the faulty hoverpads; they had thrown great gusts of earth — and insects — into Sanyul's face. He'd needed to change into a clean navy suit behind a large mgunga tree before knocking on his parents' door.

Anywhere else in the galaxy, his chosen garb would have garnered him respectful glances instead of suspicious ones. Here on Sundafar, a planet that favoured colour and comfort, he knew he stood out, like some clumsy mark. But he had no interest in impressing anyone in this town by wearing something more acceptable — even if the unusually thick lining of his suit made him sweat.

Sanyul released a grateful sigh as the climate-controlled air inside his parents' house washed over him. There were solar panels on the roof and so the brownouts that frequently beset the town didn't affect his family — one of the many improvements Sanyul had paid for. Though he would have liked to send water, the liquid was prohibitively expensive to ship and usually it was stolen at the spaceport in Tanza, the planet's capital city, before it could even move one step in the town's direction.

Sanyul had seen withered fields and the bleached skeletons of stock as he'd ridden in on his hoverbike. It seemed his parents' neighbours were faring just as badly after five years of punishing drought. In times like these, the town's children were either in Tanza or off-world, making money wherever they could.

Just as Sanyul did. Just as he had done for half his life, ever since he'd turned fifteen.

It had been his decision. One born from witnessing the tail end of a severe drought that had decimated his town and bankrupted many of its families.

Sanyul had spent years in the Arms Academy on Leeds, learning to become an assassin and racking up an awful debt in the process. But it had been worth it; he'd managed to pay off his tuition fees after only two jobs. Sanyul's parents had been horrified by his chosen profession, and still were, but they never refused the coin-chips he sent them to keep their mbege business running.

'Aren't you glad to see me, Mama, suit or no suit?' Sanyul asked, lowering his beer.

Malikar sighed, hands braced on her hips.

'I only brought one lasrifle with me — and Baba said he'd lock it up,' Sanyul assured her.

He had found his father in the equipment shed, worn out from travelling back from Tanza on foot, no doubt having gone there to see if he could purchase anything from the city's water importers. Sanyul's baba hadn't been conscious enough to speak to him, so Sanyul had locked the weapon up himself. But Malikar still thought of him as a teenager, frozen in time from the moment his feet had first left Sundafarian soil. She didn't trust the boy he had been. She trusted the lie.

'Mama, come on, stop sulking,' Ablar spoke up. 'It's been years since Sanyul was last here and there's so much to talk about — he doesn't even know I have a husband yet!'

'I do now,' Sanyul said with a laugh. 'Maybe I'll go stay in your house, Ablar.'

'No! You will do no such thing!' Malikar told him, horror widening her brown eyes. 'Everyone saw you ride in just now! What will my neighbours say if my own son does not stay beneath my roof? And what will they say if he does not stand beside me at tomorrow's rain meeting? It's bad enough that Bibi never comes to these things!'

'Don't stress so much, Mama.' Sanyul moved over to Malikar and wrapped her up in a hug. Her head barely cleared his collarbone. 'You know they will say nothing. They will be too busy thinking about it.'

'Thinking might do those wretches some good,' Malikar

muttered, then stiffened inside Sanyul's arms. 'By The Goddess, please don't tell them I said that. What will they think?'

Ablar visibly shook with the effort to keep from laughing. She waved a hand in front of her face, tears streaming down her cheeks, and then ducked out of the room before she could incriminate herself any further.

'Ablar! You should stay for dinner — your brother's not here for very long!' Malikar called after her. 'Your husband can survive one evening without you, surely. He has kept you from me enough times this month!'

Sanyul dropped a kiss onto Malikar's head. 'Don't worry, Mama. I will go speak to her.'

He followed his sister into the kitchen. Ablar tensed, then sighed in relief when she saw that it was Sanyul darkening the doorway. She took a second beer out of the fridge and gave it to him. The bottle began to sweat immediately in his grip.

'For Bibi,' she instructed.

'Mama still not letting her have any mbege?' Sanyul asked.

Ablar chuckled. 'Mama *thinks* that Bibi hasn't had any for a while. Let's keep it that away.'

'It's best if she doesn't think any more than she already does,' Sanyul said, smiling.

He left the house and walked up the rise towards his grandmother's mud-walled shack; she still refused to live inside the house, distrustful of the unfamiliar tech that Sanyul's money had bought. As he'd expected, Bibi was sitting in the shade of the ailing banana trees. Even they, hardy though they were, had gone from green to yellow and were in the process of becoming ugly brown husks, just like the fruit they grew did if abandoned long enough.

Sanyul's grandmother was wearing two orange kanga as a dress, both pieces filled with diamond-shaped patches that were various shades of red and yellow. She looked like a sunset incarnated as a woman, a striking contrast to the dying plants around her. More than a hundred Old Earth years had passed since she'd been born. Though she had outlasted many trees and many droughts, she had never left Sundafar. She would probably die here, in this very spot, but to Sanyul that was always in some distant future.

'Why are you here, Sanyul?' Bibi asked once they were both seated, mbege in their bellies.

'To help with the rainmaking, like I told you in my last vid,' Sanyul reminded her. He had a communicator, but it seemed strange to contact his family in such an impersonal way when they could exchange footage of their faces instead. 'This drought has gone on long enough. I must do what I can to help end it.'

'Fala! You think I'd fall for that?'

Sanyul smiled against the lip of his empty bottle. 'Maybe I came home to take a wife.'

'Don't continue to insult me, Sanyul. I know you have no interest in marriage.'

Sanyul lobbed his bottle at a banana tree several metres away. He missed.

Annoyed that one beer had affected his aim, he muttered a curse he had learned from his fellow students at the academy. He hastily apologised when he remembered who was sitting beside him, but his grandmother was chuckling. His frown lodged firmly on her instead.

'When did I ever say that?' Sanyul demanded. 'I've got no problem with marriage. It's the other things the girls in this town would want from me once we got married — things I'm definitely not interested in doing.'

'Ahh yes, many of us *girls* do enjoy being kissed and touched and made love to,' Bibi said lightly, though she didn't manage to mask the sigh. Her husband had died forty years ago. She was lonely. 'But we can live without these things, Sanyul, even if we do think of them from time to time. Didn't you date a Lentarian who wasn't completely awful?'

'Eli-Tra,' Sanyul supplied. 'She was fine with not doing anything physical, but that was the only reason I kept seeing her. I didn't feel anything for Eli — I just liked that it didn't bother her. It's hard to find someone like that.' Sanyul shook his head, resigned. 'I haven't found anyone else willing to give those things up. Not anyone I care about, anyway.'

'You are very good at distracting your poor old grandmother,' his companion mused.

'Oh, Bibi, I knew I couldn't distract you for long.'

'So. Tell me.' She leaned forward, the sharp morning light from Sundafar's nearest star shooting sparks through her deep brown eyes. 'Why did you come home after so many years?'

Sanyul refused to break his gaze away from hers. She had taught him to never back down, to never apologise for his decisions. It was something that had earned him the respect of his peers at the academy. And this decision meant the galaxy to him. If he succeeded, his family would prosper, no longer crushed beneath the heel of some invisible figure who withheld joy far more than she granted it. If he failed, they would be no worse off. He had to at least try.

'I came to kill The Goddess,' Sanyul said.

Bibi stared at him for a long moment, then pointed back

down towards the house. 'You had better get us both another bottle of mbege, Sanyul. You have some explaining to do.'

***

Isabis, the goddess of savannah and third eldest daughter of the Creator God, smiled as she picked up the small wooden figure, recognising it as a child's toy. It had smooth brown cheeks, specks of glass for eyes and two dark braids running from its crown into a knot at the nape of its neck — much like her own hairstyle. A tiny little goddess.

It appealed to the Savine (her official title in the Galactic Pantheon) so much more than the pots of strange-smelling herbs that most of her people had placed on the shelves inside the shrine. Each item was an offering or a plea, sacrificed out of the expectation that something would be given in return. The herbs, though they might be missed come dinnertime, held no special place in the hearts of those who had left them there. But this toy, loved and worn, had been brought to the shrine by a child whose intentions were still pure, still unsullied by selfishness.

Isabis knew her people were desperate for rain. Their minds were full of wild chaos and pure poison, a tumult that she could no longer ignore. This was usually the sign that her presence was required, that the mortals' needs had finally outstripped their own abilities. She relied on their thoughts, potent though they were, to alert her to problems like this.

But those same thoughts made her temples throb fiercely. She would have to leave soon.

Isabis glanced towards the town, unsurprised to find that its streets were completely deserted. None of her people would see her here at the shrine; they were too busy in their so-called rain meeting, brainstorming ways to please her, or denouncing those they deemed to have upset The Goddess. As if simply talking about the drought could somehow lift it.

The Savine's teeth cut into her bottom lip. She would love to give the mortals some rain with a simple wave of her hands. But those hands were useless, and tied.

She would have to rely on another. And here he was.

The air stung her skin and tasted of salt, even though the nearest shore was many hours away by hoverbike. But the sub-level god who administered the oceans, rivers, lakes and other bodies of water had indeed left his domain and come to a landlocked town on the precipice of disaster.

Isabis straightened her spine and narrowed her golden eyes, infecting them with disdain. This was not the time to plead or show any other signs of weakness.

'You are late, brother,' she said as a spout of water shot up in front of her. Immediately she became aware of his turbulent mind and didn't try to fight the grimace that slashed across her features. She would bear this pain for her people, for their survival.

And it wasn't like her brother meant to hurt her. He couldn't help it. He wasn't even aware of what his presence did to her, because it never affected his other siblings. Only the Savine had mind-reading abilities so sensitive that another's thoughts and feelings caused her physical discomfort.

Fayay, the Watine and god of water, adjusted the rotting seaweed that made up his cloak, straightening it. Tiny droplets of water slid down each oily strand, glistening in the sunshine, a dazzling sight that contrasted with the dourness of the rest of him.

He sniffed at the offerings lined up along the shelves. 'This smells foul.'

'Indeed, it smells worse than you,' Isabis agreed.

Fayay's lip curled. It might have been a smile or a sneer. Either way, it made the scar that Finara, the goddess of fire, had lashed into his cheek stretch towards his ear.

'Surely you are not going to cave at the first demand these mortals make of you?' he asked.

'It has been five Old Earth years since the drought began,' Isabis said. 'Usually they would make private offerings in their own homes, just before planting begins. But now they're holding an abominably noisy meeting and are accusing each other of angering me.'

'And did they anger you, sister?'

'No,' Isabis replied. 'But it makes them feel better if they think the drought is due to some slight, something they actually have control over.'

'Foolish, gullible mortals.' The Watine smirked. 'They deserve to perish.'

'Be that as it may, I'd rather not rule over desiccated corpses.'

Fayay slicked his dark hair behind his ears, his pallid features twisting beneath a frown. 'I do not know why you won't tell them to move elsewhere.'

'And risk them leaving my domain? They might settle on a planet belonging to one of our siblings.' Isabis shook her head, annoyed. She couldn't trust any of her brothers or sisters to care for her people in her stead. 'Worse still, they may end up inside the Desine's grip. I cannot allow him to expand his destructive influence any more than he has already.'

'*Sandsa,*' Fayay hissed, his hatred of the desert god palpable.

Isabis also disliked her eldest brother. Their domains shared too many borders and there was always a risk that the Savine might lose some of her followers to him. Sandsa did not mistreat his people — he loved and cared for them greatly — but he instilled in them the belief that they were apart from the rest of the galaxy, somehow different and *better* than everyone else. It was divisive and led to conflicts with those of other faiths. Often those conflicts became physical.

'My people here on Sundafar need rain this season,' Isabis said, once Fayay's pale blue eyes were focused on her instead of midair. He often slipped into unhappy memories involving Sandsa and she had little patience for these lapses, especially since they made the ache inside her skull even more acute. 'Will you provide it, brother?'

Fayay's chin tilted forward. 'Yes. It is cruel that Father did not give you the ability to bring rain to your people. He makes you suffer as much as they do.'

'The Ine has been like this for all eternity,' Isabis remarked. 'We should expect no better from the mortals' *Creator God*, the one who created and then abandoned them, expecting us to do his dirty work for him.'

The Savine did not thank her brother. She knew what came next.

'What will you give me in return?' Fayay asked.

It was fair. He did not have to help her. And he rarely refused to do so.

'I know what you're up to,' Isabis said. When Fayay darted a frantic look at her, she held up a placating hand — not the one clutching the wooden figure; she kept that safely out of sight behind her back. 'Relax, Fayay. I happen to agree with you. This galaxy is in chaos. It needs to be unified. But you cannot do it alone, with only your small collection of followers to back you up. Have you forgotten how many loyal mortals I have inside *my* domain?'

Fayay's smile was cold and calculating. 'A generous offer. Too generous. I will give your people many years of good rain.'

Isabis bit down on the laugh. *He does not want to remain in my debt. Wise.*

'I must go,' the Watine said, taking a step back. 'There is much to do before my plans can be put into motion.'

His mind was now feverish, stirred up by the prospect of approaching another sibling, the one he cared about the most. Isabis snarled as his own pain magnified hers, but she wasn't angry. She pitied him. While many of the sub-level gods could read his thoughts, Fayay could read no one's; his lack of mind-reading abilities isolated him from the rest of his siblings. Isabis was not sure she would be any less disagreeable in his position.

'Don't go to Rasson,' she warned, naming the Watine's beloved brother. 'I have felt his mind. He does not wish to see you.'

I'm sorry was left unsaid. It was pointless. It would do nothing to ease Fayay's distress — and it might even delay his departure. Isabis would prefer her brother to take his emotions away with him, somewhere they did not hurt her so much.

Fayay turned his back on his sister. 'I must still speak to him, regardless.'

Then he was gone.

Isabis exhaled, her headache slowly dimming in his absence.

When she could finally move without wincing, she left the shrine, allowing the long grasses to tickle her knees and bare feet.

Her dress fell to her thighs and clung there, black and sleek, nothing like what the people on Sundafar wore. She enjoyed the simple elegance of the dress and the lines it gave her.

But she detested the way the mortals looked at her if they saw her wearing it — as if she was an object. As if she had dressed this way for some mating ritual. She dressed this way because she liked it.

As for mating, she had never felt the urge to indulge the way many of her brothers and sisters had over the years. For a time she had been perplexed by their behaviour, but then she had perused their minds while they looked at mortals and realised they experienced a physical attraction that she never had. Instead of becoming concerned, she had relaxed. Because she was glad to be unlike them, in all aspects.

Isabis stood there on the warm soil, a gentle breeze sliding over her cheeks, her smile aimed at the sky. For a moment, she was happy — blissful, even.

But then the nearby whispers rose into a roar.

Agony cleaved through the Savine. Hundreds of mortals, those messy tornadoes of emotion, were gathered in one place for that useless rain meeting. And though the cacophony was nowhere near as bad as something she might encounter outside a city like Tanza, it still threatened to overwhelm her.

Isabis held a hand to the side of her face, gasping out, 'Shut up! Why can't you mortals just shut up!? I don't want to hurt anyone, but if death is the only way to silence you...'

Breathe out, empty your lungs, hold, a mortal thought somewhere close by, interrupting her.

The man responsible was three hundred paces away, lying as

still as a corpse in the browning grass. The image in his mind was of her — through a sniper scope.

Isabis turned towards him, furious, her shoulders rigid. How dare this mortal aim a weapon at her? How dare he, this follower of hers? And how had she failed to hear his thoughts before now?

Their eyes connected through the scope.

And then he pulled the trigger.

CHAPTER TWO

Maintaining a routine was a sure way to end up dead.

Was it arrogance or a complete disregard for her own safety that saw The Goddess visit a town's shrine, as she always did, during the first rain meeting of a major drought? Was she aware that she had been spotted on hundreds of different worlds doing this same thing? Did she even care?

When she stepped out onto the soil, Sanyul's decision to lie unmoving for hours in the long grass, his lasrifle propped up on its tripod, finally bore fruit. He hadn't seen her enter the shrine and had begun to doubt the information he'd gathered over the years, but there she was — doubling over for some reason, an offering clenched inside her fist. There was something he liked about the way the leaf-strained sunlight glanced over her skin, which was the same rich brown as the mgunga trees surrounding her. If Sanyul was an artist, he might have tried to capture such beauty with a vidcam, not a sniper scope.

Breathe out, empty your lungs, hold, he reminded himself.

That was when she looked right at the scope, as though she could somehow see him.

He fired.

A single lasbolt, unhindered by the wind that had plagued the marksmen of Old Earth, burst from his weapon and drew a steady line that would bend for no one. It was the perfect shot. It should have punctured her chest.

The Goddess wasted no time in escaping her fate.

She exploded into specks of dirt just before the lasbolt dashed through the space where her torso had been. The bolt instead struck the trunk of a nearby mgunga tree, burning a hole right through the centre, announcing his failure for all to see.

Sanyul remained frozen in place, unsure if he could trust his eyes. He allowed a slow blink and drew the breath that his lungs demanded (he had denied them during that crucial moment of firing, to maintain accuracy), but this did nothing to change the empty scene in front of him. Sanyul's heart faltered and he inwardly cursed the organ for evading his control.

Where had The Goddess gone? Was she coming to kill him?

There was no way he could outrun a sub-level god.

The yellowed grass that had shielded him began to whip back and forth, frenzied and furious, the sharp blades tearing into his suit like paper and only stopping when they hit the lasproof panels underneath. This form of attack was more inconvenient than deadly, but he had a feeling The Goddess wasn't done with exacting her vengeance. This was only the start.

Sanyul knelt, his lasrifle on the ground and his hands laced behind his head. Doing this wouldn't save him. He knew that. But he refused to meet death with anything but dignity.

'Goodbye, Bibi; goodbye, Ablar,' Sanyul murmured, wanting his last words to be full of love, not fear or hatred.

The nearest clumps of grass violently uprooted themselves, throwing dirt into his eyes and pressing in around him, creating a tightly-wound cocoon that would surely compress his chest and steal his breath —

He bent over, wheezing. But his tiny attackers had already retreated. The hands he'd flung out to support himself touched ice-crusted rocks instead of grass and the air in his lungs was cold, thin and unforgiving. He shivered. His suit was better at blocking lasbolts than the temperatures that reigned here in the mountains.

Sanyul found his eyes drawn to the low, flat plain beneath him, where Tanza glinted and beckoned, a rapidly spreading metropolis that might very well encase his hometown one day. He realised that he was now kneeling hundreds of klicks away from where he'd been a moment ago. It would take most of the day, but he'd be able to reach the city at a steady walking pace. Clearly The Goddess didn't wish him to starve or die of thirst.

'Why did you bring me here?' he demanded as he got to his feet.

'I thought it would give us an opportunity to talk,' a woman answered him.

Sanyul turned towards her, his arms loose by his sides, ensuring that The Goddess saw no physical tell of what he planned to do. The blade at the small of his back was archaic in style, not powered by anything except the arm of its wielder, but it was silent —

— and suddenly gone, teleported to the ground at her feet.

'Really, I would like to talk,' The Goddess said, frowning.

Sanyul lowered his stance and lifted his hands, flattened instead of fisted, into a defensive position in front of him. 'You could have killed me by now. Perhaps you are only keeping me alive to find out if I was working with others. I was not. This decision was my own.'

The Goddess sighed and rubbed her temples, a surprisingly mortal-like gesture. 'I know you were working alone. I can see your thoughts, Sanyul Bello.'

Well, *that* explained his failure. He mentally berated himself for this gap in his knowledge.

While he did this, The Goddess turned her back to him. Because she could. She had nothing to fear from him. He was powerless, just as he always had been.

'You are not powerless,' she told him in a tone that was too gentle, too understanding.

'All your people are,' Sanyul bit out and advanced on The Goddess, not to harm her because there was no chance of that, but to make sure she at least felt his presence. 'We can do nothing — *nothing* that helps — when you decide to toy with us. We perform meaningless rituals, give great speeches and make offerings we cannot spare, just in the off-chance that you will feel generous enough to spare us some rain. You watch — and do nothing. You enjoy our suffering.'

The Goddess spun back around. A fierce scowl warped her face, erasing its beauty and making her look as frightening as she sounded in the tales told about her in Sundafar's schoolyards.

Her voice now dripped with unrestrained venom. 'Do you know what I must do to get you that rain? No, you don't.' A dark laugh. 'You mortals. Always expecting someone else to suffer for you. Always asking someone to *save* you. Always wanting to give up at the slightest hardship.'

'*Slightest* hardship?' Sanyul spat. He had already accepted that his death was imminent; courting her ire couldn't possibly do any more damage. He hoped. 'There hasn't been a planting in five Old Earth years! We are one heartbeat away from disaster.'

The Goddess gave him an imperious stare. 'That is why I'm here.'

'You could have done something earlier!'

She marched forward and speared his chest with a finger, her golden eyes lit with fury. 'Your people know how to prepare for the worst. They store food, they store water, and they never use more than they should. Centuries ago, well before you were born, they opened trading routes to Tanza, even to other planets, in case of a drought such as this. They *survive*. They always have. But now, when things are desperate, when their thoughts are piercing cries instead of whispers...*this is the right time for me to intervene.* Not before.'

She holstered her hand at her side, chin held high as though daring him to disagree. Sanyul rubbed his chest. She had known to strike him through his shirt, without the reinforced suit in the way to soften the blow.

'I would die for my town to see rain more often,' Sanyul told her. 'And I would gladly die if it meant my family could prosper without having to rely on you.'

'Do you think I wouldn't die for these things either?' she asked him, her expression pained.

Sanyul hated himself for believing her, for being persuaded by the body language that could so easily be performed. He took a step back.

'You would prefer to leave us to rot,' he accused, managing to keep the uncertainty from bleeding into his words.

The Goddess sighed. 'I did not say that. You know I didn't.'

'But it would be easier for you to ignore us,' Sanyul said. 'And maybe it would be better for us if you did. You're right. We can deal with this drought on our own.'

'You cannot.'

'*Yes, we can.*'

'No, you can't, not this one!' The Goddess cried, then swiftly clapped a hand over her mouth, eyes wide. After a moment, she peeled her fingers away from her lips to let the laugh escape. 'I cannot believe this — I am arguing like a child! I have not felt this young in thousands of Old Earth years.'

Sanyul frowned. 'You are not taking our plight seriously.'

'Foolish mortal,' she said, now wearing a patronising smile. 'Sanyul, I am the one responsible for the rain that will fall tomorrow. I had to ask my brother, the god of water, for that boon. If I left your people alone, there would be no rain at all for a full decade. Would you rather the drought forced your family to flee their farm entirely?'

'I can't trust anything you tell me,' Sanyul said flatly.

A strange look came over face. 'I suppose you can't. What if I could show you?'

'Why don't you just kill me?'

The Goddess bit her lip, looking down at the small wooden figure cradled in one of her hands. Sanyul remembered making a similar one when he and Ablar had been children. They'd been desperate for some way to pass the time during the tedious wet season — when there *had* been a wet season in these parts.

'Because I'd like someone to see me as I am,' The Goddess said at last.

'You're a child of the Creator God, a mere child who discards her toys when she is tired of them,' Sanyul snapped, jerking his head at the figure she held. 'See? I know exactly who you are!'

The Goddess meet his eyes squarely. 'No. You don't. But you will.'

A nearby shrub threw out a branch that ensnared Sanyul's ankles and dumped him onto his back. Sharp rocks cut into his palms as he struggled to rise, but even the ground was his enemy.

The rusty soil writhed and buried his limbs until he was trapped, The Goddess kneeling beside him.

She lowered a hand to his forehead, her thumb and forefinger braced against his temples.

'What are you doing!?' he demanded.

'Making you see,' she said. 'Making you see what it's like to be me.'

The agony began as white-hot sparks inside his skull and quickly spread throughout his entire body, making him arch and cry out in a way he hadn't done since that training session at the academy, when his sparring partner had snapped his arms and legs in several places. But at least back then he'd been able to put up a fight.

The Goddess slashed her way into the deepest crevices of Sanyul's mind and planted something inside him, something powerful, something that had no place there —

When dark oblivion came to take him, Sanyul didn't even try to resist it.

CHAPTER THREE

Isabis teleported Sanyul's supine form into the spare bedroom in his parents' house, where he could remain out of harm's way until his family returned from the rain meeting. His mother was already planning to scold him for disappearing when he should have been helping her make a case against her neighbour — a woman who had obviously asked The Goddess to give them a drought out of spite, because her daughters were nowhere near as beautiful as anyone else's.

When Sanyul finally woke, no doubt to his mother's voice, it wouldn't take him long to discover the mind-reading abilities that Isabis had given him. And once he was on his knees, driven to the brink of insanity by his family's thoughts...she would be there to laugh at him, to mock him for thinking her life any easier than his.

Isabis used the coordinates she had scoured from Sanyul's mind to locate his starship, which he'd stashed inside a cave some distance from his hometown. Even though it was cramped, the ship wanted for nothing — for a single-minded assassin, that is.

Two seats were wedged together inside the small cabin that served as cockpit, study and sleeping area. The ship's onboard toilet and shower shared one tiny cubicle that looked, from the outside, no different from the storage lockers beside it. Isabis wasn't surprised to discover that Sanyul kept no personal items or frivolous clutter in the limited cargo space underneath the cockpit; he had turned it into a charging bay for his hoverbike.

Bending over to avoid brushing her tight braids against the ceiling, Isabis moved through the cabin and took the pilot's seat. Every password the console asked for she was able to give and soon she was watching the vids Sanyul had recorded for his family, vids she knew she had no right to watch — but she hoped to glean information from them that even Sanyul's mind had not yielded to her. It was exhausting to dig that deep into someone's thoughts and she was still vulnerable from the act, incapable of defending herself.

But she was more than capable of learning about this strange mortal without resorting to her powers.

'Ablar, don't you dare have a go at me,' Sanyul told the vidcam attached to the ship's console, skating a hand over his recently shorn hair. 'I know it's a month later than I promised, but here I am. Checking in. Alive. And I've got good news — I'm coming home. I know, *I know*, I've only done that in the past to lie low between certain jobs, but I swear this time I've got a better reason for showing my face down there. Just wait and see.'

He spoke so tenderly, making sure his sister knew he loved her — all while plotting Isabis' murder behind that smiling face. He was a killer. A master of deceit. And he thought he knew everything because he spent weeks, sometimes even years, studying his marks and their movements.

Foolish, ignorant, *dangerous* man.

Isabis flicked through the hours of footage stored on the console, watching Sanyul grow younger and younger. Some vids were boring, others vaguely interesting, and then there were the ones showing him covered in bruises, cuts and plasters — trophies he had earned from his training at the Arms Academy on Leeds.

'I completed my first commission today,' Sanyul declared in

yet another vid, his brown eyes gleaming with pride. 'I nailed the mark at six hundred paces. My instructors didn't think I'd manage it inside a month, much less a week. But it was easy. He was too predictable. Even a thick head like that can't repel a lasbolt, especially if you've taken off your armour to go swimming like you always do just before dawn. At least I stopped him going to that Jezlo café afterwards. He always got indigestion from there.'

Isabis laughed, delighted. There were times when the assassin delivered, straight-faced, an unexpected moment of humour. Perhaps this was his way of reminding his family that he had no reservations about his career. He didn't apologise for the decisions he'd made.

Just like he hadn't apologised to Isabis for trying to kill her. And he probably never would.

She flipped to the next vid. Sanyul was still a teenager in this one and the footage had been captured inside a dim square-shaped room instead of a starship.

'I don't know why I put myself through this, Bibi,' he muttered, downcast. He was never this vulnerable or honest in the vids he sent to the other members of his family. His grandmother he trusted the most. 'It was going so well. I really thought she might be the one. Anyway, we were up to our seventh date and I was walking Dahlia home like always when she turns to me and asks if I'll kiss her this time. So I did it, because it's not hard to kiss someone on the cheek, especially if you know they'll like it in a way you can't. But then she wanted me to go in and have sex with her.'

Sanyul sighed, rubbing a hand over his stubble-ridden face. 'I tried to fob her off, but she was just so insistent, kept demanding to know why. So I had to tell her it's not my thing, I'm not into sex. She accused me of leading her on, told me I should have said something earlier. Maybe she's right. But I was so afraid she wouldn't go out with me if she knew. And now she knows.'

The shadows around him deepened, almost as dark as the despair he was clearly feeling. Isabis bit her lip, annoyed, when unwanted sympathy ached inside her chest.

'Stark, I want kids — one day,' Sanyul added quickly. 'Don't you start getting ideas, Bibi. But how am I supposed to find the right mother for my children? Someone who actually gets me?'

Isabis looked down at the small toy in her lap. She stroked her thumbs over its cheeks, imagining that the grainy wood was skin, that this was a child of her own. Someone to give her love and attention to, someone who accepted and loved her in return.

Sanyul's voice abruptly lost all inflection. 'Bibi, I've got to cut this short. I need to go shoot some shit up at the firing range. My instructor says I show promise as a sniper but only if I keep at it.'

Isabis waved a hand over the console, pausing the vid. He was so *angry*. Angry at the universe, at her, at any convenient subject. But she understood. She felt that unaimed anger herself often enough, even if hers was caused by the abilities she had inherited from her father, the Ine and Creator God. But somehow Sanyul could switch his anger off, along with his thoughts, until his mind became as still as stone. She hadn't felt his presence at the shrine, nor any of the agony that usually came from being so close to a mortal. He'd lost control after that, understandably.

Why was he taking so long to wake up? She needed to ask him how he did it.

Isabis glanced down as something fluttered onto the floor from the seat beside her. She bent over, startled to find scattered pieces of flimsy paper, an outrageously archaic form of keeping records. Paper was made from trees, which meant that plants had to die in order to create it. But anything written on the thin sheets was impossible to find on the Web, impossible to hack.

And that was definitely why he'd used paper, she realised, her eyebrows shooting up as she read the information on the pages.

Dossiers. He was compiling dossiers on each of the sub-level gods, assessing if they were harmful or beneficial to mortals and deciding how best to go about assassinating them if they proved unworthy.

He had even gone to the trouble of printing off two-dimensional images of some of the gods. There was a fuzzy picture of the Desine standing before a sandstorm, obviously threatening the people in his path; there was a clear shot of Finara, the fire goddess, waving towards whoever was holding the vidcam aimed at her; and there was even a close-up of the Tirine, the tundra goddess.

Renaei. Once Isabis' closest companion. But no longer.

Her heart squeezing painfully, Isabis forced herself to read that dossier *very* closely.

***

He was a teenage girl, bouncing across the grass and laughing, his hand held firm in Renaei's. The Tirine was round and smooth and beautiful — and so much more vibrant in real life than in the footage Sanyul had managed to locate of the tundra goddess over the years.

With ivory skin so unlike his own and golden tresses that fell past her shoulders, Renaei wasn't unaware of her beauty but she didn't care for it. No, the things she cared about the most were the insignificant mortals in her domain — and her immortal sisters, especially this new goddess she had taken under her wing.

'Oh!' Renaei said, smiling down at — *Isabis*. 'Someone's calling my name. I need to go to them. Will you come with me?'

'Yes!' Sanyul/Isabis cried. 'Do we always have to go when they call us?'

'Indeed we do. The mortals are so vulnerable. They need so much help!'

Sanyul/Isabis laughed and laughed. *Silly mortals.*

The young savannah goddess assumed her godly form, remaining invisible as she watched her older sister attend to her duties. Renaei answered as many as pleas she could, even stopping to help fifty mortals who were perched on the edge of an eroding cliff. The Tirine teleported them somewhere more stable, somewhere they could rebuild the town that had crashed onto the rocks below. They had waited so long for her to come to them, long after they could have saved their own lives and all the possessions they had lost.

The pain began as a dull throb and at first Isabis didn't know what was causing it. But as she continued to watch the Tirine help those who clearly could have helped themselves, and as the thoughts of the mortals became a howling maelstrom that threatened to overwhelm her entire being, Isabis realised that those desperate little minds hurt her.

She recoiled, frightened.

Later, when the sisters sat by a fire inside a hidden cave, Renaei leaned against the wall, exhaustion flitting over her perfect features.

'Sometimes I wish we did not have to help them so often,' the Tirine said. 'It is difficult to always be listening for their cries —

especially for you, Isabis, because of your unique powers. But this is what we were created for. We cannot ignore the duties Father has given us.'

'It feels awful being near them, Ren,' Isabis said frankly. 'Why should we put ourselves through this?'

Renaei laughed. 'Give it a few more centuries. You will understand eventually.'

Isabis soon grew into a woman and lost the carefree spirit she had possessed as a child. Her title, the Savine, now came with responsibilities instead of just a place in the Galactic Pantheon. She kept in touch with Renaei, always worried about the sister who felt too deeply, always trying to please Renaei by adopting the same attitude in her own domain. Even if doing so hurt Isabis so much she couldn't take human form without curling up into a ball and sobbing until her eyes ran dry.

The mortals didn't like being told what to do. Once, the Savine outright spoke to them, trying to avert a war, but her people ignored her and chose to fight to the bitter end.

Many died that day. And Isabis fled, unable to bear their agony when hers seemed so much worse.

Decades later, a man hurled himself off a cliff inside her domain. She teleported him to safety and took human form, wanting to see if her words could do what her powers could not; she might not be there to save him the next time he tried. But he yelled at her, told her that she shouldn't have bothered. His fury was like a blunt knife hacking into her skull.

The next time she let him fall.

He cursed her with his dying breath. Because he'd expected her to save him.

From that day on, Isabis left the mortals to it. Let them live and die however they chose. She would not interfere, not unless she absolutely had to.

Hundreds of Old Earth years later, the bot uprisings that tore the galaxy apart and destroyed the lives of so many were eventually suppressed — by mortals. Including her own. Some of her siblings, the other sub-level gods, had actually helped the mortals win those bloody battles, but Isabis had refused to involve herself in any of it.

'You let them suffer!' Renaei cried when the last bot was rendered useless, tears streaming down her porcelain cheeks. 'Your people died when you could have prevented it!'

Isabis shrugged off the stinging moss that grew across her shoulders, a weak attack by Renaei's standards. 'They died *proud*, knowing that their sacrifices would lead to victory. Your people died screaming, because they expected you to save them. Mine fought until they could fight no more. They would not have thanked me for making them reliant on some invisible being.'

Isabis and Renaei stared at each other, the rocks and trees around them splintering and even exploding. Their domains were similarly bare and sparse, but the climates and the species that grew and lived within them had always set the sisters apart.

Now something greater had become between them.

'You don't care enough!' Renaei hurled at the Savine. 'You don't even care about me!'

'I hope one day you care so much it kills you,' Isabis hissed in response.

The Savine left rather than take on a goddess who was so much older, so much more powerful and so unwilling to listen. Isabis found herself standing by an ocean on one of her worlds, fists clenched, so angry she thought she might burst.

'She sees my thoughts and thinks she knows me — well, she's *wrong*,' Isabis snarled.

'Many of our siblings are like that,' Fayav, the water god and Watine, said as he rose from the waves to stand beside her. 'You will have to be more specific about which one has offended you, sister.'

Isabis eyed him. He was callous and cruel and that was no secret, even among the mortals, but this ensured that he never had too many followers relying on him. He would never care to the point of poisoning himself. And he could make it rain if she bargained with him. It was a boon to be used sparingly — and use it she did.

Because she couldn't stop caring about those foolish mortals. Couldn't block out their thoughts or panic when a drought set in.

She would have to protect the very minds that hurt her.

Forever. And alone.

CHAPTER FOUR

'Forever and alone,' Sanyul repeated in a parched whisper as he opened his eyes.

He breathed deeply and lay there in the dying afternoon light, stunned to find himself alive. When he touched his chest, checking for wounds, he felt his shirt gaping as though someone had undone a few buttons before giving up. The Goddess, most likely. Hanging on the door of his childhood bedroom was one of his spare suits, free of tears and soil stains. She must have found it in his starship.

Sanyul rubbed his aching temples. What had Isabis done to him? Implanted her memories? They were vivid and awful — but the things she had seen! He had watched, through her golden eyes, as Sundafar had changed from an empty planet colonised by his ancestors into a growing galactic power. His people had accomplished so much with so little. This had filled Sanyul with pride, something he had never thought he would feel for his homeworld.

He glanced up, frowning. His family's voices were so loud it was as though they were in the room with him, but they had to be in the kitchen. They always gathered around the counter, squeezed in between the cupboards and the stove. The much wider lounge room lacked both intimacy and the convenient snacks that were required to fill the many awkward silences that his mama inspired.

Sanyul strained his ears, curious to know how the rain meeting had gone, but all he heard was a confusing mess of half-finished sentences. The three of them — Mama, Baba and Ablar — were speaking over the top of each other, not even pausing to acknowledge what the others were saying.

'They saw that he wasn't there, why wasn't he there!?' Malikar wailed. 'They will say it is *our* fault the rain didn't come — they will blame us, they will say we told The Goddess to pass us by, when we suffer just as much as anyone — !'

'And in an unexpected turn of events, the rebels on Frossi have managed to overthrow their planet's government practically overnight,' droned Baba's voice, as though he was trying his best to sound like a half-asleep mediaist.

'I hope it rains soon, if only to make Mama shut up,' was Ablar's contribution.

'Oh for stark's sake!' Malikar exploded, but instead of rebuking her daughter, as she normally would have, she said, 'Are we all just going to sit here and pretend nothing's wrong or are we going to talk about Bibi? She's only got three months left — the doctor on the medical app said so!'

Sanyul jerked out of bed and stabbed his feet into the shoes on the floor (they were scuffed and filled with dirt — The Goddess had not replaced those as she had done with his suit, but he hadn't expected that from someone who went barefoot). Still buttoning up his navy jacket, he marched into the kitchen and glowered at the trio clustered around the counter.

His baba dropped the techpad he'd been holding, though not before Sanyul noticed that the device's screen was displaying a recent article written by Grace Pendergast, the galaxy's most famous e-paper reporter. The article had indeed been about

Frossi's change in leadership, Sanyul remembered. He'd read it on the way to Sundafar while his ship's leapdrive had been engaged.

'When were you going to tell me that Bibi's dying?' he demanded of his family.

Ablar sighed. 'Mama, you were so loud even the corpses in the burial plain heard you.'

'It's nothing,' Malikar said with a violent jerk of her head. Her lips sealed but Sanyul kept hearing her voice, as though she was still speaking. *Oh, it's horrible. The cancer got into her bones. Why didn't Bibi tell us something was wrong? We could have taken her to a clinic, before it was too late — but would the stubborn old popo have gone? Stark her for doing this to me!*

Sanyul opened his mouth then quickly closed it, confused — and worried.

'Fine, I'll tell him,' Ablar muttered, rising from her stool. Her eyes were full of sorrow. 'Bibi's got cancer. And it's gone into —'

'Her bones,' Sanyul finished.

Ablar's shoulders relaxed, her burden taken off them. 'Oh. Bibi told you.'

Sanyul stared at her.

What did you expect — tears? From him? Ablar's voice exclaimed inside his head. She sounded so much like Mama all of a sudden. *He doesn't even feel anything when he looks at a woman. No wonder no one wants him.*

'What did you say?' Sanyul snapped.

'Bibi...told you?' Ablar repeated, eyes wide as he advanced on her.

'No! That other thing — about me not feeling anything!'

Ablar backed up against the cupboards, trembling. 'I...I said nothing.'

'I can feel love, you know,' he said, swiftly tempering his fury and loosening his stance. He had not meant to frighten her. 'Sure, there are times when I can't afford to feel anything — it could mean *death* for me, you get that, right? But when the job's over, when the money hits my account, I'm as human as you, Ablar. And I can still get hurt. I just don't show it as much.'

'Sanyul, I didn't say...'

'No, but you thought it,' he realised.

The Goddess had wanted him to see what it was like to be her. His lesson had begun with the dream, but it hadn't stopped there. He could hear everything: Malikar's horror as she considered a future without the mother-in-law who had helped her raise a family, Ablar's shame that Sanyul had known what she was thinking, Baba's focus drifting as his eyes found the article on his techpad again.

And that wasn't all.

Sanyul could hear *everyone* inside the town.

Hundreds of minds accosted him with their worries about the rain, their annoyance that Bibi, the town elder, hadn't bothered to show up to the rain meeting and their suspicions about her strange grandson who hadn't come either. Their shrill words scratched their way into Sanyul's skull, stealing a surprised draw of breath from him, a physical tell he had never failed to conceal. Until now.

Stark, it hurt. It hurt *so much* —

'I have to get out of here!' Sanyul cried, a hand clapped to his aching forehead.

He ran — past his family and their open mouths, out the door and onto the soil that was still warm from the day's heat, then through the lines of dying banana trees. He thought, perhaps in vain, that Bibi might be able to help him. But he never made it to her shack on the rise.

Sanyul collapsed onto his knees, his silent scream aimed at the dirt.

The voices crowded in around him, more insistent than before, seemingly intent on ripping him apart. But he wasn't some useless first-year student at the academy.

He could handle this. He just had to...had to...

Breathe in, breathe out, he reminded himself. *Breathe in. Breathe out.*

He continued this silent chant, his breaths long and even, until he found the strength to stand. Furiously massaging his temples, he began to stagger away from his family's farm. The further he went the less painful it became, so he kept going, heading towards his hidden hoverbike. He just had to get to his starship, then he could get the stark off this rock. Space would be silent. He hoped.

But Sanyul's head was throbbing so badly he wasn't sure if he could ride his hoverbike without crashing it.

This was insane. He had to put an end to it. Now.

'Isabis!' he called, a hand braced on a tree as he tried to keep himself upright. 'Isabis! I understand. I have learned my lesson. Can you please take this...this *thing* from me?'

The Goddess swirled into being, a cocoon of broad green mgunga leaves blowing apart to reveal her scowl. 'How you do know my name? I did not give it to you.'

'But the dream...' Sanyul began.

Her golden eyes widened.

He has seen too much, she thought. *Isabis, you fool!*

Sanyul grimaced. 'I can hear you, you know. Ouch.'

'Yes, I am aware that you can hear my thoughts.' Isabis tossed her head from side to side, as though aggravated by a mistake he had made instead of one of her own. 'It was a punishment as much as a lesson. But...' Her gaze roved over him, her forehead creasing even further. 'I did not mean for this to happen.'

'Isabis, what did you *do?*' Sanyul demanded.

She bared her teeth. Grass fronds began to lash his ankles.

'Goddess, I meant to say Goddess,' Sanyul amended quickly. He wouldn't bow or get to his knees, as her mind was suggesting he do, but it *was* offensive of him to use a name that only her siblings and her father — *the Creator God* — knew.

Isabis glanced at the ground and the restless grass stilled. 'My mind-reading abilities have always been...unique. And uniquely strong. I can affect dreams. My past has been on my mind lately and some of my memories must have transferred to you. It appears I lost control of my powers.'

Some goddess you are, Sanyul thought.

Isabis' head jerked up.

Well, there's no point pretending I didn't think that, he mused. *I will not apologise. My thoughts will never be pleasant in regards to you and you have done nothing to change that.*

She threw her head back and laughed.

Sanyul basked in her amusement for several long seconds, enjoying the warmth of her presence. It was strange, talking to The Goddess this way. But he liked it. There were no secrets, no hidden thoughts. She had seen his past. And he had seen hers.

Stark, she was always in *so much pain.* What she felt was so powerful it could very well kill him if he let it.

He forced himself to breathe.

'How do you do that?' she asked.

'Do what?'

Isabis growled in frustration and gestured at his forehead with a slashing motion. 'You can close yourself off until the thoughts don't hurt you anymore. How?'

'Oh, they hurt me,' Sanyul corrected. 'But I won't let someone else's thoughts rule me. And I've had training.'

'I haven't had any training.' Isabis blinked, as though startled by this revelation. 'But none of my siblings, not even Renaei, have the same trouble that I do. How could they have taught me?'

'But the Creator God...' Sanyul tried.

'He never has any time for his children,' Isabis said flatly. She had drawn closer to Sanyul, but there was no malice in her stance or her mind. In fact, she felt *envious*. 'Your family always has time for you. And you tried to run for your grandmother first. Why?'

Sanyul wasn't sure if he should bother speaking out loud — The Goddess had to have already seen the answer in his mind — but he made himself say it anyway. 'Bibi has always cared for me, always understood me. Once she's gone I will have no one I can really talk to. No one who *gets* me.'

'Oh,' Isabis murmured, her eyes travelling past him, back towards the town.

'You didn't know,' Sanyul realised. 'Don't you know everything about your followers?'

Isabis shook her head. 'It would be intrusive if I stayed in everyone's minds all the time. And exhausting.' She hesitated. 'I'm sorry. There is nothing I can do. I cannot heal.'

'Bibi would have refused your help anyway,' Sanyul said.

'She'd probably try to kill me if I went near her,' Isabis agreed. 'She approved of your plan, even though she did not think you would succeed. She was right. You failed. And here I am again, within your grasp, and you have made no move to end my life.'

'I have no weapon on me right now,' Sanyul informed her.

'That shouldn't stop you. You graduated at the top of your class at the Arms Academy on Leeds.'

Sanyul raised his eyebrows. That hadn't been on his mind. At all.

'You've obviously been inside my ship,' he said, hands patting the fresh suit she'd left out for him. 'And it sounds like you've been on my console.'

'Sometimes even The Goddess must stoop to using mortal tech.' Isabis sighed. 'Perhaps I should kill you before you reveal to the galaxy that we sub-level gods are not as omniscient as everyone thinks we are.'

It wasn't a threat. It was a joke. He knew that even before he saw her grin.

Sanyul found himself smiling in response. Swirling around them were the thoughts of tens of thousands of people from all across the planet. But they were unimportant compared to the goddess standing in front of him.

She was already thinking about taking it away, the punishment that allowed him to understand her as no one else ever had, immortal or otherwise. But to him it was a privilege and the very opposite of a punishment. Because he could see her, all of her, and he knew that she was like him, that she had no interest in the physical activities that most of his dates demanded.

It made him bold. And reckless.

'Do you want to get out of here?' Sanyul blurted.

He didn't duck his head or perform any other gesture that someone else might have done out of shame or embarrassment.

He felt neither. Sanyul knew he was never going to get another chance like this — and he didn't regret asking.

'Was that a pick-up line?' Isabis asked, sounding intrigued.

'You don't get out much, do you?'

Her lips twitched. 'I do get out. A lot. There's little in this galaxy I *haven't* seen.'

'But you've never seen The Bolthole on Leeds, have you?' Sanyul asked with a smirk. 'You could take us there right now.'

Isabis tipped her head to the side, thinking it through. He saw her veer very closely to refusing him.

'It's a bar near the Arms Academy,' Sanyul explained, trying not to blur his words together in his haste to get them off his chest. 'Most of the patrons are my fellow alumni; they can keep their thoughts and emotions in check. We don't have to stay if it hurts —'

'Alright,' Isabis said out loud, barely a nanosecond after she'd made the decision.

She had considered the discomfort that visiting a bar might cause her, but only briefly. Sanyul could see that she was hesitant to leave Sundafar because her people might still need her. But the rain was coming in a day or so. And if there was an emergency, she could dispatch an invisible part of her presence to deal with it.

'You're buying,' Isabis told Sanyul. 'I don't have any coin-chips. We gods have little use for those.'

Sanyul didn't have time to respond; grass and chunks of soil were already dancing around them. He felt no fear, however. This was just her method of transportation, showy and strange though it was.

But he still held his breath as Isabis took him from one world to the next.

CHAPTER FIVE

Isabis lifted the plexiglass cup, caught Sanyul's encouraging nod, then threw the shot back in one seamless glide. The alcohol slid down her throat, torrid and foul, but when it hit her gut she felt a surge of warmth in her veins. For one moment, one brief moment, she actually understood why the mortals were so attracted to the disgusting liquid. But then that moment was over — and her tastebuds did not thank her.

'And this is what you mortals do on dates?' she asked, curling her lip.

Draped across the seat on the opposite side of the booth, Sanyul laughed. 'Apparently. It's what always happens when I ask someone out on Leeds. I suppose there isn't much else to do here.'

'Clearly you have low standards for what constitutes a date,' Isabis said dryly.

'I can't really be choosy.' Sanyul abruptly sat up, his expression stricken. 'I — I didn't mean...Goddess, that's not...'

Isabis winced as his horror cut into her, but it was gone just as quickly as it had come. He had managed to stamp down on his feelings the moment he'd realised what had happened. It embarrassed her that he was getting a handle on the mind-reading abilities a lot faster than she ever had. Sanyul's mental discipline was impressive.

And he hadn't been wrong about his fellow alumni; most of The Bolthole's patrons were also adept at keeping their minds closed, except for those few who were clearly inebriated. But it was oddly easy to ignore them at the moment.

'If all your dates are this bad,' Isabis commented, 'then perhaps you really did need a goddess to attend this one. And call me Isabis. Unless you want to alert the other mortals here to your good fortune...'

'I'm happy to keep my good fortune to myself,' Sanyul said, his shoulders losing their rigid line as he relaxed again. 'It's not every day I get to go on a date with someone who already knows everything about me. This is a nice change — not having to put up a front, not waiting for you to find me out.'

'It's a good thing you didn't shoot me then.'

Sanyul had just opened his mouth — no, he wasn't going to apologise for trying to kill her; he was preparing to make a jibe about the night being young — when another body dropped into the booth, interrupting him. A handful of unopened beers hit the table, some of them skidding and coming to a stop on their sides. The plexiglass bottles failed to shatter. Clearly The Bolthole had a sound reason for not supplying their customers with breakable items.

'A friend of yours, this one,' Isabis commented, edging away from the newcomer. She could feel the camaraderie bleeding off this man and it was being reluctantly answered inside Sanyul, though he managed to mask his feelings within a nanosecond this time.

'Unfortunately,' Sanyul said with a sigh, but one that was more performed than annoyed. 'Len, can't you see I'm on a date?'

'Obviously I can't let you enter a dangerous situation without some backup — that and I'm curious,' Len added, winking. He was dark-skinned, like Sanyul and Isabis, but his face bore laugh lines instead of wariness. 'She's new. And she's not from the academy. So that means she doesn't know about our...uh...*charms* yet. Should we warn her now so she doesn't break our hearts later?'

Sanyul leaned over and swiped a bottle from Len before his friend could open it. Waving away Len's weak attempts to retrieve the beer, he told Isabis, 'Len's a pacifist. I've no interest in sex. Since everyone else in here graduated from the academy, they know us — and they know we're not worth their time.'

Isabis smiled. 'And so you two have bonded in the corner, drinking your woes away together.'

'There are worse ways to make friends,' Sanyul remarked.

And worse ways to get a date, he added mentally, his dark eyes glittering.

'Are you an assassin as well?' Isabis asked Len. She already knew from his mind that he wasn't, but she thought she should act like a mortal date would.

Sanyul threw her an amused glance.

I am being civil to your friend out of deference to you — you haven't shot him yet, so you must like him, Isabis said, straight-faced. *Or perhaps he still lives because you like having someone around who makes you feel competent by comparison.*

Sanyul coughed violently and clapped himself on the chest, as though congested.

'Nope, currently doing mixed freelance jobs,' Len answered, completely unaware of this exchange. 'But my aim is to get into bodyguard work.'

'The Goddess help us,' Sanyul said a shake of his head. 'Let's hope you don't get as attached to your clients as you do your one-night stands.'

Len grinned. 'I can't help it if I have a lot of love to give.'

Sanyul popped the seal on the beer he had stolen from Len and drawled, 'Love, riiight. So it was love you and that woman from the Advanced Seduction class were getting up to in the alley out back.'

'Well, I must do the work of two men,' Len said solemnly, 'since you've generously allocated me your duties in this matter.'

Isabis didn't even try to suppress her laugh. She hadn't enjoyed herself this much in the company of others in more than two millennia. It was tempting to forget why she usually kept away from people. But she didn't have to wait long for a reminder.

Len's mind was full of despair that grew until it was as thick as sludge, an overwhelming darkness that threatened to drown Isabis. He felt everything so keenly and deeply, and it hurt him. He tried so hard to numb the pain with alcohol, but it didn't work. It *never* worked.

Isabis gasped and slumped in her seat.

She couldn't teleport away. Not now. Not in front of the mortals.

Sanyul whacked Len's arm none-too-gently. 'Piss off. Isabis is my date and I'm not interested in sharing. Go, Len — go get drunk somewhere else!' he added sharply, casting a worried glance at Isabis.

Len rolled his eyes, apparently used to such abrupt dismissals from his friend, then wobbled onto his feet and swerved back towards the bar.

'He's okay most days,' Sanyul said, sounding pained. His mind was now so difficult to read that Isabis found herself having to rely on his intonation to know what he was feeling. 'He's also not a terrible shot. And his hand-to-hand is hard to beat.'

'But he is often drunk,' Isabis observed.

'Only after he's had to kill someone. It's hard on him when that happens.'

'Why did he go to the Arms Academy if he's a pacifist?'

'Len's a *militant* pacifist,' Sanyul replied, his eyes tracking Len, concern creasing his expression. 'He says that the best way to save lives is to know how to end the fighting before it gets too bad. It makes sense. I get it. But I hope he lands a defensive gig soon. He doesn't like having to make ends meet this way.'

'Do you like doing it?' Isabis asked.

'You've seen into my mind. You should know.'

'I can't tell. Not right now. But I don't think you have any strong feelings about it.' Isabis tilted her head to the side, watching him closely. 'You turn off your emotions to kill, otherwise you wouldn't be able to complete your task. I think it's admirable that you can easily detach yourself from your work. Unlike...some people I know.'

'Renaei, your sister,' Sanyul guessed. 'Being too attached can literally kill you.'

'Yes,' Isabis agreed in a whisper.

Sanyul grimaced. 'I shouldn't have accused you of abandoning us. You were right. My people learned long ago to prepare for droughts. If we always expected you to come to our aid, especially when it hurts you so much...'

'And sometimes there are more urgent matters that I must attend to,' Isabis added.

They held each other's eyes for a heartbeat that seemed to last an eternity. Isabis heard nothing from him, not a single distracting thought, and felt herself relax for the first time in centuries.

I could stay in his presence forever, she thought.

Too bad I won't live that long, he retorted, a laugh leaving his lips in lieu of words.

Isabis smirked. There was a way to ensure that a mortal lived forever, but she kept *that* thought to herself.

'Well, that's me done.' Sanyul threw a handful of coin-chips onto the table. 'Got any better ideas for this date of ours?'

Isabis didn't, truthfully, but she nodded, not wanting to leave his side. Not just yet.

They had barely left the booth when the carbon fibre doors of the bar blew apart, thrown across the room by explosives — nothing too high-powered, obviously, since The Bolthole's owner billed anyone who damaged his establishment. Better to do it on the cheap. Isabis blinked; this knowledge was not her own. It had been delivered to her by an unemotional voice from inside Sanyul's mind.

He was already reacting to the threat, darting over to Len to swipe a lasgun from the back of his friend's belt. Len fell off his stool, drunk and unbalanced, but even he grabbed a weapon when he saw what was happening. The doorless opening in the wall had quickly filled in with a line of men and women, all of them wearing the same silver jumpsuits — and all of them armed to the teeth.

They're from the Leeds Quarter, a rival academy, probably trying to prove that they're ready for graduation, Sanyul noted. *They thought they could take us? In our own den? Mafala!*

Sanyul and his peers were always prepared to deal with an unexpected attack. Their minds became even quieter than before as they took cover, drinks and conversations forgotten. But the newcomers didn't have the strict mental training that their rivals from the Arms Academy had enjoyed — their fear and turbulent thoughts clamped around Isabis' throat as surely as a hand, choking the air out of her.

Isabis staggered backwards into the table, her mouth opening soundlessly.

Sanyul! she cried.

The ringleader of the Leeds Quarter group stepped forward. 'You will no longer use this place. It is now ours — '

Both his kneecaps exploded into red clouds of blood. Sanyul had taken the shots. Calmly. Without a single thought or a single doubt.

'You will pay for this!' the ringleader screamed from the floor. His agony tore through Isabis' mind, causing her to fall forward onto her hands and knees.

The bar descended into controlled chaos. Sanyul and Len's fellow alumni were cool and collected, almost like machines, as they dealt with their rivals. Sanyul could have kept fighting, as Len was, to help defend the honour of the Arms Academy — but he didn't. He ducked and crawled his way back over to Isabis, tugging her underneath the table with him. By now she was panting, her vision close to whiting out.

'Why didn't you leave?' Sanyul demanded. 'Don't you have somewhere you can go to clear your head? Answer me, Isabis.'

'I don't...I don't want to...' Isabis gasped.

'You need to go. Now.'

She glared at him, but it wasn't anger she felt. It was fear.

And he could sense it. He could sense why.

'You won't be alone this time,' Sanyul promised, his gaze serious. 'I'm coming with you. But we have to get out of here. *Now*, Isabis.'

She drew a shuddering breath, forcing herself to focus — and then she exhaled.

At her command, mgunga leaves swept up from the floor, concealing the pair and taking both of them to safety.

CHAPTER SIX

'Completely uninhabited,' Isabis confirmed out loud. 'Completely mine.'

Above them, in the hazy periwinkle atmosphere, were a handful of silver moons that hung dangerously close to the planet. They glowed beneath throbbing starlight, reflecting unsteady shadows onto the golden grass below. The tips of each grass stem were bright purple and, when the wind picked up, they looked like tiny fists being waved by millions of skinny arms.

'No minds,' Sanyul commented when he realised that his head was no longer aching, that he was no longer scrunching up his forehead as though to armour himself against an onslaught of thoughts and feelings. 'No mortals. No distractions.'

Isabis smeared a palm over the tears sliding down her cheeks. 'I wish I could feel like this all the time. Empty.'

'Empty?' he echoed. 'Oh. Just like I did in the bar.'

Isabis turned to him, those strange silken shadows writing symbols over her features until he was sure he could read about her sorrow in them.

'Yes,' she said softly. 'I want to stop feeling my people's pain so they don't sway me with their emotions, so that I know if I should help them now or later or *at all* — and so that I can go near them without hating them. Can you teach me?'

'It takes more than a single day to master it,' he warned her.

'Then we should start now. Unless you have a better idea for our date...?' she teased.

Sanyul laughed and dropped into a crouch, patting the grass beside him. 'Alright, you've got me there. Sit down. We need to clear your mind.'

'I must clear my own thoughts as well?' she asked.

'Yes. But first we're going to whittle it down to one thought. It's easier.'

Isabis carefully crossed her legs as she sat down. 'Very well.'

Sanyul lowered his voice to a murmur. 'I want you to think this as you breathe — and only this. *Breathe in, breathe out. Breathe in, breathe out, breathe in...*'

He silenced when she took up the chant, her mind filled with nothing but those words. Before now, the pain from her past had been vivid in her memories, like a burning infection that had never seen treatment. But slowly, with each breath she drew, it began to ease, that weight she had carried throughout the millennia — and the last twinges in Sanyul's temples finally faded.

Isabis gasped and opened her eyes. 'Oh! That was wonderful. Should I have done it longer?'

'Don't worry about it; the time's not important,' Sanyul told her. 'How do you *feel?*'

She blinked. 'Better. Lighter. A child is calling for The Goddess because her brother pushed her into the dirt. But this is a matter for her mother, not me.'

'Does it hurt?'

'No...no, it doesn't!' Isabis' face abruptly fell. 'But it's already coming back — *breathe in, breathe out,*' she repeated, until the chaos became background noise once more.

Together they sat in silence, the grass whispering around

them, their minds completely bare. For several uncountable minutes, they simply existed.

'I don't want to feel again,' Isabis said at length.

'But you must — you need to take the time to feel,' Sanyul cautioned her. 'If you stay like this for too long, your feelings will break through eventually. They'll destroy your focus — and usually at the worst possible moment. Believe me, I know.'

He made sure she saw *that* particular memory, of the job he'd almost failed to complete. All because the mark had looked a fraction too much like Ablar when his scope had landed on her.

That was the day he'd decided to never hesitate on the trigger.

'But how can I feel without feeling *them?*' Isabis asked.

'I listen to Sundafarian music,' Sanyul offered.

She glanced at him. 'Music?'

'Yeah. It's a good way to feel something without actually putting yourself in harm's way. I usually play it between jobs, when I'm in leapspace.'

'I would like to hear some of this music,' Isabis said.

'I'd play my favourite tracks for you, but my techpad's back on Sundafar,' Sanyul said, smiling. 'If you promise not to laugh, I'll sing for you.'

Her expression grew solemn. 'No laughing. I promise.'

The wind tickling his cheeks, Sanyul closed his eyes and began to sing, his voice trembling its way through the notes. The song was both hymn and lament, for the rain had not come and the time to plant was over. There were no seeds in the soil, no promise of growth. But on the horizon, glinting like diamonds, were the droplets of water that would surely come next year.

'So please The Goddess, please and praise her,' Sanyul finished, meeting the Savine's gaze once more.

'Of course they would sing about me,' Isabis sighed.

Sanyul shook his head. 'No. It's not about you. It's about hope. We don't see you, because you help us out of sight — I should have noticed that earlier. Without you appearing on command to soothe our worries, we have to make our own hope. We're good at that, us mortals.'

'Hope helps you live with uncertainty without going mad,' Isabis said, her golden eyes distant.

'Yeah, despair's a killer in its own right,' Sanyul agreed. 'I guess that's why I like the song — it's about what tomorrow might bring, not what today doesn't have. Uh, I could sing you another if you'd like.'

'What's this one about?' she asked.

She could have read it straight from his mind. But no, she had stayed inside her own skull. It meant more to him than he could say, that she was willing to waste the time on getting to know him, person to person, instead of moving on once she'd scoured his thoughts.

Sanyul let his gaze wander back to the moons above them. 'This one's about loving a woman from far away. She's the other piece of you but she had to leave the planet to find work. And she can't return because she has to support her family.'

'Sounds lonely. And sad.'

'It isn't,' Sanyul assured her, 'because the singer is sure she'll be home one day. And he can always see her in his mind if he needs to.'

'Hope again?' Isabis said with a gentle smile.

'Hope *always*,' Sanyul countered.

And then he began to sing anew.

***

His voice was beginning to fade a fourth time when roiling emotions from halfway across the galaxy clawed into Isabis and ripped through her mind, again and again. An immediate problem then. One she couldn't ignore. She was on her feet in moments, Sanyul not far behind her.

'Croanz,' Isabis said tersely before he could ask. 'My people there are about to attack each other. If they are willing to lose their lives over something so stupid, I shouldn't have to...' She drew a breath. 'I have to go.'

'Croanz?' Sanyul repeated.

Without the time to explain, she threw the necessary information into his mind. As small as a moon but following the required path that marked it as a solar satellite, Croanz was home to a colony comprised of vastly different cultural groups that had been knitted together by mutual isolation. A recent discovery of a n'radian deposit was threatening to undo years of peaceful compromise.

N'radian was strong, rare and expensive — it should have given the colony a stable future. But instead two factions led by twin brothers had arisen. One brother wanted to hire mercenaries to protect the n'radian; the other thought the colony should learn to defend themselves instead.

The colonists were about to spill blood over this ridiculous debate.

'There won't be anyone left to enjoy their windfall if they keep this up,' Sanyul muttered. He glanced at Isabis. 'Take me with you. I might be able to help.'

She didn't hesitate. Isabis called up the golden grass from

beneath their feet and spun it into a vortex that, for a moment, reminded her uncomfortably of Renaei's hair whenever a gust of wind blew it back from the Tirine's beautiful face.

Isabis' heart stuttered and she nearly lost focus, but then she heard Sanyul's unspoken words: *Breathe in. Breathe out. You can do this.*

I can do this, Isabis thought — no, she knew she could. *Breathe in. Breathe out.*

The vortex dropped away, leaving them standing on a burnt-orange outcropping above the colony, which was half the size of Sanyul's hometown and protected by boulders instead of twisted mgunga trees. Clustered in front of the n'radian mine's entrance were the tight-lipped colonists, all of them armed with mining equipment and all of them prepared to misuse it.

Sanyul immediately dropped onto his stomach. He was recalling his lessons from the Arms Academy: make yourself as small a target as possible, don't give any sniper a clear shot at your centre mass and evaluate the situation from a distance, both physically and mentally. Isabis found herself acting on this knowledge, as though she too had sat in on Sanyul's classes during those years on Leeds.

'Their minds are so noisy; it is difficult to know who is right and who is wrong,' Isabis murmured as she lowered herself to the ground beside Sanyul. *Breathe in,* she told herself. *Breathe out.* The stabbing headache swiftly became a distant nuisance. 'I have no idea who to punish. And I do not wish to humiliate myself by speaking to them.'

'You've had trouble in the past when attempting to make mortals see reason,' Sanyul said, accessing the memory a moment before she found and presented it to him. 'They've wanted to kill you when you were only trying to help? Mafala!'

'Mafala indeed,' Isabis agreed, smiling.

Sanyul gave her an unabashed grin in return. 'Yeah. I can take a hint.' He paused for a moment, his forehead creasing. 'We use a lot of words on Sundafar that aren't in the galaxy's main dialect. Did we make them up? Or are they so old that people stopped using them?'

'They're old. Very old. Older than me.'

'Good,' Sanyul said. 'Then I won't let anyone forget them. Too much of our past has been lost already.'

Isabis had always loved that the people on Sundafar had not completely forgotten their old ways. Many other mortals had. The bot uprisings had destroyed more records than there were stars in the sky and patchy oral tradition was all that remained of thousands of years of human history.

Sanyul squinted down into the valley beneath them. 'The colonists stand to make a lot of coin-chips from n'radian sales. They could easily pay for both mercenaries *and* training.'

'I agree,' Isabis said.

'They need a common enemy,' Sanyul decided. 'Someone to make them look outwards instead of inwards.'

His mind was back on Sundafar, recalling where he'd left his lasrifle. He would have no trouble taking out the faction leaders with this particular weapon; the laser setting was the highest on the market and it could slice through lasproofing like butter. Well, the common kind of lasproofing anyway. Sanyul's suit was filled in with panels made of n'radian, which was impervious to laser-based weapons. Hence why it was so coveted.

'Sanyul...' Isabis trailed off, not sure if she was cautioning or encouraging him.

'You're needed elsewhere — I can hear those other voices calling you away,' Sanyul said. 'Let me handle this one. I have a plan. But I need my lasrifle, the one I tried to shoot you with. And I'll also need...'

She listened to him, gave him his weapon as well as a promise to supply whatever else he required, and then shed her body. In an instant, she was on thousands of different worlds, able to watch every single one of her followers and help them if she had to. Even though she did not need to draw breath in this form, she repeated the chant — *breathe in/breathe out/breathe in* — and separated herself from the countless feelings and thoughts accosting her.

Isabis made sure she kept a large portion of herself behind with Sanyul on Croanz, wanting to keep him safe and curious to see if his plan would work.

Sanyul was methodical as he set up his weapon, using a tripod to keep it steady. The lasrifle's scope was digital and could alter one's perception when it was zoomed in over great distances, especially if one failed to factor in the curvature of the planet they were on. This could put off anyone's aim, he silently informed Isabis, but not his. Even if his equipment hadn't compensated for this, there were ways to do it manually.

Isabis was about to respond when Sanyul was suddenly lost to her, like a lifesign that had blinked out of existence on a ship's sensors. His mind was still there, still intact, but it seemed to lack any signals or thoughts.

Only his lasrifle and his targets existed in that moment.

He pulled the trigger — once, twice, then two more times. Within seconds he was lowering the lasrifle.

'Now,' Sanyul breathed.

The rusty soil he was lying on rose into man-sized waves that swiftly buried him. The vortex dropped Sanyul onto his feet a moment later, allowing him to emerge from behind a rock close to where his shots had hit their marks.

Sanyul smirked as he went out to meet the two opposing sides who were now cowering on the ground, their leaders clutching blown kneecaps. With his lasrifle slung over his shoulder and his suit jacket sharp and buttoned, Sanyul exuded danger and confidence. Compared to him, in their dirty utilitarian clothes, the colonists seemed insignificant — and powerless.

'I have more people up on the ridge,' Sanyul informed his audience, his shadow smothering the two brothers who had torn their colony apart. 'They're all armed. And they're all aiming this way.'

The Croanzans gasped in horror.

Sanyul gave them a mirthless smile. 'We like the look of your n'radian mine. Nice set-up.'

One of the colonists rose to his feet and thrust his chin forward. 'The mine is not for sale —'

'I don't give a shit,' Sanyul cut in. 'Consider it up for grabs. Now I don't have the...*resources* to snatch it off you today. But we'll be back to stake our claim in one Old Earth month. Any questions?'

'But...' the colonist tried.

'Don't make yourself sound as stupid as you look,' Sanyul told him.

The man glanced at the fallen brothers, his mind racing.

Isabis saw him decide to hire mercenaries, because there wasn't time for anything else. But after that initial month, it would be a simple matter of paying those mercenaries to teach the colonists to defend themselves.

His fellow Croanzans were already nursing similar thoughts. This so-called attack had united them in a way that nothing else ever could. It had been a brilliant plan. And it had yielded the intended result within minutes.

Isabis wondered if anyone would ever impress her as much as Sanyul just had.

'We'll see you in one Old Earth month,' the colonist said with a bow of his head.

'No later,' Sanyul warned, then turned and walked away.

Once he was safely out of sight, Isabis retrieved him with a vortex.

CHAPTER SEVEN

Sanyul clipped his lasrifle back into its designated storage locker then sealed the door, his retinal scan and a whispered password keeping the weapon out of unauthorised hands (well, those hands that couldn't use a vortex to whisk it away). He glanced at the co-pilot seat, where Isabis had made herself comfortable, and wondered what it would be like to always have someone sitting there as he travelled throughout the galaxy.

Len had ridden with him a time or two, but it wasn't the same. Sanyul's heart didn't ache at the thought of Len's absence.

'Do you mean to assassinate all of the gods?' Isabis asked, a hand stroking the dossiers lying in her lap. 'Or just the ones who have personally offended you?'

Sanyul crossed his arms and leaned back against the locker, carefully disentangling his thoughts from hers. He could drown in her mind if he wasn't careful. If he couldn't stop himself. Sometimes he didn't want to.

Isabis narrowed her eyes. She wasn't sure she liked affecting him that much.

He assured the goddess that he was more than capable of handling it.

Isabis smiled. She liked his mind. It was orderly and logical, just as she'd want her companion's mind to be. She aspired to be more like him.

Realising that neither of them had spoken an actual word in

over a minute, Sanyul cleared his throat. 'I don't care about the majority of the sub-level gods. It's just a few of them I think the galaxy can do without. And I'm sure there's a lot more gods out there than I'm aware of.'

'About forty more,' Isabis agreed with an unrestrained laugh. 'You thought the water god, Oceania, was also in charge of ice. That is incorrect.'

Sanyul rubbed a hand over the bristles shadowing his jaw. 'Ouch. The academy's intelligence tutors would have failed me for making such an inference.'

Isabis picked up a clean sheet of paper and teleported a stylus into her grip. Mentally assuring Sanyul that she was aware of his exacting standards, she kept her handwriting small and neat as she created a new dossier for him.

'Rasson is the Iceine,' Isabis continued out loud. 'Fayay — that is Oceania's true name — was counting on him to join our side, but Fayay mistreated him one too many times. I understand Rasson's reluctance.'

'Our side?' Sanyul repeated.

Isabis lowered the Iceine's dossier. 'You know there are gods who interfere too much, the Desine among them. They create divisions between people where there should be none. And the mortals in this galaxy don't need much of an excuse to turn on each other as it is! There wasn't any of this dissension before, when there were fewer of us — gods and mortals both.'

Sanyul took a few meandering steps forward, barely aware that his feet were moving. 'You're saying that we should go back to a time...when we were all united under one god. The Creator God.'

'No,' Isabis said sharply. 'My father has charged me and my

siblings with the duty of caring for his creation and I will not disobey him. But we need to unite the mortals under something. I just wish we had some idea of how to do it.'

'You'll come up with something,' Sanyul said. He believed she could. She was smart and she knew how to play a long game, even if she didn't believe him as soon as he thought this.

'What would you do in our place?' Isabis asked.

It didn't occur to him how absurd it was that a goddess was asking for his advice until he was sitting in the opposite chair, his eyes locked onto hers. 'You have to make them want it, to want to work together despite their differences. And you have to ensure that your side has enough power to entice others to join you. Usually to a mortal like me power means weapons, soldiers, starships — *especially* starships.'

Isabis' gaze grew distant. 'So a sub-level god appearing out of nowhere and demanding that people unite, because it's for their own good...'

'You'll get a rebellion on your hands, Isabis, if you do that,' Sanyul warned her. 'We mortals hold grudges and we'd probably demand to know why you hadn't dealt with this or that. No, I wouldn't try it. You saw how the people on Croanz responded to my weapon — and my threats. This is the kind of thing that makes us pay attention.'

'You have given me many things to consider,' Isabis said.

And many things to discuss with my brother, she thought and smiled sheepishly, apparently remembering that she had an eavesdropper. *Fayay's company is nowhere near as tolerable as your own, of course.*

Sanyul grinned. 'Glad to be of service. I should add that I

enjoy your company a lot more than Len's. Or anyone else's, for that matter.'

Her forehead creased. 'I could have used your company thousands of Old Earth years ago.'

'That's not my fault,' he told her. 'I'm not in control of when your father spits my soul into a body.'

'I wonder...' Isabis trailed off. 'Was your soul in another body before this time and I foolishly did not look for you? I hope not.'

Sanyul shrugged. 'Doesn't matter. I'm here now. We're both here.' He paused, then forced out the words he was sure he was meant to say. 'I'm sorry for trying to kill you.'

'No, you're not,' Isabis corrected, her lips twitching. 'You're only sorry you tried to carry out your mission without being fully aware of your target's abilities.'

'I'm glad of that oversight,' he said. 'Because we wouldn't be sitting here and enjoying each other's company if I'd succeeded.'

They said nothing more for a time, merely sat there and let their thoughts vanish into Sundafar's deep night. Sometimes Sanyul could feel Isabis dealing with an emergency or some other problem on planets scattered across the galaxy, but for the most part her attention was free to wander — and she kept most of it with him.

It's going to be hard to look at that chair and not see her, he realised.

'I should be heading back now,' was what he said out loud.

To his relief, the ensuing vortex encased them both. She wasn't leaving him.

Not yet, anyway.

***

Sanyul was immensely glad that he had never been prone to a sweaty grip. He had once thought it useful, because he didn't need to coat his hands in powders or buy special attachments to accommodate slippery alien appendages — but now he decided it was useful for a very different reason. Isabis' hand remained firm inside his as they walked, side by side, the sunrise warming their backs and forming a single shadow on the ground ahead of them.

He took her to his family's property, taking a circuitous route so he could show her the trees that would soon see rain, judging by the heavy clouds gathering over the mountains. Sanyul knew he'd have to leave before those clouds arrived. His ship could withstand many turbulent atmospheres, but a Sundafarian storm, as ionised as they came, might destroy it.

But he couldn't think of any good reason to leave right now.

He watched as Isabis' other hand lingered on the bark of the nearest banana trees. One of the plants bent gently towards its mistress, brushing a dry leaf over her cheek.

They're happy to see you, Sanyul noted.

Isabis smiled. *They are even happier that you came back. They miss your steady hands. Your sister is not so deft with her blade.*

Sanyul was about to respond when he came to a complete stop, startled to see his grandmother sitting up against a banana tree. 'Bibi! Shouldn't you be resting?'

Bibi waved a dismissive hand at him. 'Don't frown so much, Sanyul, not in front of your lovely companion. So you know I'm dying, do you. Well, I don't mind. It will be nice to see Nuru again. He said he'd wait for me in the afterlife. He always did keep his promises.'

'But if you'd just gone to a clinic...' Sanyul began.

'Go get us something to drink, Sanyul,' his grandmother said, interrupting him and giving Isabis a significant look. 'It would be rude not to provide for your guest. Mbege, if you will.'

Sanyul obeyed, the back of his neck itching with anxiety. He wondered what Bibi might say, what offence the goddess might take. But Isabis' mind thrummed with amusement as Bibi warned this stranger not to break her grandson's heart, because if that happened she'd have to dig her way out of the burial plain to take her revenge. But of course, her grandson could take his own revenge if he had to. He was a professional assassin, you know.

Sanyul has already told me everything I need to know about him, Isabis replied, her thoughts echoing the words she spoke out loud. *And though he might be able to locate me with his scope, he'd have a hard time hitting me.*

Chuckling quietly, Sanyul entered the kitchen and grabbed the required amount of mbege before creeping back out. When he returned, the bottles snug in his hands, the women were sitting side by side and wearing identical grins of mischief. Bibi clearly didn't know who she was brushing knees with otherwise she would have gone for the small blade she kept hidden underneath her kanga. Or maybe she would have stayed her hand, because right then she was thinking that Sanyul had chosen a decent romantic interest for once.

Sanyul slowed as he neared the pair, wishing this wasn't the last time he'd see them together.

'Sanyul, stop staring and bring those bottles here before we both die of thirst!' Bibi called. 'And tell me where you found your companion. You aren't from here, are you, Isabis? I know all the young women in this town and I would allow none of them near Sanyul, much less give them free mbege.'

Sanyul handed them a beer each and dropped into a crouch on Isabis' other side. 'Isabis is just passing through. She's a rainmaker.'

'A rainmaker,' Bibi mused as she took in the darkening horizon. 'A profession of lies and deceit. But look at that.'

Isabis shrugged modestly. 'It is a difficult task, but I succeeded on this occasion.'

'How did you two meet?' Bibi asked.

Isabis didn't look at Sanyul but her hand was in his again, a firm pressure that let him know this was his responsibility, his answer to provide.

'I mistook her for someone else and nearly shot her,' Sanyul said.

Bibi snorted, mbege slopping out of the bottle she held. 'You thought *she* was The Goddess? Did you know that Sanyul is trying to kill our goddess? Well. I can see why he made that mistake. You're uncommonly beautiful, Isabis. But you are too likeable to be a sub-level god. And you have yet to offend me.'

Isabis' lips twitched. 'I am sure it is only a matter of time before I offend you.'

'I'll be dead in a few weeks, don't you worry!' Bibi chuckled. 'And if I annoy Sanyul too much, he might decide to end my life sooner rather than later.'

'Hey!' Sanyul cried, laughing. 'I only do that if someone's paying me. I'm a professional assassin, you know!'

Bibi continued to tease them for a time, until the sky lost its orange hue and Ablar's figure appeared at the end of the road as she made her way towards the property. Sanyul knew he'd have to go into his parents' house shortly, to make his farewells, and yet...

Isabis squeezed his hand.

Bibi caught sight of Ablar then looked back at her grandson, frowning. 'Isabis told me about your little disagreement. Sanyul, your sister didn't mean to hurt you. She can't help what pops into her head — she was raised by *that* woman in *this* town, after all. But I am surprised that Ablar said such a thing out loud. That isn't like her at all. Many people never say the first thoughts that occur to them, because they know they're wrong. It's just what's been beaten into them over the years.'

'Doesn't mean it doesn't hurt,' Sanyul murmured.

'You should still say goodbye to her,' Bibi said tartly. 'And are you going to say goodbye to Isabis? Not for good, I hope.'

Sanyul smiled sideways at his immortal companion. 'I like Isabis. A lot. I want to take her out again — if she'll permit me.'

'Permit him, Isabis!' Bibi commanded.

Isabis held Sanyul's eyes. Gone was the laughter. Gone was the carefree woman he had spent the night with. In her place was The Goddess.

Sanyul's heart was poised to shatter.

'It would be nice to go on another date,' Isabis said at last.

'You can have as many as dates you'd like,' Sanyul promised.

Bibi set her bottle down and released a groan, slowly getting to her feet. 'Well, I'm not going to waste my morning sitting around and waiting to die. I think I'll go into town and give them all something to gossip about. Isabis, walk my grandson back to his door. And you'd better give him your communicator details or I'll haunt you 'til the end of your days. Don't think I won't.'

Bibi turned her back to them, her gentle stroll taking her towards the centre of town. There would definitely be gossip later, Sanyul was sure of it. He couldn't help but smile.

Once Bibi was out of sight, Sanyul and Isabis rose as one and headed for the front door of his family's home. As they walked, fingers still entwined, Sanyul said, 'We should probably find out now if we're compatible or not. Make sure there's no deal-breakers. For one, I'd like children.'

'As would I,' Isabis replied. 'I would love to have a family to care for.'

Sanyul wondered if he was glowing. Probably.

'I should tell you that anyone who marries me will live for eternity,' she added with a sly glance at him. 'Is that agreeable to you?'

'Uh,' Sanyul said, taken back.

'You find it daunting.'

'Well, yeah. But I won't worry about it unless things get serious between us.'

'And then?' Isabis prompted.

'If I fall in love with you, then I doubt it will be as daunting as it is now,' he decided. 'But it's good to know. It would complicate things too much if I found out later.'

Isabis nodded, accepting his answer. 'We'll see, then.'

They stood outside the door, toe to toe, her bare feet and his shoes crusted with the dirt and grime of other worlds, worlds they had explored together. Here was the moment he'd usually have to reveal to his date that he wouldn't be inviting her into his bed. But he didn't need to say anything. She already knew. And she felt the same way he did.

'I'd better go in and say goodbye,' Sanyul said.

'And I had better return to my duties.' Isabis hesitated. 'Do you want me to remove the mind-reading abilities now or after you leave Sundafar?'

'Remove...? And let you put us on uneven footing for the rest of our dates?' Sanyul shook his head. 'No. I'll keep it. For now.'

'Then this is goodbye,' she said, smiling. 'For now.'

She vanished moments later, becoming nothing more than a bundle of grass that fell to his feet and disintegrated. His heart light, Sanyul opened the door and waved aside his sister's apology, embracing her instead. Ablar's thoughts sounded much more like her own voice this time.

'I love you too, Ablar,' Sanyul said, replying to what he saw inside her mind. 'But I'll love you even more if you get me some mbege to take back to my ship.'

Laughing, Ablar wiped her cheeks and hurried into the kitchen.

CHAPTER EIGHT

Five Old Earth years later

'Thank you for meeting with me,' Isabis said. 'I was not sure you would grant me an audience, given who I am.'

The e-paper reporter on the other side of the table didn't even flinch. She had no powers, nothing with which to fight a god — but her silver prosthetic leg, the scar slashed through her left eyebrow and the determination etched into her features made it very clear that she had been in situations far more dangerous than this.

Grace Pendergast laced her fingers together on the table's grimy surface, two cups of coffein and a generous amount of space dividing her from the goddess. 'I couldn't refuse this opportunity. It's not every day that I am able to speak to someone on Fayay's side. I'm something of a family historian — it's more than a hobby, more like a second job. So meeting you is an unexpected bonus.'

Isabis glanced around the café, a location she would never have chosen before she had learned how to shield herself against incessant thoughts.

'Is Finara listening?' she asked.

The goddess of fire had chosen this woman as her eternal wife, something Isabis had understood the moment they'd sat down across from one another. Grace's mind was a fortress of secrets, almost impenetrable, and she was admired throughout the galaxy for exposing the truth without harming her sources.

Grace shook her head. 'No. Finara doesn't know about this. You've probably noticed that I'm good at keeping my thoughts to myself.'

Isabis frowned. She would have to use more energy than she'd like to check if the reporter was lying to her. But oddly enough, she didn't feel the need to intrude on Grace's thoughts.

'I believe you,' Isabis finally said. 'I'll tell my sniper to hold his fire.'

She waited for Grace's reaction.

The reporter lifted one of the cups of coffein to her lips, grimacing. 'Stark, this is bitter. I wish you'd picked a bar. So now that we've got the measure of each other...what can I do for you, Savine? That's your title in the Galactic Pantheon, I believe. I won't presume to use your name.'

'Finara hasn't told you what my true name is,' Isabis guessed, pleased by Grace's nonchalance.

Grace's lips twitched. 'No. She hasn't. But I have my sources.'

'You may use it instead of my title.'

'Isabis — I'll call you Isabis then,' Grace rushed out, as though she had been biting down on her tongue in an attempt to keep the name inside her mouth. 'How can I help you? Because you wouldn't have come to me unless you needed something. I'm pretty sure I'd be dead otherwise.'

'You are much too useful to kill,' Isabis told her. 'But only for now.'

'Yes, and it's Renaei you dislike the most,' Grace mused.

Isabis kept her lips sealed, accusations burning inside her throat like bile. The goddess of fire could have fed her wife that information within seconds. But Grace was a reporter...she had her sources. And it was entirely possible that she had met Renaei.

'You can speak freely, I promise,' Grace said, making an open gesture that invited Isabis to partake in more than just coffein. 'This conversation will remain completely confidential.'

Do you trust her, Isabis? Sanyul asked. He was lying on the roof of a nearby building, the scope on his weapon giving him a clear view of everything that was happening inside the café.

Isabis tilted her head to the side, watching Grace closely. *I trust that she does not mean me any harm.*

That decided, Isabis reached for the other cup of coffein and sipped carefully. Not poisoned, but certainly as foul as the e-paper reporter had made it out to be. Grace grinned at her obvious distaste which Isabis did not appreciate, but the symbolism of the act was more important than some facial expression.

Isabis released a hiss of air. 'Very well. I recently wed a mortal.'

She then spread her hands, allowing Grace to see the binding scars on her palms. They looked years old when in fact they had been slashed and healed the previous night, while she and Sanyul had stood beneath his family's banana trees, right where Bibi's ashes had been scattered.

'Congratulations,' Grace said, taking another draw of coffein from her cup. Her face twisted when she swallowed the acrid mouthful, but she seemed genuinely pleased. 'It's not easy to find someone who can handle eternity. Although, some of your siblings' spouses are a little *too* keen about eternity, if you ask me...'

'I do not wish to bond with you over idle chitchat,' Isabis interrupted. 'My husband and I would like to have a child and we have no interest in the traditional method. I understand that you and Finara used a private mortal clinic to merge your DNA. This generated an embryo that my sister carried to term.'

Grace nodded shortly. 'That's correct. We had to pay the doctor a considerable fee for his discretion and he destroyed all of the DNA samples afterwards. I take it you want to get in touch with him. Do you need the coin-chips as well?'

'My husband's job provides us with an adequate amount of money,' Isabis replied. 'I just need the clinic. The doctor. The results.'

'You'll have them,' Grace said, reaching for the techpad nestled in a pouch on her belt. 'Where do I send the details?'

Isabis stared at her. 'But what do I give you in return?'

'Nothing.'

'Nothing,' Isabis repeated, dubious.

Grace sighed and set her techpad down on the table. 'You came to me for help. I don't care what *side* you're on — it would be cruel to deny you the joy that Finara and I share.'

'This makes me uncomfortable,' Isabis said. 'Surely I should owe you for this.'

Grace gave her a pained smile. 'There's a lot about being married to a goddess that makes me uncomfortable. But if you really love someone and you want to make them happy, you can learn to live with that uncomfortable feeling.'

'I see,' Isabis said, recalling Sanyul's unease with eternity and how that unease had slowly shrunk into an insignificant shadow. 'But I won't let this go unrewarded.'

'You don't need to — '

'*Be quiet,*' Isabis ordered, disturbed by Grace's willingness to help. When the reporter fell silent, Isabis continued, 'In return, you will be given a favour. And believe me, Ms Pendergast, you'll need to use it sooner rather than later.'

Grace went very still. 'It's really happening, isn't it.'

'*Sooner rather than later*,' Isabis repeated.

Grace bowed her head, accepting this, then used her techpad to send the information that Isabis required. When the reporter stood to leave, she said, 'I hope you realise just how much you have to lose, Isabis.'

Sanyul was waiting for Isabis outside, not a single weapon in sight. He had many inventive ways of hiding blades on his person, but the lasrifle she wasn't sure about — it could be back in storage for all she knew. A couple of years ago, she had given Sanyul the additional ability of being able to teleport his weapons to and from himself as he wished. It was a useful skill for an assassin, one that had helped him evade the authorities on many different worlds.

'I captured an image of the reporter through my scope,' Sanyul said. 'But it disappeared as soon as I moved it to my techpad. Someone's got a very advanced program lurking on the Web, one that's trained to find and erase her facial features.'

'Don't try that again,' Isabis instructed. 'Ms Pendergast deserves our respect.'

'Should we take her off the Kill List then?'

'No. Remove no one.' Isabis focused on her breathing for a few moments, then said, 'That's enough for now. You promised me a honeymoon, Sanyul.'

'I did, didn't I,' Sanyul agreed, holding out his hand so that she could slide her fingers through his. 'The information Ms Pendergast sent us indicates that she used a clinic on Enoc. Not a particularly exciting place for a honeymoon. I think we should hit Tiantung afterwards.'

Isabis raised her eyebrows. 'Should I trust any suggestions you make for something as important as a honeymoon? You're still terrible at choosing where we have our dates!'

'If only we could leave a planet as soon as we got bored of it,' Sanyul said, completely deadpan.

Isabis managed to swallow the laugh but knew she could not hide her amusement from him. 'You'd better hope I don't grow bored of you over the next few centuries.'

'You won't,' Sanyul promised. 'Just as you won't stop loving me.'

'Good, that means we're on even footing,' Isabis said, smiling.

Grass as golden as her eyes swirled up around them and then sent them across the stars. Together.

THE CREEPING MOSS

CHAPTER ONE

Lorne Lavine, formerly a major in the Galactic Law Enforcement Agency (GLEA for short), pulled down on the hardlight bar of his weights machine until he felt the dual pinch beneath his shoulder blades. He held that position for several seconds, breathing slowly, and then let the bar tug his arms up above his head. The next time he brought the strip of hardlight down to his thudding heart, he grimaced from annoyance instead of pain.

His head was all over the place. He couldn't focus.

Lorne released the bar, causing it to thrum angrily as it bounced back into place, and hunched forward on the padded seat, contemplating the sunrise bleeding its way across the horizon.

A red dawn. It should be considered a warning — so said the many ancient tales that humans continued to tell each other. But Old Earth, where those first red dawns had been observed by Lorne's species, had been destroyed millennia ago. Red dawns here meant it was just the start of another fifteen-hour day.

Lorne lived on Velde, a planet buried beneath dense cloud cover for eleven months out of each Old Earth year. Most days only red light made it through. Today, however, the atmospheric blanket shielding him from the nearest star was thinner than usual, a promise of better light. He wouldn't need to sit by the UV lamps this evening if he went outside. Lorne had lost his tan since coming back to Velde and he intended to work on it. At least his wavy brunette hair still had its blond highlights. That was something.

Maybe he should pull on some shoes and try to outrun this feeling…whatever it was.

Lorne dragged air into his lungs and then spat it back out again. The plexiglass dividing him from this red dawn could be set to opaque or even midnight black, but he preferred his workout sessions to be surrounded by natural serenity.

He wasn't feeling particularly serene right now.

The lonely clumps of grass outside shivered as a breeze wafted over them, the only sign of movement in a field studded with scarred and moss-strewn rocks. The mountains in the distance were capped with gleaming bronze snow and remained unmoving, unbending.

Very few large species of fauna existed up here on the endless plateaus. Usually it was as empty as a desert out there. Sometimes, if he was lucky, Lorne would spot a herd of imported muskoxen, descendants of the beasts that had roamed Old Earth.

He should have been used to the quiet by now, but today it felt different.

Someone — or something — was coming.

Lorne hissed out some choice curse words that he'd learned during his service to the Creator God and tapped two fingers to his scarred temple, where a chip had been housed underneath the skin until three Old Earth months ago. The specialised tech had made him, in slang terms, a 'Chipper' — someone who was capable of sensing and manipulating the energy of the Creator God's universe. While he'd been at the Agency, Lorne had used his chip to create defensive forcefields and to locate nearby lifeforms.

He felt naked and vulnerable without the chip. Anyone could sneak up on him now. He'd never sense them coming.

So why did he feel a presence?

'Hardlight deactivate,' Lorne snapped as he jumped off the seat.

The bar on his weights machine blinked out of existence. Cursing once more, he grabbed his coat and left the room. The coat's fur lining sealed in around his loose workout clothes at the touch of a button, but it was nowhere near as snug as the voice-activated boots he shoved his feet into. Lorne unclipped his preferred lasgun from its mount and hefted the weapon, a heavy model that required two hands to hold, and felt his shoulder ache in protest.

He gritted his teeth. It had been too long since he'd been in the field. Too long since he'd had to take on galactic criminals. Too long since he'd dug the chip out of his own temple rather than wait for the Agency to carefully remove it for him.

The door slid aside at his barked command. Cold air immediately rushed him like a stream of lasgun bolts. Unrelenting, it struck his face and swept over his lips, trying to steal the breath from his lungs.

He refused to let it.

Lorne caught his reflection in the plexiglass when he turned to make sure the door had shut behind him. He couldn't remember the last time he'd shaved and it showed. Despite this, he smiled. The dark stubble had suited him ever since he'd first started growing facial hair. He liked the way it strengthened his jaw and how it never transformed into a wild beard, no matter how long he left it.

Disgusted with his vanity, Lorne shook his head and shifted

his attention back to his surroundings, wary of the encompassing silence. He took a step down from the verandah and cast his hazel eyes across the horizon.

'Where are you, you little shit?' he muttered. 'Or are you that phantom sensation the Agency's medical personnel warned me about?'

'Well, I can be everywhere at once, if I choose to be,' a feminine-sounding voice answered him. 'But for the purposes of our conversation, I am right behind you.'

Lorne spun around and fired off a shot before he was even aware of his finger tensing on the trigger. A horrified gasp peeled his lips apart. Had he just killed someone?

But the intruder remained right where she was, amusement written over her soft features. The lasbolt hovered in the air between them for a few moments more, then sprang away into the atmosphere.

Her temples were bare of any bumps that might house a chip, but he hadn't expected to see any. No agent of GLEA could create a defensive forcefield without extending their hands to guide the output of energy — and no Chipper could manage to do that inside a single nanosecond. He was standing in the presence of one of the divine children of the Creator God.

Lorne's knees hit the ground. The lasgun swiftly followed.

'Renaei, my goddess,' he breathed. 'How may I serve you?'

'Stand up, Lorne,' she said.

His eyes burned with tears as he obeyed her. She had used his real name, the name that most of his family was incapable of remembering. Lorne's father had always been careful to use it, but Jon Lavine was long dead and his ashes were in some other relative's keeping, forever out of reach. The only thing Lorne had left of his father was this house, despite his family's attempts to steal it for themselves. They'd failed. The Galactic Database listed his name as *Lorne* Lavine and so had the will. There was no misinterpreting that. It didn't hurt that he'd had GLEA on his side at the time.

Lorne knew he should keep his gaze averted, but he couldn't. Gods, Renaei was even more beautiful in person than in his distorted childhood memories. Those stunning green eyes, as dark and mysterious as the moss growing on the nearby rocks, captured him anew. Those long golden locks that flowed down past her shoulders shone as brightly as the bangles on her wrists. That smile, so full of warmth, could have vaporised the clouds gathering overhead. And those generous curves, accentuated by the white dress clinging to her form, invited more than the caress of his eyes.

She was perfect.

'Are you capable of having a coherent conversation right now?' his goddess asked, one eyebrow raised.

'I...' Lorne cast around for something to say; nothing came to him.

He shook his head.

Laughing, Renaei flounced past him and then swung back around, a hand propped up on her hip. 'You should invite me inside and make me breakfast. It's the least you can do for the goddess who saved your life once — especially since you just tried to shoot her!'

'Yes, of course,' Lorne managed.

He barely remembered to pick up the lasgun on his way in.

***

241

Renaei, goddess of every type of tundra imaginable, took command of the gas burner after Lorne gave her the remaining ptarmigan eggs and strips of muskox meat he'd kept in his fridge. The mortal then sank onto a nearby stool, gratefully relinquishing the task of making breakfast to her.

Renaei liked the earthy colour scheme of the kitchen — even the stools and appliances complemented the muted granite benches. This made the room feel very homely despite its expansive size. Clearly it was intended for a party consisting of more than just one man.

Renaei set a plate loaded with food in front of Lorne. When he stared at it, she gestured impatiently. 'I believe it's edible. This isn't my first time with a spatula, Lorne.'

Lorne sighed and relented. 'I didn't mean to offend you, Renaei.'

She rewarded him with a smile. Renaei was known in the Galactic Pantheon as the Tirine, a title given to her by the Ine (or the Creator God, as her father was known to the mortals). Her siblings used their titles or other assumed names around their followers, but Renaei hated the lack of intimacy that resulted from this practice. Every soul who worshipped her had been given her true name and knew only to use it when they desperately needed her help.

This man had adhered to that rule all his life. But he had sought her in other ways.

Just as she had sought him.

Lorne speared a strip of crispy meat with his fork and brought it to his lips. He chewed, his hazel eyes distant, then swallowed. Surprise flashed across his expression and his mind was filled with a pleasant glow. It didn't last long, but Renaei relished every moment of it.

She had always appreciated inheriting both telekinesis and mind-reading abilities from her father, but some of the heads she peered into contained some pretty nasty stuff.

Lorne's mind had never been like that.

'I hope you didn't join GLEA just because you thought being close to my father would help you get close to me,' Renaei said, allowing a frown to cut through her sunny expression. The Chippers believed they could reach the Creator God by inserting chips into their temples. The Ine, for whatever reason, had humoured them and had even allowed the tech to grant the mortals weaker versions of his lowest abilities.

'No. That's not why.' Lorne cleared his throat a couple of times. 'I mean, that's only one reason. I wanted to help people. Save people. The way you saved me.'

'And there's no other reason you enlisted?' Renaei prompted gently.

Lorne set his fork down. 'You already know.'

'Since we're going to be spending so much time together,' Renaei told him, 'we really ought to speak as equals — and not as worshipper and goddess. So let's pretend I don't know.'

The former Chipper linked his shaking hands together on the counter. He kept them anchored there as a single fist, his emotions tightening into a ball as he controlled his anger. 'My family refused to accept who I was. What I needed to do. Dad didn't have the funds to help me, Creator God knows he wanted to, so I joined GLEA. They pay for all of your medical expenses. Even the *elective* surgeries,' he added, visibly annoyed by the term. To him they had been the very opposite of elective.

'That should have told your family something,' Renaei muttered. When he looked up at her, startled, she clarified, 'Well, they insisted that you should be forced to accept the body you were born with. But GLEA, those closest to my father, had no issue with you obtaining the form that suits you best.'

Lorne's lip twisted. 'My relatives believe the Agency only helped me transition because they needed more bodies to fill out their ranks. Maybe they're right. I hope not.'

'No,' Renaei said firmly. 'That's not why the Chippers helped you. I *know*.'

'Doesn't matter now, does it? I had my own problems with GLEA in the end.'

Renaei inclined her head towards him. 'It also upsets me that the Agency now pressures its agents into marrying and breeding. I imagine it's because they want a steady supply of recruits.'

'Yeah, your contribution to that *supply* is the most important thing in your file when they consider you for promotion,' Lorne said in disgust. He blinked. 'Shit. How is it I'm speaking to you so casually? You're my starking goddess.'

She laughed and danced around the counter towards him, reaching over to swipe some of the food from his plate. He flinched. Renaei swiftly took several steps back until he relaxed. Reminding herself to be patient with him, she said, 'My sisters say I'm too friendly with you mortals. But I'd rather treat you as dear friends instead of servants.'

'You said...we would be spending time together,' Lorne said quietly.

'Yes! Oh yes, I should get to that.' Renaei licked the grease from her fingers. She didn't miss his eyes following the movement of her tongue. 'I need a bodyguard.'

He stared at her.

Renaei stared right back.

Finally, he said, 'But you're a goddess. You don't need a bodyguard. You don't need...me.'

'I hate to ruin this perfect image you have of me, but we sub-level gods are not invulnerable,' Renaei said, chuckling. 'Immortal, sure. But a well-aimed lasbolt can actually take us out.'

Lorne's eyes widened. He wasn't just surprised by this new knowledge; he was surprised that she'd shared it with him. His pride at being given her trust created a warm thrum inside his mind, but it didn't quite manage to unseat the feeling that he was not worthy of her attention or her presence — her gorgeous, distracting presence. Despite all his attempts not to, he was imagining her naked.

'Please tell me you can't read minds,' he said after a moment.

Renaei grinned. 'I can't tell you that. But I can assure you that I look way more awesome than you've pictured since you were a teenager with your hand beneath the covers.'

'Why do you need a bodyguard, Renaei?' he asked, holding her gaze, his breakfast forgotten. 'You have telekinetic abilities that outstrip anything a Chipper could simulate with their forcefields.'

Renaei nodded. 'But I can still be overwhelmed.'

'And are you heading into a situation where you might be overwhelmed?'

Renaei appraised him for a long moment. His tone was now very similar to the one he'd used when delivering orders to the agents under his command. And he was already sorting through the scraps of information she had given him, trying to assemble them in his mind.

Good. She needed him functional.

'My enemy's powers are more than a match for my own,' she answered vaguely.

He wasn't fooled for a nanosecond. 'Another sub-level god? Then you're going to need more than just one bodyguard. You're going to need several.'

'It's a good thing I picked someone with a background of training others,' Renaei remarked.

'Funny that,' Lorne said, humour threading through his words. He slid off the stool. 'I'll need to pack some clothes. Equipment. Weapons.'

'Just a moment, Lorne,' Renaei said. 'You'll need something else first.'

He waited patiently, arms loose by his sides, and didn't move away when she reached for him, two fingers aimed for each temple.

Skin met skin. She whispered an apology.

And then she flooded her power into him, raw and potent, enough to make him gasp in pain.

It wasn't unheard of, to do something like this. Sandsa, the Desine and god of the deserts, gave a small measure of power to every single follower born inside his domain. Most sub-level gods refused to share themselves in this way. Sandsa did it because he wanted his people to be able to defend themselves against the Chippers, whom he regarded with disdain and sometimes fury because of their connection to his father.

Renaei had many reasons to choose Lorne, some of which she wouldn't admit to, but she was quite willing to justify her choice by pointing out that he had already learned discipline and was no stranger to mental-based abilities.

But even he was overwhelmed by the sudden influx of power. He fell against her, a dead weight. Startled, Renaei used her abilities to catch him and quickly stepped aside, holding him up telekinetically until his limbs regained their strength.

When he could finally move, he sagged onto his knees, a cute mixture of bewilderment and awe sweeping over his face. 'My goddess...how can I thank you?'

'By doing your job,' Renaei said.

'I can do that,' he promised.

CHAPTER TWO

Rain slapped his head and shoulders with the force of relentless hands. Not to be outdone, the cold cyclonic wind howled and struck him so hard it was like being hit with a hovercar.

He kept his lips sealed, refusing to unleash the scream buried inside him. For over an hour, he had survived on a boulder smothered with slippery lichen, but if the water rose any higher it would reach his ankles or, worse, his knees. The raging torrent was strong enough to yank him down and carry him away, battering his tiny body against the rocks as it went.

His long brown pigtails, kept attached to his scalp by the will of his mother, lashed his back as he swung his gaze around, desperate for the clouds to break apart, for the storm to stop.

But it had no intention of stopping.

And his fear might claim him before the inky water ever did.

He was a thin, pale waif, so insignificant compared to the gales that were trying to topple him. The dress he wore beneath his coat was tattered and torn and now so wet it was only making him colder. He should have stayed inside, with his siblings and his cousins, but he'd had to show them, had to prove he could survive a night alone in the wilderness.

They'd said he couldn't do it, because he was the youngest of them, only nine years old — and he was weak because he was a girl. Lorne had tried to argue that on other planets far from Velde it didn't matter, that girls could fight and even pilot starships, but that wasn't the real reason they taunted Lorne.

He had dared to say he wasn't a girl at all. They had laughed and bruised him.

So he had marched out into the icy darkness, armed only with a coat, oversized boots and a pair of gloves. Lorne knew he'd lasted longer out here than any of his relatives ever had. He didn't need a tent when he could use tiny outcroppings for shelter. He didn't need a pack of provisions when he could scrape moss from the rocks for his dinner. And that same moss could become a warm blanket if you found a thick enough patch of it.

He had hoped that his family would realise he was missing. They were supposed to come find him and be so impressed with his skills that they would finally stop calling him Lorna.

But the storm had found him instead.

Gritting his teeth, he told himself he wasn't giving up. It stung his pride to do this, but he'd rather fail than lose his life.

He would use Renaei's name, just as he'd been taught to do ever since he was a baby. Everyone in his family knew they lived under the protection of a goddess who loved and cared for them all. Human, Jezlo, Unandan, boy, girl, whoever you were — it didn't matter. Her love knew no bounds.

And that's why he loved her back.

'Renaei!' he cried. 'Renaei! Save me!'

She appeared so suddenly that he nearly fell off the boulder. Moving to stand beside him, she wrapped an arm around his shoulders and shouted into the night, 'No, Fayay, he is mine! He's under my protection! Now shoo!'

Grudgingly, the rain eased — not by much, but just enough. For hours they stood together, the goddess shielding Lorne as the flood waters spun dizzyingly around them. She even conjured a cocoon of moss that wrapped around his entire body, warming him from head to toe and smothering his fear. He'd heard that she could instantly teleport people to safety, but somehow she knew he didn't want that. Somehow she knew he needed to do this, to see the whole night through.

Renaei stayed by his side until the red dawn broke and the water began to recede.

'R — Renaei,' he said through trembling lips. 'Y — you can go now. I'll be okay.'

She gave him a radiant smile. 'Yes, I think you will be. Do you know what else I think?'

'N — no?' He was mystified.

'I think you're going to be a very handsome man one day,' she said.

And then she was gone, along with the moss that had embraced him.

Lorne fell to his knees and praised her, removing his gloves to press his bare hands to the very place where her feet had been mere moments ago. When his fingers began to ache, he stood and ran for the safety and warmth of his home.

His mother fussed over him, so worried, so frightened — and then the scolding started. Lorne wished his father was home instead of halfway across the galaxy on some interplanetary freighting job. No one else would believe that Lorne had met their goddess. No one. He knew this for certain.

Because his father was the only one who believed Lorne when he said he wasn't a girl.

***

The strip lighting overhead blasted away the last vestiges of Lorne's dream and the memories it contained. He fumbled for the techpad he'd dropped when he'd fallen asleep the previous night and checked the time. His eyebrows bunched together. He'd never slept his long while at the Agency. It was well past dawn and he needed to wake the others for their training.

But his Guards of the Goddess weren't exactly GLEA — they hadn't even been around for six full months yet. And they hadn't seen a single day of action. He'd styled himself as their captain, a rank that GLEA no longer used because they wanted to avoid any association with the numerous starship captains running around the galaxy. Renaei had also told Lorne that GLEA's ranking system was only a pale imitation of the ones that had been used by military groups millennia ago, so he'd decided it really didn't matter what he did with his own rank.

Lorne's eyelids snapped shut and refused to budge when he commanded them to open. He cursed. 'Stark! Someone turn the lights down — it's too starking bright.'

'Is that an order, Captain?' chortled Merryn Lee from the bunk above him. He'd never given anyone a proper rank in the group, mostly because no one else had his level of power or experience, but everyone knew she was his Second. They'd served together during their time at GLEA.

'Or you could ask Renaei to do it for you,' Merryn added, a smirk tainting her words. 'She's the one closest to the panel right now.'

Lorne shot out of bed, his head narrowly avoiding a collision with Merryn's bunk — then he remembered that he was only wearing boxers. He snagged the sheet from his bed and twisted it around himself, ignoring the snickers of the fourteen men and women who shared the sleeping quarters inside the grounded vessel.

They'd make fun of his sudden shyness later, probably even suggest he had a crush on his boss. Lorne had spent years toning and building up muscle so he wasn't ashamed to show off his hard work in the showers. But this was different. He'd had no warning, no chance to prepare himself for the goddess' arrival. No time to hide his obvious reaction to her presence.

Renaei, his powerful patron, was in her usual form-hugging dress and its thin fabric left very little to the imagination. She seemed unaware — or simply didn't care — that this was the sort of dress favoured by a woman several sizes smaller.

Lorne swallowed. He was unable to suppress the heat that had gathered inside his abdomen. The lift of her eyebrow suggested she'd read his desire straight from him.

'Captain, come outside so I can speak to you privately,' Renaei invited.

Lorne cleared his throat. 'Can I get some clothes on first?'

'No, the goddess wants you go out naked and freeze to death,' Merryn said with a snort as she dropped down from her bunk. 'So while you're off doing secret Captain-y things, d'you want us to hit the showers then practice the Trip and Rush?'

She was referring to a drill which began with them using their goddess-given abilities to turn rock and moss and anything else from their surroundings into snares. This would then be followed by the Guards of the Goddess racing in with their lasguns to subdue their fallen opponents. The manoeuvre lacked finesse, but Lorne hoped it would provide enough of a surprise to give them an advantage in battle. His guards would also be carrying personal shielding devices to protect themselves from lasbolts or any debris a sub-level god might hurl their way.

'Sounds good, Second,' he said, keeping his voice even. 'Now can you all fuck off and give me a few moments to myself?'

Lorne waited for Renaei to slip out and for his people to start filing off to the large shower bay before reaching for his clothes. It wasn't a uniform but he'd had enough of those to last a lifetime. He preferred jeans these days, even though he always cursed under his breath as he pulled on the cotton stockings he had to wear underneath them in colder climates.

He didn't think it was a bad thing to have an extra layer separating him from the goddess he couldn't stop thinking about. And in ways that were entirely inappropriate.

Stark. She had to know how often he did that.

***

The starship was parked in a gully that shivered each time a breath of air passed through the blood-red grasses that grew there. Despite the ship's impressive size — squeezed inside the hull were sleeping quarters, showers, toilets, an armoury and even a kitchen with tables and chairs — it was dwarfed by the ridges rising up around it.

Renaei was waiting on top of one of these ridges, peering off into the distance. Lorne wasn't sure what she could see in that horizon. He only saw an unfamiliar blue sky (he still couldn't pronounce the planet's name, so hadn't bothered remembering it) and though he knew that most worlds were terraformed to look this way, it seemed glaringly bright and overly optimistic.

Lorne jogged up to Renaei, deliberately taking his time and wondering — with no small amount of dread — if this was the day she would finally order them to leave their temporary base and head for enemy territory. When he reached the ridge, she turned to him and smiled. He tried to tell himself it was the run that had taken his breath away.

But he knew he wasn't that unfit. It was all her.

'Are my Guards of the Goddess ready?' Renaei asked him.

Lorne slicked his tongue around inside his mouth, moistening it. 'To fight? Sure. To win? I don't know. Chippers take years to reach their full potential. You only gave me six months to find people, convince them to join us and then train them to use their new powers.'

Lorne had remained in contact with a few agents who'd left GLEA for one reason or another — they'd been the easy ones to track down and trust. Finding other people who could wield a lasgun and weren't complete crooks — that had been slightly more difficult.

The mind-reading abilities Renaei had given Lorne had helped him ascertain the likelihood of a person betraying them. It was also a lot easier to spot a negative reaction when he casually mentioned some childhood incident that revealed how he'd spent his earlier years. Though Lorne knew that his family was the exception and not the rule, he'd wanted to avoid recruiting anyone who would refuse to take orders from him.

Some of the guards he had picked because they were worshippers of Renaei already. Even though they weren't particularly good shots to start with, they had the right amount of awe and respect for their goddess. The coin-chips Renaei spirited in from somewhere (Lorne suspected they were stolen) to pay the guards certainly helped to curate loyalty. In addition to this, the Guards of the Goddess enjoyed powers that gave them control over tundra-based terrain.

So far none of Lorne's choices had let him down. All of them were decent people, even if their jokes were crude and they didn't seem to feel ashamed about cracking them in front of their goddess.

Renaei, for her part, always seemed to laugh the loudest. Once she even mentioned a sexual escapade which had impressed several of the guards, mostly because that incident had involved a public location and a fair amount of risk. They'd laughed and congratulated her. But Lorne had needed to leave the room.

He didn't like the swell of jealousy in his gut when she spoke of things like that.

Renaei sighed. 'Lorne, I can't give you more time. I need you and the others to travel to New Sydney within the week.'

'I was afraid of that.'

'I know. Are they able to protect me?'

'They'd do a better job if you'd give the telekinesis to all of us, not just me,' Lorne pointed out. 'That way we could link up like the Chippers do and create a shield big enough for all of us.'

'I'll take that into consideration,' Renaei said.

'Will you.'

The frown added shadows to her face. 'Lorne, you are my chosen leader. I wanted your gifts to match how special you are to me. The telekinesis and mind-reading abilities — they are for you alone. You deserve them.'

Lorne looked away. 'I don't know what it is you think you see...'

'Read my thoughts and you'll know,' she interrupted. 'See through my eyes. See how much I admire you.'

'I can't do that, Renaei,' he said, pained.

'Why not?'

'Because...' He groaned in frustration and managed not to kick a nearby stone down into the gully. 'Because I'm a mortal, a piece of shit compared to you. I can't look into your mind. It would be wrong. Disrespectful.'

'I understand,' she said after a moment. 'So I will say it instead.'

'Renaei, I'm not sure you...'

She rested her hands on his shoulders, her eyes boring into his. 'What you have been through has made you into this remarkable man I see before me. I can trust no one else with my innermost thoughts. I know you'll never betray me, no matter what happens to you, because you can endure anything.'

'I'm not sure I can endure any more of Merryn's sarcasm,' Lorne commented, relieved when his voice didn't waver.

Renaei's lips quirked into a short-lived smile. 'I am not the one who chose her, so the blame for that lies with you. But listen. I'm not embarrassed by your thoughts. There's no need to feel embarrassed about mine. All you'd discover is that your goddess adores you as much as you do her.'

Moments later, she vanished inside a swirl of burgundy-streaked moss, teleporting away and leaving him alone on the ridge. Lorne stood there, frozen in place, unable to fight the tears gathering in his eyes. If she'd stayed, he would have demanded that she retract her words or explain them. A part of him was glad that he hadn't had the chance.

Lorne crushed his eyelids together and cursed.

CHAPTER THREE

There was a sharp pain inside her chest, as though one of her ribs had torn right into her heart. Renaei clasped a palm over the affected area and felt the steady beat of the organ beneath her skin, but how could that be when it was broken? How could Isabis still refuse to speak to her, even after all this time? How could her beautiful little sister hate her so much?

'You're sure?' she whispered.

Finara, her oldest sister and the goddess of fire, grimaced. 'Yes. Isabis means to kill you when she gets the chance. It wasn't an empty threat.'

'I will continue to avoid her, since that is her wish,' Renaei murmured. She had promised her mortal-born mother millennia ago that she would look after Isabis and help the savannah goddess with the unusually strong mind-reading abilities that hurt her so much.

But their mother was gone. And so was any chance that Renaei might have had of keeping her promise.

'There's more,' the third woman inside the cave said, stepping forward. Her silver prosthetic leg glinted in the firelight. This was Grace, Finara's eternal wife. 'Isabis has joined Faycy's side. Part of the agreement binding them is his promise to help her end your life. You need to be careful.'

Renaei lifted her chin. 'I am a goddess. I can take care of myself.'

'Renaei...' Finara hesitated.

'You think I failed her, don't you?' Renaei demanded, letting her anger stitch its way through her words. 'I know I did! But it's not as though you ever helped me. You never even tried!'

Renaei flattened herself to the ground, shed her human form and tore across countless worlds in a single heartbeat. Her silent screams shook uninhabited mountains, dislodging rocks and causing destructive avalanches. She tried to find comfort in helping her people and answering their prayers, but they gave nothing in return, only asked and asked and asked. She was a goddess to them, not a person. They might love her from afar but it wasn't enough. It never would be.

No one was truly there for her, to hold her, to wipe away the tears she shed when she was alone.

She was desperate for a companion, someone who would treat her as an equal instead of an object to be worshipped. Finara had Grace. Kuja had Fei. Renaei's other siblings were beginning to find and marry those mortals who completed them.

But where was her equal? Did such a person even exist?

And then she heard him. The boy she had once saved was now a man, a man who still thought of her with longing when he knew he shouldn't.

'Merryn, we didn't betray Renaei by joining GLEA and serving the Creator God,' Major Lorne Lavine insisted. His stool listed alarmingly beneath him as he leaned forward to make himself heard over the screeching noise emanating from the band. 'We're protecting those who don't worship Renaei, those who don't know to call her name. We're helping our goddess look after the galaxy, don't you see? We're sharing her burden.'

Sergeant Merryn Lee rolled her eyes. 'Next you'll tell me Renaei is just like us and hangs around in bars with her friends. Fuck that. You can't assume the gods think like us, Lorne. You just can't.' She flicked a hand at the bartender. 'Get me a Minty Madness.'

'You'll put your chip out for a day if you have any alcohol,' Lorne warned her.

Merryn yanked her hair over her temple, hiding the chip that connected her to her powers. 'I'm off duty. And you have no starking right to lecture me. You're not perfect. If GLEA knew you still worshipped a sub-level god...' Merryn didn't finish her sentence. Drink in hand, she slapped Lorne's shoulder and headed for the back of the bar.

Now alone at the counter, Lorne murmured, 'I hope I'm helping you, Renaei. It's the least I can do after what you did for me.'

Renaei didn't think about what she was doing; she just did it. She assumed human form in the bathroom and teleported wigs and prosthetic enhancements into her hands. Once she had created a look she was comfortable with, she left the bathroom and approached the counter, her heart thudding erratically. She slid onto the stool beside Lorne, then quickly used her powers to break the lamp swinging overhead, just in case her disguise wasn't enough.

When Lorne glanced sideways at Renaei, he didn't recognise her but there was a brief hesitation before he acknowledged her with a nod. Renaei wasn't offended when she saw that he was already thinking of a way to escape her presence. He was too tired to spend the night trying to find the best time to tell a prospective date about his past. Most people in the galaxy didn't care, but there was always a chance she was someone who'd grown up on a backwater planet like Velde, someone who had blindly accepted what they'd been told.

'Will you buy me a drink, Major?' she asked before he could leave. 'Something without alcohol. You might need your chip working if this crowd becomes any rowdier.'

Lorne stared at her, then his lips slowly curled. 'I hope you like jenz water.'

The band played for hours, unheeded and unheard while Renaei and Lorne drank and talked about many things — Atsan politics, their mutual love of the planet he now owned a house on, and his reluctance to *leave GLEA because being an agent allowed him to help people. With a pang, she realised that he would never speak so candidly with his goddess. She kept her name to herself.*

When the music faded and the band began to pack up their instruments, Renaei leaned in and kissed Lorne, the muscles beneath her abdomen clenching when she felt his desire to take it further.

'I want to walk you home,' he told her. 'But there's something I haven't...'

Renaei curled her hand around his neck, pulling him closer and stilling his lips with her own. She drew back to smile at him. 'I have my own secrets. Let us part now before we have to share them. Just know this...when you eventually do leave GLEA, I will come find you.'

'I'll be waiting,' he whispered against her neck.

Even now, nearly a full year later, Renaei still shivered whenever she remembered his words.

***

Renaei had meant to rejoin Lorne and his subordinates on New Sydney, but it was a rare for her to sleep and rarer still to dream, especially about the past. She found Lorne alone in the cockpit, watching the distorted stars dance across the viewport while the rest of the guards passed the leapspace journey in slumber. With his leg leaning against the console and his elbow propped up on his knee, he looked thoughtful, almost brooding.

Lorne glanced over at her the moment she appeared. He remained where he was, tiredness and familiarity deciding for him that standing and bowing was unnecessary.

He smiled instead. And her knees immediately weakened.

She wanted to bring up that night in the bar, but she knew he rarely thought about it. He'd made a promise to a stranger without even giving her his name or his communicator details. The matter was as ancient as Old Earth history to him.

Renaei resisted the urge to admire his sculpted form and forced herself to hold his gaze. 'I need to tell you about the situation on New Sydney.'

His smile was gone now, replaced by intense focus. 'Alright. Let's hear it.'

'The god of water is attempting to destroy me by sending his people to attack mine,' she informed him and lowered herself into the co-pilot's seat.

'Makes sense,' Lorne said, his leg sliding off the console as he straightened to face her. 'It's common knowledge that you physically appear when someone calls your name. He's taking advantage of this. Doesn't sound very brotherly to me. You all share a father in the Creator God, don't you?'

'The Watine, or Oceania as his followers know him, is...' Renaei tried to think of a description that had less sting, but couldn't. 'He's a cruel, vicious man eaten alive by his own jealousy.'

Lorne raised his eyebrows. 'Sounds a lot like a mortal.'

'Our mother was a mortal,' she said patiently. 'But I do not blame her for Oceania's less-than-desirable traits.'

Renaei had never spoken so openly to a mortal about the Galactic Pantheon before. It should have been overwhelming. But Lorne had accepted everything she'd told him and was already devising ways to deal with the problem.

'Cruel and vicious, that's not surprising,' he said at last. 'I heard a lot about Oceania during my time at GLEA. He seems to punish his followers a lot more than he rewards them.'

Renaei nodded. 'Exactly. Some of his people moved into a zone already inhabited by my followers — a stretch of land which borders the ocean. Things became very tense very quickly, especially when Oceania threatened to bring a tsunami to the shore to eradicate my people *as well as his own*. He said their shrill voices were annoying him.'

'Why didn't he kill everyone?'

'I suggested that he wanted to murder my people simply because he was incapable of swaying them to his side. He has so few followers as it is.'

Lorne's lips twitched. 'You attacked his pride. Nice work. I'm assuming you didn't take human form when you said this.'

'I am capable of exercising *some* common sense,' Renaei assured him, curtailing her laugh. 'Though you will not agree when I tell you this next part. I offered to meet his followers in person, as a human, to discuss their cooperation or their withdrawal. My brother could not resist the opportunity.'

She felt Lorne brush her mind in his impatience to know more and she waited, waited for him to see how desperately she wanted —

'I'm sorry, I didn't mean to,' Lorne said, stricken.

'It will save a lot of time if you use your abilities, Lorne. So read my mind. Please.'

He drew a deep, shuddering breath — and then he obeyed her. Renaei mentally stepped aside, allowing him full access. He came in as a glancing strike and retreated the moment he had the information he needed. She tempered her disappointment.

'So Oceania has offered to give some pretty impressive water-based powers to whoever kills you,' Lorne stated. 'Not an unattractive award.'

Renaei sighed heavily. 'Yes. I'm hoping that when my bodyguards arrive, already gifted with my powers, my brother's people will think twice about killing me. And perhaps they may be interested in gaining my protection instead. I have a much better reputation than my brother.'

'I can't imagine how bad it'll be once Oceania's followers start setting off their own tsunamis,' Lorne muttered, his thrill of foreboding matching the one that raced down her spine. 'And if the wrong person gets those powers, they might think themselves a god — and they won't have any of the restraint you guys have built up over the centuries.'

By the Ine, he's amazing, Renaei reflected. He understood the mission she had given him and he was already translating it in his mind, to better explain it to his people. She'd tried her best to become friends with the Guards of the Goddess but they looked askance at her, never daring to speak to her unless she started a conversation. Lorne was still the only one who gazed directly into her eyes.

'I'm going to get some sleep before we drop out of leapspace,' Lorne said and shifted to the edge of his seat, about to rise. He froze when she cupped his face in her hands. 'Renaei...'

'I found you, just like I said I would,' she whispered and showed him her memories of that night.

He blinked. 'That was you?'

Before he could see her intentions in her thoughts, Renaei moved forward and kissed him, renewing that moment, that perfect memory. But his lips remained sealed. When she leaned back, his gaze was hard and full of betrayal.

'Yes, fuck you, of course I have a problem with this,' he said curtly, answering her unspoken question as he stood and retreated to the doorway. 'I thought you chose me because I was the best man for the job — '

'You are!' she said swiftly.

Lorne scowled. 'Really, Renaei? It's not because one night when you were lonely I spoke to you as though we were friends? I wouldn't have let you kiss me if I'd known who you were! Do you get that? I only kissed you because I thought you were a mortal, like me!'

'Lorne — '

'Stop talking, just stop,' he pleaded. 'And look into my mind. Really look.'

She didn't. He would know that she hadn't, but she just couldn't.

'There is mutual love and respect between us, Lorne,' she said instead.

'I don't love you, not like that!' he said, his voice throbbing with fury. 'Adoration from far away isn't the same thing. I can't give you what you really deserve.'

'If this is about the body you once wore — '

'It's not!' he snapped. 'Don't you dare assume that. You want to know what's wrong with this? Fine. I'll tell you so you don't have to go digging around in my head. Sure, I find you attractive, you'd have to be blind not to. But I see you as a follower sees his goddess, not as a man sees his lover. I can't fill that hole in your heart, I can't hold you the way you want me to — and even if I tried it wouldn't be fair to you, because I don't...I don't have the feelings you need me to have.'

He turned away from her, his hands braced on the octagonal frame of the cockpit opening. 'I wish I felt that way about you. But I don't. I'm sorry.'

His shoulders straightened and he stalked down the corridor without a backwards glance.

Renaei sank further into her seat, startled, baffled — and hurt. She drifted into his mind, trying to avoid detection as he retreated to the safety of his bunk and pulled the sheet over his head.

Surely he hadn't meant what he'd said. But his thoughts were no different; he'd spoken the truth. He didn't love her that way — and he believed that she didn't love him that way either, that she had simply clung to the only mortal she'd ever had a real conversation with.

He's not wrong, Renaei realised with regret.

She closed her eyes and vanished inside a swirl of rock-studded moss.

CHAPTER FOUR

'Is Renaei planning a warm welcome for us, Captain?' Merryn asked. 'Or is she gonna make us wait?'

'She's already down there,' Lorne answered in a toneless voice.

He had felt Renaei's presence even before Merryn had begun to guide their ship past rings of debris and down to the surface of the planet below. Renaei had already flashed an apology into Lorne's mind, one that was short and abrupt, but she was not able to conceal her embarrassment. He almost wished she'd smite him.

Anger he could have understood and dealt with, because she was a goddess. Her apologising and admitting that she had been wrong when he, the mortal, had been right...it unsettled him. She shouldn't be this human, this vulnerable, this easy to hurt.

'Good thing we're not any larger,' Merryn observed while the ship pulled in its wings to squat on the rocky outcropping like a metallic bird of prey. 'But check out that view!'

Lorne nodded and made vague noises of agreement, though privately he thought the waves were too blue and too bright beneath New Sydney's cloudless sky. It looked as though someone had scrubbed the atmosphere until the planet had lost all traces of its unique personality. Another victim of terraforming, no doubt. Lorne directed his gaze to the dunes below and watched a group of people scatter back towards the shore, where they had parked their small sea-bound vessels.

He supposed the starship was the largest thing they'd ever seen drop out of the sky. It probably didn't help that the ship was packed with more lascannons than was standard for its model.

'Look at that, we've already got Oceania's followers on the run,' Merryn noted, squinting through the viewport. 'Think they'll fuck off entirely?'

Lorne grimaced. 'They have a compelling reason to stay.'

'So they're not just here for the view then? That's a shame.' Merryn flopped back in the pilot's seat and turned her head towards him. 'I've seen Oceania drown his own followers by filling up their lungs with sea water. Must be a *really* compelling reason.'

Lorne gave her an even stare.

Merryn smirked. 'Oh, I get it. This is one of those little secrets between you and the goddess. And you've got a compelling reason not to share this one.'

'Get yourself to the armoury and put your starking gear on,' Lorne ordered her.

He definitely didn't imagine the wink she threw at him as she bounded out of the cockpit.

***

Renaei ceased pacing the moment the ship landed and clenched her hands behind her back. She had to show him that she was fine. That it didn't matter. Their working relationship was unaffected. Maybe if she believed this strongly enough then it would become true.

She couldn't afford to lose Lorne. This would all fall apart without him.

Lorne was the first one down the boarding ramp, flanked by

his people — hers, after a fashion. The Guards of the Goddess. His name for them, his idea, and it was his protection and judgement that she was relying on. Renaei remained where she was, regal and unmoving, even as the previously gentle sea breeze whipped itself into a frenzy. With her golden hair swept back behind her like a banner, she was sure she was an impressive sight — her guards' thoughts confirmed it.

Smiling, Renaei greeted them individually, then stepped back as they all bowed to her. Lorne bent over hastily when she arched an eyebrow at him. He'd been standing there with his arms crossed, stubbornly rigid and upright. Renaei regretted that she had forced the issue because she'd enjoyed the defiance in those deep hazel eyes.

She glanced across the hilly terrain, towards the village populated by mortals who still worshipped her despite their doubt that she could do anything to help them. How could she convince them otherwise? How? Would they think her a fool for being unable to kill those that threatened them? She abhorred the thought of ending anyone's life, no matter how cruel they were. But she knew Fayay had no such reservations. Not even their shared blood would save her.

Renaei fought the shivers. They threatened to overwhelm her, but then she felt Lorne's heat at her side and his hand circling her arm, as familiar to her as one of the golden bangles she always wore. Except his touch was softer, more comforting.

Lorne's voice slid into her thoughts. *Don't show any fear. You are a goddess. They won't expect fear from you or respect it.*

But I am afraid! she snapped.

His laugh in her mind was dark, bitter. *Do you think I've never been afraid? I was terrified every single day of my childhood because my brothers might go too far and beat me to death. I was afraid when I was an agent of GLEA that I'd run out of luck and get myself killed. And I'm afraid every time a beautiful woman sits next to me, since she might be the one who rejects me just because of the way I was born.*

Renaei met his gaze, her breaths quickening when she saw his eyes darken. Their close proximity wasn't just affecting her.

I am often afraid, Lorne said. *I just don't show it.*

I won't feel afraid so long as I have you to protect me, she decided.

His hand dropped away from her and he took a step back. *Good. That confidence in my abilities will help mask your fear.*

Shouldn't you tell me not to have misplaced confidence in those abilities of yours?

She saw the corner of his lips twitch as he replied, *You didn't just choose me because of a long conversation we had one night.*

His humour warred with hers until Renaei was uncertain who stopped feeling it first.

She turned on her heel and started down the winding cliff track that cut towards the sliver of grassy land beside the dunes. Renaei's guards fell in around her as she approached Blashi, a village that looked more like a bunch of misshapen mounds than a home to hundreds. The Blashians had chosen to dig into the earth to create their dwellings, a smart move given the lack of trees in the area and how icy the ocean-born wind could become in the colder months. The same method had been used to build the school, the shelters for the herd animals and the garages that contained amphibious vehicles.

The people living in Blashi had suffered a recent attack which had scoured moss from the rocks that fortified their homes and destroyed their heavy lasgun mounts. Those that were brave enough to come forward and greet the newcomers cradled both weapons and injured limbs, eyes narrowed to slits as though they were expecting another fight.

Pleased to see that no lives had been lost, Renaei beamed at them. 'I, Renaei, heard you call my name and have come to you in your time of need!'

Despite their surprise and lingering suspicion, more and more of the Blashians began filing out of their homes, their faces slack with relief. But others weren't so cowed.

'If you're Renaei, why do you have bodyguards?' someone demanded. 'And why do they carry personal shields? Can't you shield them yourself?'

'Yeah!' another Blashian cried. 'If you can't protect your guards, how can you protect us?'

Renaei wavered. She didn't dare glance back at Lorne, mindful of what it would look like to her people if she deferred to a mortal. She could not let them know how afraid she was. She had to give them a show of strength.

And she would rather die than disappoint Lorne.

Renaei drew a breath.

CHAPTER FIVE

'Steady, everyone,' Lorne ordered when he sensed the build up of power inside Renaei.

The Guards of the Goddess braced themselves and softened their stances. The Blashians weren't so prepared.

Beneath their feet the ground *writhed*. Rocks danced and bounced, finding new positions and gouging tracks into the grass. The villagers fell to their knees, though not because they had lost their balance. When the tumult finally died, they all had their heads bowed and were whispering praises that Renaei accepted with a smile before pleading her people to stand up again.

Lorne tensed, suddenly aware of nearby minds that weren't full of respect and awe — there, a handful of Oceania worshippers creeping in from the shore, weapons at the ready. Warning everyone would take too long.

He spun towards the attackers, hoping to face them before they fired, and threw up his hands. The abilities Renaei had given Lorne didn't require accompanying gestures, but as a Chipper he had always needed to use them to focus his power output. Old habits died hard. And so did he.

The lasbolts struck. His telekinetic shield easily deflected them, causing the energy beams to slam into a nearby earthen wall instead of flesh.

'Merryn,' Lorne said calmly. 'Can you deal with our uninvited guests, please?'

His Second nodded once and began advancing, flanked by six of his guards. Their personal shields hummed into life, forming faint orange spheres around each member. Unbothered by the lasbolts flying at their faces, they created tracts of slippery red lichen to encircle those who tried to flee, tripping them into undignified sprawls. The ground then swallowed the attackers' arms long enough for the Guards of the Goddess to confiscate their weapons.

Lorne stowed his proud grin. He'd congratulate them later.

'As you can see,' Renaei said, her voice cutting through the silence, 'my guards are quite capable of defending you with the powers I have granted them.'

A woman with a curved back shuffled forward, supporting herself on a staff. She looked over a century old but the hand she used to gesture at Lorne and the other guards remained steady. 'You need bodyguards now, do you, Renaei? It must be true, that even the gods can die.'

Renaei inclined her head towards the woman. 'Yes, it's true, Silvia. It's also true that I could kill you all in a heartbeat. But I won't. Because you have my love and protection. Forever.'

'I once called your name as a child, when a great storm came,' Silvia mused, her dark eyes distant. 'I lived with my parents in a house on stilts. The floor fell away and I went with it, but you caught me and took me back to my parents.'

'I always help those who call my name,' Renaei said firmly.

Silvia laughed. 'Perhaps you saved my life because you knew that one day I would become an elder with sway here on New Sydney. Just the sort of person you need on your side.'

'It would certainly suit my purposes if you believed I had such foresight.' Renaei's answering smile faded. 'Gather your people in your meeting space. I must speak to all of you.'

'And the Driftwood?' Silvia asked, indicating the shore with the tip of her staff.

Lorne figured she must be referring to Oceania's followers.

'I'll need to speak to them as well,' Renaei said, her green eyes narrow. 'I will release those who attacked us just now so that they can arrange their own meeting for me.'

With a nod, Silvia began herding the other Blashians into a nearby building. Lorne turned back to the guards and gave them their orders. His people released the so-called 'Driftwood' they had captured, though not without dark looks being passed between them. Lorne could see the thoughts they left unspoken; they disagreed with Renaei's decision to let them go.

'Renaei, just a moment,' he called and waited until she drew close to him before continuing. 'Now that you're here, Oceania's people will probably launch a full-scale attack.'

Renaei lifted her chin. 'My guards can repel any attack of theirs.'

'Won't our opponents have...similar backing?' he asked, alluding to her brother.

No, Renaei said, using her abilities to silently answer him after a furtive look around. *He won't dare show his face. He's just as afraid of dying as I am.*

Lorne frowned and also switched to thoughts instead of spoken words. *He won't come? Then this won't end with New Sydney.*

What do you mean, Lorne?

There's a reason we try to take out the leader of a group in a fight, Lorne told her. *Oceania's the head of this animal and he'll keep attacking you and your people all across the galaxy.*

'I will protect my people from any harm that comes their way,' Renaei declared out loud and then marched towards the large hovel the Blashians used for their meetings. The doorway was so low that the goddess had to duck to follow Silvia inside.

Lorne watched Renaei go, grinding his molars together. *Don't make promises you can't keep, Renaei. You yourself told me that Oceania has other gods on his side. Even if you spread your fifteen Guards of the Goddess across the stars, we can't protect everyone.*

She didn't answer him but he felt the tendril of fear that she quickly coiled up inside her. He remained a spectator in her mind, listening to the speech she was giving her people — words to placate, words that omitted instead of explaining, words that held the empty promises they had all heard before.

'We'll be easy pickings once you abandon us and take your guards with you,' Silvia pointed out. Through Renaei's eyes, Lorne could see that the elder was pacing, her staff drifting beside her, almost like an afterthought. The other villagers packed into the room nodded their agreement.

Lorne? Renaei called. *Please help me. What do I offer them?*

So he told her. He told her exactly what he would do in her place.

Moments later, Renaei's words echoed his. 'I will leave some of my guards here to protect you and they'll also train you to defend yourselves. Anyone who wishes to learn from them will be given my powers as well as countless brothers and sisters to fight alongside. Who among you is willing to volunteer?'

The response was immediate: cheers, applause, bows, even whispered reverence.

You didn't need to use my idea, Lorne said, not bothering to hide his pleasure that his goddess trusted his opinion so much.

And you didn't need to help me, Renaei countered.

Yes, I did.

Because I am your goddess?

He swallowed a laugh. *Give your ego a rest, Renaei. If your people can defend themselves, you won't have to physically appear so often. It's safer. I guess today it was my turn to exercise some common sense.*

Her amusement spiking briefly, Renaei did not reply and instead shooed him out of her mind so that she could concentrate. Lorne obeyed her, already preoccupied with the ramifications of her speech. She would need him to travel across the galaxy and teach her people how to use their new powers. The thought of leaving someone else at Renaei's side while he did this rankled. But it was something he'd have to live with.

A hand fell on his shoulder. Lorne started — and looked around at his Second, who had managed to sneak up on him. There was a smirk twisting her lips.

'Stopped talking to the boss in your head yet?' Merryn asked.

'I shouldn't have lost focus,' he said, annoyed with himself. 'Thank you.'

Merryn snickered. 'Happy to help, Captain. Who'd have thought when you were teaching me about forcefields back at GLEA that you'd need me this much?'

'Merryn...' Lorne sighed, rubbing his scarred temple. 'We need to be alert and ready for a fight, not reminiscing.'

'Stark, you're as much fun as Colonel Vasquez,' she complained, naming the agent she'd been paired with before she'd left the Agency.

'Hopefully I was a much better agent than him,' Lorne muttered.

One of the nearby guards shouted a warning, interrupting whatever smart comment Merryn was about to make.

'The Driftwood are converging on the beach and they're all heavily armed!' Rejos Michson announced from his position on one of the mounds that constituted a building. 'Shouldn't have let those fuckers go. We're outnumbered now, Captain.'

Merryn clapped her personal shield back onto her chest, reactivating the device.

'He's right, you know,' she said aside to Lorne.

'Don't question your orders! You're not being paid to do that.'

'And here I thought I was being paid to watch you make eyes at our boss,' Merryn drawled, then danced away before Lorne could take her to task.

***

Renaei emerged from the meeting hovel when the fighting had already started, a smile playing over her face as she watched the Guards of the Goddess build a solid wall of soil, moss and rock in front of Blashi. The altered terrain shook but held. Mere lasbolts wouldn't be able to punch their way through. But Oceania's people had more than lasguns in their arsenal.

'Get back inside!' Lorne roared at the villagers who had followed Renaei.

Broad lascannon fire sailed down from the sky. Lorne was already moving, his hands thrown up in front of him and lines of concentration cutting into his face. Renaei felt him effortlessly take command of the powers she had given him, powers that were so much stronger than what he'd had when he'd been a Chipper. She was stunned. His mastery was nearly a match for her own.

The Blashians could do little but stare at each other in horror as death fell towards them. But they were safe — thanks to Lorne. He used his telekinesis to encase them instead of himself, relying on his personal shielding device to protect him. Its small forcefield wavered ominously after two large beams struck it, then grew seamless once more. His relief swiftly gave way to annoyance.

Lorne spun to face Renaei. 'Are you done watching us show off? I know you can teleport a whole bunch of people at once, so get rid of these starkers' weapons and send them back to shore. You can talk to them there.'

But I don't know what to say to them! Renaei cried silently. *And would they even listen to me if I appeared with armed guards?*

Leave the others and take me with you, Lorne ordered.

Oceania's followers shouted in fear as swirls of moss and grass smothered them, teleporting them away from Blashi and back to their beached vessels. Renaei then moved up beside Lorne, including him in her personal vortex. He was used to this method of transportation now and barely blinked when it happened.

The second their faces were obscured from those inside the village, Lorne murmured, 'I'm here, Renaei. And I'm not going anywhere.'

The words were unnecessary. He didn't need to say them.

But they stilled the rapid beating of her heart.

Side by side, the goddess and her bodyguard walked out onto wave-licked sand. Lorne immediately fell behind a pace. His personal shield was still active, even if it was giving off uneven whirs of discontent. It sounded as though the device was only a handful of lasbolts away from failing altogether.

Renaei kept her telekinetic defences in place and could also feel Lorne's touch on her shield, bolstering and strengthening it. He was using all of his powers to protect her while continuing to trust his safety to malfunctioning tech.

She would have to remonstrate him for this later.

'People of Oceania!' Renaei called, advancing on the people crowded together on the shore.

Now lacking their lasguns, they began to grab rocks and seashells to throw at Renaei. She flinched. It wasn't a dangerous attack, merely an inconvenient one, but it made her want to take Lorne's hand for reassurance.

His mind pulsed with warning. A goddess shouldn't need to rely on her subject.

But I do need you, she thought.

Focus, Ren, Lorne told her firmly.

Renaei glanced at him, startled. No one had used her nickname in over a millennia. Somehow Lorne had found it inside her mind and had known that the surprise of hearing it would distract her from her fear.

Lorne's shielding device failed after another minute of the primitive onslaught. Without missing a beat, he dropped the smoking tech and stepped in behind Renaei, taking advantage of their combined defences. Nothing came through. Nothing struck them. They were untouchable.

When their opponents realised this, the rocks stopped coming.

Still wary, Oceania's followers maintained a loose circle around the pair. Renaei held up her hands and waggled them threateningly, a reminder that she could attack at any moment. Lorne stayed at her back, protecting her, ready to offer her any insight.

But he believed she could do this without him. She had every intention of proving to him that his faith was not misplaced.

Renaei lowered her arms to her sides. 'People of Oceania, I don't want to hurt you. I would rather speak to you instead.'

'We'd rather kill you!' a man cried, throwing one last rock that bounced harmlessly away. 'Oceania said he'd give us powers if we handed him your body. He promised!'

'Has Oceania ever answered any of your prayers?' Renaei asked. 'Has he even bothered to show you his face? Oceania, my own brother, sent you against me, knowing that you might perish in the attempt.'

'If we don't obey him, he'll slaughter us!' someone else shouted.

Renaei shook her head. 'No. I'll protect you from him. And the fact that he hasn't shown up means he's either afraid of me...or he doesn't care about your wellbeing.'

She hadn't wanted to inflict the pain she saw in their eyes, nor the uncertainty. Many of them looked to the sea, remembering how their god had ignored or punished them when they dared to ask for help. They had grown jealous of those ashore, having heard that the goddess of tundra always answered her followers' pleas when they used her name. She let them see her, let them know that she was watching over them. It had been a story, a rumour, but now Oceania's people knew it to be true.

One by one, their shoulders slumped, the fight in them fading to nothing.

Renaei softened her voice. 'I will make you an offer. Any of you who need help, at any point in the future, please call my name. I would never send you against a powerful being that you have no hope of defeating. And I would never leave you without some way of defending yourselves. If it's powers you want, I'll give them to you — but in return, you must save lives instead of ending them.'

Mutters spread amongst Oceania's people. They didn't trust her. Everyone knew the sub-level gods would do anything to grow their followings and expand their influence.

'I won't even demand your worship,' Renaei added quickly, hoping she didn't sound as desperate as she felt. 'All I ask is that you come to Blashi when you're ready to trade war for peace. If you ever are.'

She turned her back to them and strode towards the village, Lorne at her heels.

'You didn't need me as much as you thought you did,' he said after a few moments.

Renaei glanced at him, catching the flash of fear before he buried it. 'Is that a bad thing?'

'I'm not sure. I guess I like being needed.'

'I suspect I'll always need you,' she said gently. 'A goddess has few friends, especially ones who will scold her to her face. It's been so long since that happened I had begun to believe I was flawless. Clearly I am not.'

Lorne's eyes glittered. 'I don't know. You look pretty flawless to me.'

'Are you sure you're not just saying that because I pay you?' Renaei teased.

'Oh, I wish that was the real reason,' he said, his expression suddenly serious. 'But it's not.'

Before she could form any coherent thoughts, much less

conjure something to say to that, he sped up and left her standing there, lost in a maelstrom of confusion and hope.

CHAPTER SIX

'Well, you're obviously her favourite, Captain,' Merryn said, smothering a yawn.

Crammed into one of the Blashians' spare buildings, which reeked as though it was usually populated by the village's smelliest beasts, the Guards of the Goddess were enjoying the apparent ceasefire. They sat around a solar-charged heater and ate an array of seafood that their hosts had provided for them. Four of their number remained outside, patrolling the village's perimeter.

Renaei had disappeared earlier but Lorne knew she was still nearby, albeit no longer in human form. He could feel her presence emanating from the very ground beneath him. She was monitoring Oceania's followers, concerned that they might attack. Through her, Lorne could hear their muted, sober conversations. Some continued to argue in favour of killing her.

Lorne wasn't surprised to find that Renaei was preoccupied with his earlier comments. She wasn't alone. He kept replaying them in his mind, wondering if he had meant to flirt with her.

He cleared his throat. 'Merryn, this is not about favourites. Renaei chose me as your leader — that's why I speak to her so often. While she did give me some extra powers, I assume that was only done to emphasise my position. I should warn you all that I can read minds, though frankly I could do without that ability.'

'Oh shit, Captain,' one of the guards said immediately. 'I

didn't really mean it when I thought those things about you earlier. But you do have a nice arse.'

The hovel exploded with laughter.

'I don't always look at your thoughts,' Lorne said when his subordinates had quietened again. 'It takes effort. And I'd rather not gain a headache and lose respect for you lot in the same breath.'

'That telekinesis I've seen you do, that's pretty awesome,' Rejos Michson piped up. He could be a brat sometimes, but Lorne liked him, liked how committed the teenager was to learning his powers. 'It'd make more sense if we all had it.'

Lorne rubbed his temples, hoping his guards would mistake his frustration for exhaustion. 'I've brought that up with the goddess. But she has her reasons. And anyway, I don't have millennia of practice behind me. Her control is superior to mine.'

'Still, it's a useful ability to have,' Rejos said, sounding wistful.

'Definitely useful if you want to start taking someone's clothes off without touching them,' Merryn commented. 'That's a lot of fun.'

Everyone stared at her.

Merryn grinned. 'Just speaking from experience. I used to be in GLEA, you know. But since the captain's got telekinesis and we don't, I guess he'll be the only one taking Renaei's clothes off.'

Lorne tossed an empty oyster shell onto the ground, avoiding everyone's eyes. 'I'm not going to discuss this.'

'You're not even tempted to bed the goddess?' another guard asked with an incredulous hoot. 'Stark, she's beautiful. Maybe I'll have a crack at her.'

'You will *not*,' Lorne said, fury singeing his words. 'None of you will. She is your goddess and you will give her all due respect. That's enough on the matter.'

The hovel fell silent. Someone coughed awkwardly. Several giggles followed.

Shaking her head, Merryn stood up and trudged over to the doorway. She turned back to Lorne, her lips firmly sealed. He didn't need his mind-reading abilities to know that she wanted to speak to him in private. Reluctantly, he rose to his feet and followed her out.

'What is it, Second?' he demanded, using a hand to shield his face against the icy wind.

Strands of Merryn's dark hair whipped over her pinched expression. 'Warning us off her, Captain? You're pretty much claiming your territory.'

'That's not — ' he started.

'Oh yes it starking is,' Merryn interrupted. 'Why don't you just come out and tell us she's yours, Lorne? We'd respect that boundary.'

'She's not mine! She can't be. She can't *ever* be.'

'Why not?' Merryn asked flatly. 'Because she's a goddess? So what? I worship her too, you know. But that doesn't stop me laughing at her jokes. It shouldn't stop you falling in love with her.'

'I'm not falling in love with Renaei,' he insisted.

'Then maybe you should stop acting so starking jealous whenever someone else goes near her, huh?'

Lorne opened his mouth, then quickly sealed it.

He wasn't sure how to defend himself. Because Merryn wasn't wrong. He *was* jealous. But he couldn't be. He'd shared Renaei with hundreds of thousands of mortals before and he had been content with that for most of his life. Why did it matter now? She was still his goddess. That hadn't changed.

But maybe something else had. Maybe it was him.

The ground rumbled, cutting into his thoughts. Lorne looked down at the grass trembling beneath his boots, frowning — and then his gaze flew to the four guards who came running in from the shore, their faces as white as bleached coral.

'Captain,' one of them panted. 'The water's gone out. It's just sand for as far as the eye can see.'

'Oh shit,' Merryn said.

Lorne hissed out a breath. 'A tsunami. Let Silvia and the others know. And start building up a wall again, but make it higher and get it to encircle the entire village. Do it now!' he added when his guards hesitated, their fearful eyes darting back to the shore. 'One of you has to warn those camped further down the spit. We need to bring them back here.'

'We're saving the Driftwood?' a guard asked, scowling. 'They don't deserve it.'

'Renaei promised to help them,' Lorne snapped. 'So don't fucking argue. In fact, you've just volunteered for that task. Activate your shield and go get them!'

Ren! he called inside his mind. *A tsunami's headed this way!*

When he looked at the beach he saw that she was already there, a lone figure too far out for him to reach on foot.

My brother, Oceania, Renaei explained tersely. *He knows some of his people were swayed by my speech. Now he's going to kill us all.*

With effort, Lorne turned towards the villagers gathering nearby. He kept his voice firm. 'Your goddess has gone to fight Oceania while we protect you in her stead. She extends this protection to those who do not worship her as well. Listen!' he added before they could waste any of his time with indignant questions. 'You will accept the so-called Driftwood or you can find someone else to save you. Got it?'

They scuttled away from him, not wholly convinced but not prepared to argue either.

Lorne watched his guards erect a bowl-shaped barrier around the village, knowing it was pointless. Their powers were sourced from Renaei — if she died, they'd have nothing and Blashi would be wiped from the planet's surface. Renaei might be able to hold her own against Oceania with her telekinesis, since apparently his ability was no greater than hers, but water was his domain. It could crush her.

Lorne closed his eyes. *Ren. I need to be at your side.*

A short laugh bounced back at him. *Is that a statement or an order?*

Both, he answered and a vortex instantly swirled up around him, dropping him a mere pace from the goddess who needed him so much.

Lorne drew in line with Renaei and fixed his gaze on the tsunami. The immense wave was now so close he could hear it, a roar that sent terror pooling into his stomach where he hoped he could contain it. Filling his lungs with air, Lorne plunged inside himself and tore out every skerrick of power he could find, then lashed it to the shield Renaei had already erected. Their minds merged together until Lorne wasn't sure where his thoughts ended and hers began.

The wave soared up into the sky and crested there almost lazily, as though taunting them.

I'm here/I'm here, Renaei and Lorne assured each other.

And then it hit, slamming into their shield and howling

angrily when they failed to fall to its might. The tsunami went against its nature and hurled itself at them again and again, driven by the hand of a malevolent god.

'Stark!' Lorne cried, skidding back a pace. 'Ren, we can't hold this!'

'Suggestions?' she gasped.

'We need to let it come — slowly! Release a little bit at a time!'

She didn't answer but he felt her agreement. Within moments the sand beneath their feet became sludge as the sea dribbled back to claim its territory. The pressure continued to mount and leaks sprang in their shield, causing more and more fingers of salty liquid to crawl past them. Lorne glanced down when he felt his feet lose their purchase on the sand and saw that Renaei was using her powers to lift them above the rising waters.

Give in, cajoled a voice dripping with muck. *It's pointless to resist.*

'Leave him be, Fayay!' Renaei shouted.

Give in, insisted the voice.

Through the wall of water assaulting them, Lorne saw the slim silhouette of a man steadily approaching. Oceania did not need to show his human form to control the wave. But he *wanted* them to see him, to know that their death was imminent.

'Where's your backup, Fayay?' Lorne taunted. He had used his mind-reading abilities to confirm that Fayay was indeed the god's true name and mused that it wasn't particularly fearsome. 'Are you all by yourself?'

Fayay snarled. Jets of water, solid enough to shatter glass, savagely smacked the shield instead of Lorne's face. The telekinetic defences held — but they would probably only last another handful of minutes judging by the strain Lorne felt, an echo of what was causing Renaei's face to turn white.

Lorne forced himself laugh at Oceania's failure.

As he'd predicted, the water god threw more fury behind the tsunami, but not more power. In fact, this attack was unaimed and much less effective.

Ha, Lorne thought. *His anger is his weakness.*

'Lorne, I can't...I can't keep doing this,' Renaei pleaded, her voice fading in and out. 'The shield will fail and he'll kill me.'

Lorne grunted. 'Not if I stop him.'

'You think you can defeat me, mortal?' Fayay hissed, now close enough for Lorne to see the spite in his pale blue eyes.

'I think your name is stupid and it suits you, *Fayay*,' Lorne hurled back. He dropped one hand to his belt and grabbed his lasgun, using it to fire a bolt right past Fayay's ear. A warning shot, nothing more. Lorne knew how Renaei felt about taking someone's life...even if that life belonged to her murderous brother.

Startled, Fayay fell to his knees. The pressure behind the tsunami eased just slightly and Lorne dared to hope. But then Oceania sprang back onto his feet, his expression eerily calm instead of furious. 'I would have spared you, mortal. Now you will have to die.'

The god's human form abruptly misted into thin air.

'Shit,' Lorne said. He'd overestimated the effect Fayay's anger had on his focus.

Something very large and invisible struck the shield. It came back around for another pass — and this time it had friends. The sea vessels that had been grounded on the shore were now being tossed towards Lorne and Renaei like toys in the hands of a petulant child.

Slam. Slam. Slam. *Slam.*

Lorne staggered sideways into Renaei, nearly toppling her, and his eyes flew up to the large circular hill his guards had erected around Blashi. He didn't know if it would be enough to save the village. But his and Renaei's shield was going to shatter if they didn't shrink it soon.

We will keep the mortals safe from harm, an unfamiliar voice spoke up. It was cool, measured and carried with it a patience born of countless aeons.

What — Lorne began, confused.

We are the grass, the creeping moss, the rocks and dirt that lie beneath your feet, the voice told him. It sounded as though every facet of the nearby tundra biome was speaking as one entity. *Trust us. And trust the abilities of those you have trained.*

'Ren, your — your domain is talking to me,' Lorne gasped.

His goddess didn't answer. She was consumed with keeping them alive.

Their shield jolted again and a spike of agony lanced down Lorne's spine. He screamed until his throat became raw. *Ren! Drop the shield to cover just us! Trust me!*

As though waiting for this exact moment, the tsunami plunged down one last time, hard and determined. With it came the might of the water god, a double punch that almost crushed them. Renaei fell into Lorne's arms, limp and unmoving. He shouted at her, begged and cursed her, then felt her feebly reach for her powers.

Together they shored up a shield that didn't have the strength or size to save Blashi — but it didn't need to. The village was safe.

Fayay kept circling, jabbing at their defences without retaking human form.

'Coward!' Lorne snarled. 'Fight me like a mortal, if you're brave enough!'

Is it cowardice, Fayay mused, *or do I merely have more important business elsewhere?*

Then he was gone, his presence lingering like an oily film left on glass. Lorne chanced a look around — and saw only water. He couldn't sense Fayay anymore either. He and Renaei were alone once more, still protected by their tiny shield. Seaweed floated aimlessly by, ripped free from its home and heading towards the shore where it would wash up and rot.

They are alive, all of them, the moss growing in Blashi informed Lorne.

'No offence, but I'd rather see that for myself,' he said. 'Ren, can you take us there?'

'Lorne, I can't...' Renaei's skin was pale and her eyes were deep and hollow. 'I can't let them see me like this.'

Lorne cupped her chin in his hand. 'You need to teleport us away before our shield gives out completely. Can you do that? We don't need to appear near anyone.'

'I...can't...'

He pressed a chaste kiss against her shivering mouth. 'Yes, you can. Because we mortals? We don't fucking quit. If it gets hard, we just keep going. And if you want me to respect you the way I respect the men and women under my command, you'll fight to the end, because that's we do.'

Renaei closed her eyes, grimacing in pain —

— and then he was holding her on that rocky outcropping above the village, the ship standing over them. Lorne eased them both to the ground, keeping her close to his chest even as colour returned to her cheeks.

'I need to go reassure the others,' Lorne murmured, pausing to kiss her again. 'Don't come back until you look invincible.' This time he gave her a firm squeeze, just to make sure she was there. 'You were amazing, Ren. I'd be happy to have you in my Guards of the Goddess, if that wasn't so redundant.'

'Go, Lorne,' she whispered.

He hesitated.

'Go,' Renaei repeated, a weak smile creeping along her lips. 'Unless you want to kiss me some more. I wouldn't stop you.'

Lorne gazed down at her for several agonising moments, torn, then swiftly stood and walked back to Blashi, his body trembling with exertion — and unfulfilled need.

CHAPTER SEVEN

Renaei watched the Blashians and her brother's people dance together around the bonfire. They were celebrating her victory over the tsunami and their agreement to sit down and discuss future relations in the morning. Most of the Driftwood had chosen to stay here, inside the village, instead of returning to the shore and the god that had tried to kill them. Some had pledged themselves to Renaei already. She wasn't sure what the rest of them would do; an inherited way of life wasn't easy to shed after one day.

The two parties at this bonfire may have worshipped different deities, but they could still laugh and dance and even love. Renaei was well aware of new or temporary couples sneaking away from the festivities, some of her guards among them.

Her chest ached. Lorne might eventually agree to share her bed, the way he shared his mind with her. Any more than that, however...she could not ask for it.

Renaei turned and walked into the deep night. But she wasn't alone. Lorne was following several paces behind her. He didn't mention what was on both their minds: the kisses he had never meant to give her, the kisses he would only give her when he wasn't thinking or preoccupied with what she was.

She dropped into a cross-legged position on the grass and smiled when he sat beside her, close enough that she could feel the warmth of him. It reminded her of those nights when Isabis, her sister, had been in his place, silently waiting for Renaei to speak.

But that was centuries ago. Before Isabis had decided to kill her.

'Do you want to talk about it?' Lorne asked.

The wind tugged at his coat, revealing the dress shirt he'd worn underneath it. Renaei's eyes traced the V-shape of exposed skin that dove to the first button. Lorne followed her gaze down with his own, then glanced back at her. Renaei wet her lips.

'Stop trying to distract me, Ren,' he said. His words were soft but his thoughts were firm. He wasn't going to let her retreat or hide. She needed to discuss this. And he was willing to listen.

Renaei drew a breath, then another. 'I...I have never spoken about what happened with Isabis. Most of my siblings can read my thoughts and they already know how I feel, so why should they bother asking if I'm alright?'

'It could be that your brothers and sisters are too busy dealing with their own messes,' Lorne suggested. 'And if they all have terrible names like Fayay, I'd say that's only the start of their problems.'

Renaei laughed, but her amusement was short-lived. 'The desert god's name is *Sandsa*, so perhaps you have a point. Get comfortable, Lorne. This is quite a tale.'

He lay back against a moss-covered boulder and linked his arms beneath his head. A grin flitted along his lips. 'I'm as comfortable as I can be out here.'

Pressing herself flush against his side, Renaei reached over and stroked both of his temples with her thumb and smallest finger. Her heart soared when he didn't move away.

'This is how my mother helped me to sleep, when I was young

and had no duties or mortals to worry about,' she murmured. 'I loved her so much. I'm not saying my father was terrible to me, but...well. He's the Creator God. How do you compete for attention when you have more than fifty siblings and your father has billions of mortal children?'

'Can't say I've ever felt that attention,' Lorne said. Sensing her thoughts, he answered, 'No. I don't mind. You're the one I really care about. I've seen you with my own eyes, so I don't need to see or feel your father.'

Renaei leaned her head on his shoulder, closing her eyes as she drifted into her memories. 'I stopped caring about my father's absence after Isabis was born. She smiled so much when she was younger. I enjoyed her presence then; she was always full of light. But she has such a terrible gift — her ability to read minds is so strong it causes her physical pain. She was too afraid to use it. She even stopped smiling.'

A gentle breeze nestled into her hair, a soothing gesture from her domain. Renaei paused and drew strength from it before continuing. 'I wanted to show Isabis all the good she could do with her powers. So I took her with me when I tended to my duties. I told her how I constantly listen to mortals in case they need me. And I told her to do the same. I thought it would help. I thought that if she was exposed to their minds more often, it would become easier for her.'

'It didn't get easier,' Lorne surmised.

'No. It didn't.' Renaei's voice fractured and faded. She swallowed. 'I didn't understand her. I just assumed I knew best, because I'm older than her. I promised my mother I would look after Isabis. I failed. Maybe I do deserve to die at my sister's hand.'

'It's not your fault, Ren. You're her sister, not her mother. Or her father. Your parents should have helped her. It shouldn't have fallen to you alone.'

Renaei trembled, wishing she could believe Lorne's words. She wasn't sure she could. 'My mother might have been able to help, but she was only immortal as long as she was married to my father. She left him. When I went looking for her, after Isabis threatened me...she was gone.'

'Gone, as in...' He didn't finish the sentence.

'She was my heart,' Renaei said softly. 'My mother told me not to be afraid to care for you mortals, that you need comfort and support when your own strength fails.'

Lorne turned to the side, his hazel eyes caressing her. 'You didn't realise how much you needed that comfort and support for yourself until your mother died.'

'Yes — it makes sense. I'm half mortal.' Renaei tasted the bitterness on her tongue before it infected her words. 'Isabis often said that I'm *too* mortal, that I care too much. But I can't stop caring. And I don't want to. My people will always need me.'

'It's not a weakness to care, to be mortal,' Lorne said. His hand sought hers; their fingers entwined.

Renaei smiled up at the stars that would never burn as bright as the soul lying beside her. 'I know this because you've shown me that strength can come from despair. Your ability to overcome loss, to conquer the worst odds, to succeed even without help — it's inspiring. You can stand alone if you need to.'

'But stark it's nice to have someone with you anyway,' Lorne murmured.

Renaei agreed with him mentally, a pulse of thought, not even a word. She was too afraid to ask for it, but he sensed her need and engulfed her in his embrace, offering her a solid rock that she could cling to as she began to cry against his shoulder. Each tear that dampened the shirt beneath his coat represented a year of despair, a year of loneliness and a year of yearning. His arms kept her intact, kept her from breaking apart as she released it all.

Renaei allowed herself to *feel* the loss of her mother and the loss of her sister's love. And then she allowed herself to focus instead on the man who had finally freed her. He gave her a firm squeeze and vowed, *I won't let anyone hurt you ever again. You're safe with me.*

Very subtly, something between them shifted. She wondered if he felt it.

Lorne made a soft sound in his throat, the only warning she had before he swiftly moved her under him. His lips were cold at first, but they soon grew as hot as the kisses he unleashed on her. Renaei stole breaths when she could and then completely forgot to keep doing this when he pressed his desire against her. The grass quivered beneath them, urging them on. But its enthusiasm was too vocal and within seconds Lorne had pulled away, his eyes wide and his expression aghast.

'I — my goddess, I'm sorry,' he gasped, rolling off her. 'I...I won't let this happen again.'

Renaei ground a palm into her cheek, smearing the tears that had escaped her eyes. 'You can't keep doing this to me, Lorne. It isn't fair.'

'Renaei...' The whisper was so quiet it was barely there. 'I want to give you everything I have to give, but you're...'

'I'm not just a goddess, Lorne!' she cried. 'I'm a woman too. My heart can beat and break, just as yours does. It *hurts* when you get my hopes up only to turn away from me. Your promise to keep people from hurting me is an empty one. Because you're the one who does it the most.'

He stared at her, his mouth hanging open. But no denial escaped him.

Renaei drew a breath and stood, her eyes fixed on the invisible horizon. 'There's a hovel a little ways from here. The Blashians made it for me years ago, as a tribute to their goddess. Even though I've never used it, they've always kept a fire burning in the hearth — it's warm, isolated and perfect for our needs. That's where I'll be tonight. But don't follow me unless you intend to spend the night with me.'

She turned on her heel and walked away without waiting for his response. Lorne remained immobile on the ground behind her, mentally pleading her to take back her words. She refused.

Once she'd crawled through the low entrance of the small hovel, she slipped out of her dress and lay on the rug covering the earthen floor, enjoying the play of soft qiviut against her skin. It took hours for the Blashians to pull enough clumps of wool from the coat of a muskox to make a single rug. Traditionally, these rugs had been used as beds. Now they only served this function on a Blashian's wedding night.

Renaei shivered. The mere thought of marrying Lorne and binding herself to him for eternity caused her clitoris to swell and ache. By the Ine, she wanted him so badly. She licked the pad of one finger and began to circle a nipple, sighing in pleasure. Still more fingers crawled down her thigh to dance teasingly along her slick folds.

She was ready for him. But he wasn't there.

Renaei filled her mind with images of his body, hoarded from that brief glimpse she'd had of him back on the ship before this mission had started. His hard lines were belied by the softness of his hazel eyes and his smooth skin was crossed with pale scars, mementos from the battles he'd fought and the procedures he'd endured. He had refused to let GLEA's surgeons obscure any of them.

Each mark represented a victory. He never saw them with anything but pride. She wished she could touch them, kiss them, lick them.

Renaei groaned and slid two fingers into her throbbing core, pumping rhythmically. It wasn't enough. Her other hand abandoned her breast and slid an index finger over her clitoris, swirling the nub in time to each thrust. The need to find release grew and grew, until she could no longer refuse it. Her fingers twisted and curled up inside her, pressing against that sensitive spot.

Renaei opened her eyes just before her orgasm hit, suddenly aware of being watched.

Lorne had followed her.

She gasped as her core tunnelled around her fingers, sending out waves of pleasure that spread into each limb, each finger and toe, and then into each sensitive follicle of hair on her scalp. Renaei lay still for several moments, smiling, until her breasts tingled, impatient for another's touch.

Lorne was hunched over by the low entranceway, his breathing as hard as her own and his pants evidently too tight for comfort. As for his mind...he could barely contain the thoughts and desires that fell over each other.

Renaei stood for his inspection.

His eyes darkened until they could have reflected the depths of the ocean.

She felt her folds clench again, desperate to be parted by something much more satisfying than her own fingers. Renaei took one step towards Lorne, knowing that he could take her there, to oblivion, where their souls could join and bask in the radiance of each other.

Lorne's lips parted. She saw him consider leaving.

But he didn't. He shed his coat and stayed right where he was.

CHAPTER EIGHT

She stood before him, clad only in golden bangles and matching tresses of hair that fell over her breasts. Her skin glowed in the uneven firelight — no shadow dared to linger on her for too long — and above her hips ran slender faded lines, the perfect tracks for his trembling fingers.

Lorne straightened to his full height, unable to shift his eyes from the divine body of his goddess. He wasn't sure he would even if he could. She was an amazing sight.

'Lorne,' she said softly. 'Can I see you? All of you?'

'Ren...Renaei...' His voice failed him so he switched to mind-speech. *You don't know what you're asking. You're a goddess. You're perfect. And I'm...*

You are my equal, she insisted.

Because you made me your equal, he pointed out, his annoyance failing to chase off his arousal entirely. *You gave me all these powers. More than you gave any of the other guards.*

Renaei's forehead creased. *You were my equal long before I recruited you. And you have treated me as your equal — as your colleague, as your friend. You've cared for me in ways no one else ever has.*

You have cared so much for us, Lorne replied. *You deserve to have someone to care for you. Someone to hold you, kiss you...*

His thoughts scattered as his mind filled with what he wanted to do her, all night, every night. But he couldn't, he just couldn't.

This isn't my first time with a mortal, she said, smiling. *And past worship hasn't stopped Fei, my sister-in-law, from bedding her husband, the rainforest god.*

Lorne supposed it shouldn't surprise him that the sub-level gods had chosen mortal spouses.

His heart faltered. *Spouses.*

'I'm not asking for *that*, Lorne.' Renaei slid her hands down her form in a mesmerising fashion, pausing to cup the mounds hidden beneath her hair. 'All I ask of you is one night, not thousands.'

He didn't interrupt, didn't call her on the lie. She needed comfort and he was the only one in the entire galaxy who could give it to her. This was a duty that no one else should be allowed to fulfil. She was his and his alone.

'But Ren...' He drew a long, deep breath. 'I need to tell you something first. Make sure you've got the right expectations.'

'It's alright, I know this won't happen again,' she said quickly.

'This isn't about that,' he assured her, wetting his lips. Gods, how he wished he was brave enough to think about tomorrow. But he wasn't. 'Look, there have been advancements in the past few centuries. GLEA's surgeons were able to give me the best equipment out there — I can get hard and find my pleasure, but no one's invented a procedure that lets me create semen.'

And why would they? he thought. Doctors in specialised clinics were able to merge the DNA of two people, regardless of their sex or species, to create children with relatively little fuss. *Why would they bother when they can do that instead?*

Renaei's hips swayed as she closed the distance between them and Lorne was entranced by her sensuous movements, so much so he almost didn't notice her fingers curling around the top button of his shirt. His hand closed over hers, halting her progress. 'Ren, I need to know that you understand what I've told you.'

Then he found out where her other hand had got to — cupping him through his pants, finding him already stirred by her presence. He released the moan, unable to resist.

'I understand,' Renaei said, her voice firm. 'And I don't care. Your flesh is appealing, but it's your soul that I admire. The only soul I trust with my life and my secrets.'

The warmth began in his chest, completely surrounding his heart before spreading lower into his abdomen where it settled, causing him to harden further. Lorne pressed his forehead against hers and closed his eyes. Her scent was overwhelming at this range and it made him think of early mornings spent exploring the tundra outside his home, the cold air fresh and raw in his lungs.

'I think you're the only one, apart from my dad, who's ever seen my soul,' Lorne whispered.

His fingers fumbled on his shirt buttons for a few costly seconds, but then his hands were pulled to his sides by an invisible force. A mischievous grin played over Renaei's lips. She had clearly heard the conversation he'd had with his guards earlier. Lorne glanced down in time to watch his shirt seemingly unbutton itself. His breathing became ragged as the shirt dropped to the floor, exposing his chest. His pants and thermal stockings quickly followed suit.

Lorne stepped back the moment she released him, hooking his thumbs into the hem of his boxers and yanking them down before she could use her powers on those too. He then presented himself to her with his arms spread wide, heart stammering as he waited for her reaction.

Her gaze lowered and took him in.

'Mmm,' was all she had time to say before he surged forward.

While his lips claimed hers, his fingers were busily finding those lines above her hips and stroking them. Renaei responded to his kisses with equal fervour, nipping his bottom lip and delving into his mouth. Lorne wondered what he tasted like to her.

Strength, survival, sex, she answered mentally.

A growl swelled in his throat. He skimmed his hands down her spine, then guided them lower still. She was soft and supple beneath his touch and he kneaded her backside intently, his nails marking her flesh. She gasped, her lips detaching from his.

Smirking, Lorne walked her backwards until she had nowhere else to go, the wall firmly behind her.

'I want you in me, Lorne,' she said, her words both a plea and an order.

'Gods, I've wanted that since I was a teenager,' he murmured. 'Before I even could.'

He let out a hiss of air when she took his shaft in her hand, gently working it from base to tip and back again. Pleasant tingles soon transformed into an urgent, consuming ache. Lorne dug his teeth into her shoulder. He was close, so very close, but he didn't want this to happen yet, he wanted to be buried inside her when he finally —

'That's enough,' he said hoarsely.

Renaei raised an eyebrow as her hands drifted above her head, held there by his powers. Then her lips curled and she arched her back, offering him her body and anything else he wanted to take from her.

Lorne swallowed. How could she just...give herself to him? Without a single care for the consequences? He had no idea if his confused mess of feelings matched what he could sense inside her. She deserved someone who could return that love in full measure.

Lorne, she said, cutting into his thoughts, *I'd like you to focus on this devastatingly gorgeous body you've got pinned up against the wall.*

He laughed, his chest suddenly much lighter. 'I can do that.'

Lorne gathered her hair in his hands and pulled it behind her shoulders. Her breasts, now completely bared to him, were more perfect than he'd ever imagined. He bent down and dragged his tongue over one nipple, relishing the sigh that parted her lips, and repeated this action several more times. His goddess began to make small mewling sounds as he devoted himself to worshipping each breast, loving the taste of her, loving her reactions even more.

Renaei writhed and bucked, each delicious brush of her skin against him sending sparks shooting straight into his groin. When he slid his thigh between her legs, to apply pressure to her clitoris, her slick arousal painted him with her scent. He bit her shoulder again, overcome with desire.

'I'm wet for you, Lorne,' Renaei told him in a low voice. 'Only for you.'

He grasped her broad thighs in his hands. 'I want these around me. Now.'

'Can't you use your powers to do that?' she baited.

Oh, he definitely could. Lorne chuckled lowly. His hands moved to her backside, seating her while her legs wrapped around his waist, and then he bound her ankles together with a stray thought. Satisfied with their new position, he licked and suckled his way down her throat. Her impatient moan vibrated beneath his mouth. Smiling, Lorne guided his cock to her weeping entrance, teasing her, stroking her with his tip. Renaei tugged on her hands but his powers held them fast.

She whimpered with frustration. 'Lorne, please. I need you.'

'Yes, my goddess,' he said huskily and slid inside her.

'Ah!' she cried as her walls squeezed around him, a firm and delicious pressure. Her expression became transported. 'Yes. *Yes.* Don't you dare withdraw! I'm not done!'

Lorne couldn't have disobeyed her even if he'd wanted to. Her peak had passed but the grip she had on him was still intense. With difficulty, he adjusted his hips and shifted an extra inch into her. Renaei immediately spasmed around him again and threw back her head — which he quickly cushioned with his powers so she wouldn't hurt herself on the wall. His name fell from her lips, a low, throaty exultation.

'Again?' he said breathlessly.

She laughed. 'It takes more than a few orgasms for me to reach my limit. And I'm sure you'll do your best to take me there.'

Lorne grinned into her neck. 'Oh, I will.'

He increased his thrusts, burrowing deeper inside her, feeling her clench tighter with each stroke until he could barely move. He was so close, skating along the edge, but he didn't want to let go, not yet, not when he'd rather make her cry his name all night long.

'I can see why you're proud of that cock GLEA gave you,' his goddess whispered against his ear, sending shivers straight down his spine. 'It's hitting all the right places.'

Lorne paused, panting heavily. He was seconds away from falling right off that edge.

'Ren,' he warned.

She nipped his earlobe. 'Take it, Lorne. Take your pleasure. *Take it.*'

His hips jolted forward and he rammed into her. Heat erupted low down inside him before surging along his length, gathering potency as it went. His entire being was reduced to the sensations exploding beneath his navel and he went blind from the intensity of his release. A strangled sound escaped him, something between a pained moan and a relieved sob.

Gods, how he wished he had the seed to fill her with. But there was nothing, he had nothing, so he gave her his soul instead.

When Lorne finally regained his senses, he found himself lying on an impossibly soft rug, his damp skin bathed in flickering firelight. He looked down his body to locate the source of the kisses trailing along his thigh — Renaei. She grinned up at him. 'Are you completely spent, lover?'

Lorne skirted his eyes between his arms, which were pinned to his sides by her powers.

And then he grinned back at her.

***

She woke to his lips on her shoulder and his fingers running over her back. His touch dipped lower, around her waist and across her abdomen, but he deftly avoided her most sensitive areas. Moaning, Renaei propped up her hips and thrust out her backside, exposing more of herself. His chuckle crept over her as his hands continued to move along her skin, from her stomach to her breasts.

When she huffed with impatience, Lorne kissed her neck and asked in a soft rumble, 'Should I give my goddess what she desires?'

'Lorne...'

'Yes?'

'I'm at your mercy,' she whispered. 'Completely under your control.'

'Oh, you most certainly are, my beautiful Ren.'

He twisted himself around and slid underneath her, his kisses travelling up her thigh. She arched her back to accommodate him — and so that she could watch what he was doing to her. Sensing her gaze, he delivered a quick swipe of his tongue right between her throbbing folds, causing her hips to jerk. Renaei swallowed her gasp and refused to beg, to give him the satisfaction. But her thoughts were as bare to him as her shivering skin.

Her thighs tensed. Smirking, he wrapped his lips around her aching clitoris. Sparks shot through her as he kept suckling, increasing the pressure and sending her tumbling towards the abyss. Then, just as the crescendo of pleasure had nearly fizzled out, he pressed a finger inside her, to that sweet spot — and her climax roared into something else, something completely encompassing, a hot burst that kept going and going...

'Lorne!' Renaei cried out and collapsed.

Trembling, she lay boneless on the rug and barely managed to turn her head towards Lorne when she heard him laughing. She smiled. He had such a handsome laugh.

Now propped up on his elbow, he reached over and lifted the hair out of her face. 'I enjoy making you squirm.'

'And you also enjoy having power over your goddess,' she said tartly as she rolled onto her side, mirroring his pose. 'Especially since those fantasies of me aroused you endlessly in your youth.'

Lorne raised his eyebrows. 'You weren't the only object of my arousal.'

'But I am now.'

'Yes, because now I know for sure that you are the most attractive woman in the galaxy,' he agreed, grinning briefly. Then his hazel eyes grew serious. 'Ren, where do we go from here?'

'Aside from breakfast? Don't tell me you haven't worked up an appetite.'

'*Ren...*' he scolded.

Renaei brushed a kiss over his cheek. 'What happens now? That's your decision. I wanted my night with you and you gave it to me. I will not ask anything else of you.'

'I don't want to share you, Ren,' Lorne said and pressed his lips together, seemingly incapable of saying more.

'You won't have to,' she assured him. 'Why wouldn't I devote myself to you? You're amazing.'

'Not just in bed?' he asked.

Her chest tightened when she felt his urgency, his need to know. 'You give me so much more than sex, Lorne. I hope I give you more than that too.'

Lorne ran a hand through his hair, his frustration obvious. 'Of course you do. I lo — I like your company. A lot.'

Please say what you were going to, she pleaded silently.

He said nothing.

Renaei looked down at her lap, her eyes burning as they filled with tears. His gentle fingers curled around her chin and pulled her gaze back up to his.

'I'm sorry, Ren,' he murmured. 'I just...I just can't. Not right now. But I'm working on it. Give me some time to adjust to what I'm feeling, okay?'

Ignoring her racing heart, Renaei nodded and allowed Lorne to kiss her instead of saying the words he couldn't.

CHAPTER NINE

It all seemed to be going well. So far.

Lorne remained at his goddess' side, standing between her and the sea as she sat down at a table with her people and those who had once been her brother's. It had been decided that formal documents were to be written up and signed, making the Driftwood and the Blashians official partners. Both of them would be pledging to guard the waves and hills. Together.

Lorne felt uneasy without his lasgun but Silvia, who was signing on behalf of the villagers, had insisted that no weapons be present in the clearing while the agreement was being ratified. It was supposed to be a moment of peace.

Despite this, Lorne had discreetly made sure that the Guards of the Goddess he'd posted outside the clearing were armed and carrying their personal shielding devices. His was still broken and he'd refused to let the other guards give him theirs. Merryn had argued with him, pointing out that he would be using his powers to shield Renaei instead of himself. But Lorne disliked the idea of anyone going unprotected in his place.

Gentle waves lapped at the shore, a glaring contrast to the tsunami that had smashed into the sand the previous day. Lorne hoped this meant that Fayay had given up on Blashi. There were other Renaei-worshipping settlements for the Watine to attack, but Lorne was confident that in time those people would be able to defend themselves, even against sub-level gods.

Stark, it was almost *too* peaceful.

Lorne realised his neck was aching. He grimaced. Tense shoulders, tense limbs, finger twitching without a trigger to rest it on — he thought of another time it had been like this, when he'd still been at the Agency. They'd sent him on a mission to a supposedly peaceful settlement. And it had been much too quiet then as well. He'd barely made it out of the ensuing ambush alive, mostly thanks to the quick thinking of Lieutenant Pina-Sai, his colleague at the time.

Renaei glanced at Lorne, distracted by his unsettled thoughts.

Lorne shook his head. *I'm sure it's nothing, Ren.*

She turned back to Silvia, satisfied that she did not need to pursue the matter or use her powers. Her trust in him was frankly terrifying.

Lorne frowned, suspicious that the stillness in the air was some sort of warning, and reaffirmed his grasp on his powers. Renaei was safe inside his telekinetic shield. Just as she had been during the tsunami. Nothing could hurt her.

He blinked rapidly, blinded by the glare bouncing off the waves. Oceania couldn't read minds, but he knew his sister could. Surely the water god would find a way to use this against her.

Renaei always accessed the thoughts of the people she met and tended to trust them after that initial probe. She didn't have the time or energy to constantly peer into everyone's heads to see if their loyalties had changed; she was more occupied with using her powers to save the lives of those in danger.

Would Fayay really give up now?

'Oh gods,' Lorne murmured and began plunging into the minds around him.

It would take too long. There were so many people in the clearing. *Hundreds* of them. Keeping his mounting fear from his face, Lorne tried to think of a way to eliminate as many suspects as possible. Oceania had already tried to use his followers against Renaei without success. Which meant his only option was to tempt someone much closer to the tundra goddess.

Fayay would have made an appearance by now if he'd failed to do this.

Lorne was sure of it.

He abandoned the minds of the Blashians and the Driftwood and dove straight into those belonging to his own people. Merryn he was able to easily dismiss as a suspect. One down, two down —

Rejos Michson. That weedy kid was paid the same as the rest of the guards and had the same abilities as them. But he was envious of Lorne's power. And that made him vulnerable.

Lorne plucked out the relevant memory he found inside Rejos' head and viewed it. Rejos had met with Oceania on the beach during the festivities the previous night and had vowed that he would kill Renaei in exchange for being gifted with telekinesis.

Rejos had eagerly volunteered to stay outside the clearing. He still had his weapon.

Stark! Lorne forced himself to breathe. Renaei was currently protected by his powers. The kid had to know that. Unless he'd decided to go after someone else first, someone who was in his way...

In the time it took Lorne to blink, Rejos had made his move.

'For Oceania!' the kid cried.

The lasbolts were like streams of fire burning their way into Lorne's back; they disintegrated vertebrae and cooked vital pieces inside him. Lorne wanted to retch at the stench of scorched, ruined flesh, but when he dropped to the ground the wind was knocked right out of him. The pain was a distant thing, utterly unimportant. He had to make sure his telekinetic shield held.

And it did. Rejos' next shots struck moss instead of the goddess.

Lorne abruptly lost control of his powers and went limp. He *felt* Renaei become a furious force of nature and heard her anguished scream, almost loud enough to rupture his eardrums. Moments later, Rejos crumpled to the ground beside Lorne, his body unmarked. It was the broken neck that had killed him.

Regret passed through Lorne. The goddess would never have forgotten her aversion to killing without his being injured. But she was safe. He wheezed out a sigh of relief.

'Lorne!' That was Renaei's voice, so far away. 'Oh, Lorne...'

Where was she? Her scent filled his nostrils and her lips were on his, wet with sweat and tears. He wished he could see her one last time. He'd closed his eyes at some point and it was a struggle to unstick them. His eyelashes seemed to be fused together.

If only... he thought.

'If only what?' Renaei demanded.

If only I could have been there for you when your mother died, if only I could stay here with you forever...

He was allowed to say the words now, he reasoned. He was dying. And even if the feelings were tainted by lifelong worship...it didn't matter. He felt them.

I love you, Ren, he finally told her.

'Lorne! You will stay here, I command you!'

But this was one order he knew could not obey.

***

The desert stretched into the horizon, baked and barren, its seamless sand broken only by a collection of flimsy buildings that had managed to weather more than sandstorm. Luckily, the residents of Carton City had an outpost of Chippers to shield them — and they enjoyed the patronage of a certain desert god. Renaei wasn't sure why she'd sensed her brother's presence on Ilbb, one of the galaxy's least populated planets, but he was here. And that was all she cared about.

Lorne's broken body lay on the ground beside her. Some of the sand was creeping up his sides already, as if it had a right to judge that this was his time to be buried, forgotten for an eternity. The rest of her guards were still back on New Sydney, anxiously awaiting the return of their true leader. She couldn't let them down.

'I will join you in your war against Fayay!' she shouted at the nearest dune. 'All I ask is that you heal this man! Please.'

What else can you offer me, sister? the Desine's voice rasped, so low and so close to being blown away by a vagrant breeze.

Renaei crouched, a hand braced on Lorne's chest.

'My hatred of Fayay,' she said. 'Feel it. Know that I won't betray you.'

I need more.

'You — you lousy piece of shit!' she exploded, leaping back onto her feet. 'The man I love is dying because of Fayay, your enemy, and you're *bargaining* with me?'

A dark laugh slid over the dunes, heralding the arrival of the Desine in his human form. Sandsa strode towards his sister, a tattered brown cloak billowing out behind him and dislodging the blond hair that had been gathered up inside the hood. He gave

Renaei an even stare, his blue eyes bright in the evening gloom. 'It means I can prise more from you in this bargain.'

'Are you now so bitter that you can't do anything out of the goodness of your heart?' Renaei demanded.

Sandsa glanced down at Lorne. 'He has barely a minute left.'

'I can give you an army,' Renaei said quickly. 'An army with my powers. Serving me, but following your orders. Is that good enough, Sandsa?'

It evidently was. Sandsa knelt and extended his hands over Lorne. Bright light gathered beneath the Desine's palms before descending, forming a cocoon that hid the mortal entirely from view. Beads of sweat gathered along Sandsa's forehead and his blue eyes began to dim.

Renaei bit her lip, forcing herself to stand still. She had to trust Sandsa with her lover's life, hard as that was.

After several tense minutes that felt like an eternity, the healing light receded and Sandsa sagged to the side, his face pale and slick in the moonlight.

Lorne woke with a gasp. 'Ren? Ren, where are you?'

I'm here, my love, I'm here, she assured him.

Lorne relaxed against the sand, his breaths slowing and growing deeper. Tears dashed down Renaei's cheeks as she collapsed onto her knees and kissed him again and again, desperate to prove to herself that he was alive. When she finally remembered to look up and thank her brother, Sandsa was standing over her, envy creasing his expression. Renaei recalled that his wife had left him a quarter of a century ago, after somehow finding a way to avoid his detection.

Sandsa's eyes fell to the scars on Lorne's temple. Renaei held her breath. Her brother's loathing of Chippers was legendary. But he surprised her.

'We do so much more for our mortals than those *Chippers* ever could,' Sandsa muttered. 'Look after him, Renaei.'

'No, Sandsa,' she corrected. 'He looks after me.'

The Desine cleared his throat. 'Mortal. Stop trying to get into my head. It is pointless to try.'

Lorne blinked up the desert god in astonishment. Sandsa had effectively blocked all attempts to peer into his mind.

'Renaei sacrificed much to save your life,' the Desine told Lorne. 'She loves you. I suggest you do not waste a single moment with her, because there is a chance that not all of us will survive the upcoming conflict. Farewell.'

The Desine bowed his head, his body transforming into a figure of sand that dropped and merged with the ground. Renaei stared at the space he had vacated. She had half-expected him to refuse to help her until she had felt an unexpected surge of sympathy from him. He also had something he didn't want to lose. But his mind had been too well guarded for her to see what it was.

'Ren?' Lorne prompted.

She threw himself at him and he caught her, cradling her against his broad chest. His lips settled on her crown, a gentle pressure that sent a delightful thrill racing through her.

'Sandsa, the desert god,' she said by way of explanation.

'Was he right? Do you love me?'

'Of course.'

Lorne grimaced. 'I meant...more than a goddess loves her subject.'

Renaei buried her smile into his neck. 'Yes. I realised it last night, when you held me and took all of me. The goddess and the woman.'

'Good, I think that's when I figured it out too.' He suddenly stiffened, his voice now tight with tension. 'Ren, I'm done wasting time. And if I'm going to lose my life in this conflict or whatever it is, I don't want to have any regrets. Will you marry me? I know it's a bit sudden, but...'

'Oh, Lorne. I've wanted this for so long, even if I shouldn't have.' Renaei laughed weakly. 'But that's not the issue. Marrying me would make you immortal. I'm not sure you'd be okay with that small but significant catch.'

He lifted her hair out of her face, his thoughts warm and content. 'Catch? I'd love to spend eternity with you, my goddess. I can be *there* for you, which is my greatest wish. And I can keep you out of trouble.'

'Or help me get into it,' she added coyly.

***

The scent of sizzling muskox meat filling his nostrils and the sight of a naked woman leaning over him so that her breasts hung near his face — this was definitely how Captain Lorne Lavine wanted to wake up for the rest of eternity.

He blinked sleepily at his wife, then yelped when she yanked the blankets off him. It wouldn't be so starking cold if she hadn't insisted on fiddling with his house's climate control system. She had confessed to him that she was much more comfortable when she wasn't wearing clothes, no matter how cold her domain became.

Lorne briefly entertained himself with the thought of chasing her nude form across the nearest plateau.

'Maybe later,' Renaei told him in a low voice.

She dodged his amorous hands and danced back to the kitchen to finish making their breakfast, sorely needed after a long night of lovemaking. It had taken some doing, but Lorne had found and hit her limit. He still felt pretty smug about that.

Smirking, Lorne went hunting for boots to encase his aching feet. He paused when he caught sight of the scars on his palms. Binding scars, that's what she'd called them. Their skin had been sliced open by an invisible blade, their blood had mingled, the cuts had healed — and suddenly he'd become immortal.

He didn't feel immortal. Just vaguely irritated that all they'd had for a honeymoon was one night together — one night after him nearly *dying* — and now he was supposed to help her create an entire army so that she could join forces with the desert god against Fayay. Three guards had remained on New Sydney to train the Blashians and the rest of them had bunked down in their ship. Renaei had used her powers the previous night to teleport the vessel to a position right near Lorne's home on Velde. According to her (and Lorne had made sure to confirm it), the ground didn't mind the heavy starship being parked on top of it.

His subordinates would probably throw winks and lewd comments at him when Lorne went out to see them. He wondered if telling them he was married to their goddess would forestall some of that.

Probably not, Lorne thought, resigned.

He was very glad he'd put clothes on before wandering into the kitchen because for some reason he couldn't fathom, the Guards of the Goddess were seated on his stools and eating off his plates. Lorne transferred his stare to Renaei, who was wearing one of his bathrobes as she flounced between the stove and the counter.

'Hey, Captain!' Merryn called. 'You look like you could use a sleep-in. What did you get up to last night, huh?'

Lorne scowled. 'Ren, I was hoping to have you to myself for a little longer.'

Renaei set down the pan she was using and arched an eyebrow at him. 'We don't have a lot of time to waste, husband.'

He expected some sort of stunned reaction from his guards, but they kept right on grinning.

'You didn't knock her up, did you?' Merryn asked with a wink.

Lorne blanched. 'That's not — that's not possible, is it?' he finished, looking at Renaei. He shouldn't be able to impregnate anyone because he was effectively sterile, but his wife was a goddess and he had been heading for the afterlife less than a day ago. Nothing would surprise him at this point.

'No, it's not possible,' Renaei assured him. 'But we can merge our genetic material at one of those clinics when we want children.'

'I think we have enough children for now,' Lorne muttered, appraising his guards.

Their snickers quickly became cheers and whoops as he sprang over the counter to embrace his wife. Her green eyes sparkling, Renaei leaned in and gave him a long, lingering kiss, as though they had all the time in the galaxy. Which apparently they didn't, despite being immortal.

Lorne drew back to smile at her.

Did it matter what happened next, so long as he had this

amazing woman in his arms? So long as she had him to keep her safe?

He swooped in for another kiss, his hands sliding between the robe and her skin.

'Not in front of the children!' Renaei whispered loudly.

The Guards of the Goddess burst out laughing. More than one of their number began to make the lewd comments that Lorne had been expecting to hear from them. They soon shut up, however, when he threatened to make them clean their weapons for the rest of the morning.

ABOUT THE AUTHOR

Alyce Caswell lives in Sydney, Australia with zero cats, one husband and one son. When she isn't drinking her way through a giant pot of tea, Alyce is a keen reader and writer of science fiction and fantasy.

You can contact her via e-mail (alycecaswell@outlook.com) or on Twitter (@alycecaswell).

ALSO BY ALYCE CASWELL

The Galactic Pantheon Series
The Tortured Wind
The Twisted Vine

*The Flickering Flame**
*The Shifting Ice**
*The Whispering Grass**
*The Creeping Moss**

*The Galactic Pantheon Novellas***

*novella
**collection